THE MATRIARCH'S LEGACY

Beth Brubaker

ISBN-13: 9798999136220

Library of Congress Control Number: 2018675309
Printed in the United States of America

CONTENTS

PART I — WEATHERING THE STORM (1929–1933)

CHAPTER ONE — WHEN THE WORLD CRACKED (OCTOBER 1929)

Florence first sensed it not through the radio, but through the house.

The children's voices filled the narrow rooms more fully than usual, pressing against the walls as though the space itself were struggling to contain them. A pot on the stove simmered too quickly, the lid rattling in protest. Even the clock on the mantel ticked louder than it should have, each second insisting on its place.

Florence wiped her hands on her apron and stood still.

There were moments in a woman's life when change arrived with force—through war or death or the sharp edge of grief. But there were other moments when it slipped quietly into the ordinary and settled there, testing the seams. Florence had learned early how to recognize the difference.

This was the quiet kind.

William came in from the front room, the low murmur of the radio following him like something unfinished. Returning from work in the city, he set his hat on the sideboard and did not look at her right away. Tall and slender, his dark brown hair neatly parted on the left, he was composed and deliberate. The room seemed suddenly smaller, as though the air itself was holding its breath.

"They're saying the market's fallen," he said.

Florence nodded. She did not yet know what it would mean, only that it would mean *something*. Markets were distant things, numbers held elsewhere, by other hands, but William's voice carried weight she could not ignore.

"How far?" she asked.

He hesitated, then answered, "Far enough."

Florence turned back to the stove and lifted the lid. Steam

rose quickly, threatening to spill over. She lowered the flame without thinking, returning the pot to a steady simmer. It was a small act, but it mattered. When the world pressed too hard, you adjusted what you could—heat, portions, tone.

Outside, October light slanted across the tree-lined street in Haverford. Doors opened and closed along the block. Somewhere a laugh rang too loudly, as though trying to fill more space than it was given. Somewhere else, a man's voice broke off mid-sentence.

Florence stirred the pot slowly.

She had known instability before—known it as something that crept in quietly and stayed longer than expected. She had learned that safety was not something you assumed; it was something you created, moment by moment, by keeping certain things contained.

William sat when she told him to, grateful for the instruction.

Florence recognized the exchange without naming it. He would carry the weight outward, wrestling with what might be lost. She would hold what remained—this house, the children, this evening.

The table between them bore the marks of years already lived, small knife nicks, a pale ring from a forgotten cup, the softened grain where hands had rested night after night. Bill, newly four, traced one of those faint grooves with his finger before steadying Dean atop the wooden booster. Dean, two and restless, gripped the edge of the table as though anchoring himself to something firm. Nearby, Gerry slept in his bassinet, one month old, breathing in the warm air of stew and bread and lamplight.

Once the children were settled, flushed and hungry, Florence ladled stew into bowls, mindful of the space each portion occupied. The light above them fell gently across the table's surface, catching in the grain. She moved with quiet precision, her shapely frame steady, her dark brown curls pinned close, a simple strand of faux pearls resting at her collar, more habit than ornament, her modest dress falling neatly into place as she worked. No one needed to know why she measured carefully. Not yet.

William lifted his spoon but did not eat. He let the stew cool while they spoke.

"It won't right itself quickly," he said. "Men at the theater are already speaking of cut hours. Some have lost their positions."

Florence broke her bread and placed half on Bill's plate. The crust left a scatter of crumbs across the worn wood.

William's work had always asked for more of him than most. Long hours spent between light and shadow, guiding both the flicker on the screen and the sound that gave it life. It steadied them now, that added usefulness, though neither of them mistook it for certainty.

"Then we'll use what we have carefully."

He looked at her. "I don't want you worrying."

"I'm not," she said. "Worry scatters a house. We won't do that."

Bill studied them both. "Is the theater broken, Dad?"

William's mouth softened. "No, son. It's just ... adjusting."

"Like when Mom lets dough rest?"

"Yes," Florence said quietly. "Exactly like that."

Dean struck his spoon once against the table. "More bread."

William slid the basket toward him. "There's always more bread."

Florence reached her foot toward Gerry's bassinet, tapping it gently. The baby stirred, then settled again.

William lowered his voice. "If they reduce my hours—"

"Then we adjust," she said. "We've done more with less."

He studied her for a long moment. "You don't frighten easily."

"I do," she answered. "I just don't let it speak first."

Silence settled over the table, not heavy, only full. Two sets of small hands rested there now, and two larger ones that had learned to steady them.

William nodded. "All right then. We meet it here."

"Yes," she said. "Here."

They bowed their heads.

Florence closed her eyes and felt something steady itself inside her. Not fear. Resolve.

If the world beyond their walls was cracking open, she would not allow it to spill into this room, to this table, unchecked. Whatever was coming would be met here and held as long as it needed to be.

When she lifted her head, the lamplight caught again in the worn grain beneath her hands.

Some things survived not because they were strong, but because someone knew how to hold them.

After the meal, Bill carried the dishes carefully to the kitchen, lifting them clear of the table's edge as though it, too, required protection. William rose just in time to catch Dean as he darted toward the front room, his wooden truck rumbling softly across the floorboards.

The house settled into its evening posture. They gathered in the front room, retreating within the steady comfort of warm walls and routines that asked little more than attention. Florence cradled baby Gerry against her shoulder, feeling the familiar weight of him and the deeper reassurance it brought, proof, she thought, that some things still arrived as they always had.

Later that week, they made their monthly walk down into Bryn Mawr to the Ludington Library, the air crisp enough to sharpen thought and color. Along Lancaster Avenue the shop windows were already trimmed for autumn, and the Main Line houses stood back from the road in practiced composure.

Bill ran ahead, untroubled, his shoes scuffing the pavement in a rhythm all his own, while Dean lingered behind, stooping to collect fallen leaves, reds and golds he pressed flat between his palms as though saving what could not be kept. Florence pushed baby Gerry in the pram, humming a tune she half-remembered from her own childhood, and noticed how few leaves clung to the trees now, how easily they gave themselves to the ground.

The library doors opened with a familiar hush. Inside, the warmth settled around them like a coat. Miss Caldwell looked up from behind the desk and smiled as if she had been expecting them.

"You're right on time, Mrs. Adams," she said, lowering her voice. "I kept something aside."

Bill stopped short. "For us?"

"For all of you," she replied, reaching beneath the desk. "But it's one you'll need to share."

She placed *The Voyages of Doctor Dolittle* into his hands, its spine worn soft from use. Dean leaned in immediately, his fingers tracing the illustration on the cover.

"He talks to animals," Miss Caldwell said, conspiratorially. "I thought that might suit your household."

Florence smiled. "It suits us perfectly."

"You take your time," the librarian added, nodding toward the shelves. "I'll keep an eye on them."

Florence lingered among the stacks, running her fingers along the titles, pausing to read spines, letting herself be briefly anonymous. From where she stood, she could hear Bill whispering the words aloud and Dean correcting him amusingly, the baby stirring in the carriage at her side.

Near the front windows, a small display caught her eye—periodicals arranged in careful tiers. She lifted one, its cover illustrating the new silhouettes of the decade: longer lines, softened waists, hats angled with quiet confidence. The women inside its pages looked composed, as though the world beyond them had not shifted at all. Florence studied the hems, the collars, the careful tailoring. Not out of vanity, but curiosity. How did one dress for a decade that had begun by unraveling?

There had been a time when such questions had come more easily to her, when her days had allowed for it. Afternoons spent among shop windows and polished counters, evenings marked by music halls and the low hush before a performance began. She had known the rhythm of outings then, the careful choosing of a dress, the placement of a hat, the quiet anticipation of stepping into a world lit differently than her own.

It had not been a frivolous life, only a different one. One that moved with its own kind of order, its own expectations of beauty and presence. So much of it had been set aside, not all at once, but gradually, as other things had asked more of her hands, her time, her attention.

She turned another page, noting patterns that could be altered, seams that might be let down, fabric saved and repurposed. Even fashion, she thought, adjusted. It too, rested and reshaped.

A few shelves over, her attention drifted from hemlines to hardcovers. The bright covers of children's stories pulled her in, classics she had known as a young woman, and newer tales filled with animals who spoke plainly and forests that answered back. She drew one from the shelf and opened it at random. The paper carried that faint, comforting scent of ink and possibility.

Miss Caldwell, stationed near the reading table, offered her a small nod. "They're quite content," she murmured.

Florence returned the nod, grateful for the monthly indulgence she had begun to allow herself. An hour alone among books. An hour in which she could think without measuring flour or stretching broth. She found herself wishing it could be weekly. Perhaps someday.

For now, she held the quiet as long as it would hold her.

They returned home with the book, as they always did. This time it carried promises of distant journeys and talking animals, of worlds that listened back. Reading together in the evenings had become something Florence held close, aware, though she could not yet name why, that such rituals might soon carry more weight than pleasure alone.

On the walk back, Bill slowed suddenly and pointed toward a hedge. “There,” he whispered, as though the word itself might frighten it away.

A rabbit sat just beyond the fence line, still as a thought, its ears lifted in cautious attention. Dean tugged at Florence’s skirt. “Does he have a name?” he asked.

“Perhaps,” she said. “We just don’t know it yet.”

They stood quietly until the rabbit darted away, disappearing into the thinning October brush. A moment later, a squirrel streaked up the trunk of a maple, tail flicking indignantly as though protesting their intrusion.

Bill laughed. “Maybe he’s cross.”

“Or maybe,” Florence replied, adjusting the baby carriage with one hand, “he has something important to say.”

Dean scanned the trees. “What else can we find?”

They walked more slowly, eyes lifted. A sparrow hopped along the curb. A stray cat wound between fence posts before slipping through a narrow gate. Bill began offering names to each of them, whispering introductions as though they might answer back.

Florence listened, smiling. The world, for all its shifting, still moved with small, attentive life. Perhaps that was reason enough to keep watching.

Once the children settled down for their nap, Florence had returned to the kitchen. She pressed the dough down with practiced hands, feeling the soft resistance give way beneath her palms, then slid the loaf into the oven. The room filled with the early promise of bread. She wiped her hands on her apron, chose a chair by the window, and opened the book she had checked out, only a chapter, she told herself. A small moment, claimed.

The door opened not long after. William came in quietly, loosening his coat, pausing when he saw her seated there. A trace of city cold followed him in—iron rails, coal smoke, something metallic that clung to evenings spent in Philadelphia.

"You look settled," he said.

"For the moment," she replied, smiling. "I thought I'd borrow a little time before supper steals it back."

On the small table beside her rested the book from their walk to the Ludington Library, its spine newly creased, a paper slip tucked neatly inside. Nearby, William's folded train schedule waited, tomorrow's departure from Haverford already decided.

He pulled out the chair across from her and sat. "The theater's been ... uncertain," he said, choosing the word carefully. "Fewer showings this week. They're talking about cutting more hours."

Florence watched him a moment. Haverford held steady, hedges trimmed, lamps lit, neighbors predictable, but Philadelphia did not promise the same.

Florence glanced at the two papers without meaning to, one promising return dates and due stamps, the other bound by timetables and wages. Both measured time. Only one felt generous.

Florence closed the book, not in alarm, but attention. "We've known lean stretches before."

"I know." He reached for her hand. "I just don't want you to worry."

"I worry only if we stop talking," she said gently. "We'll make it work. We always do."

William nodded, the tension easing from his shoulders. "Together, then."

"Together," she echoed.

Footsteps broke the quiet. Bill appeared first, rubbing his eyes, Dean close behind, already asking what smelled so good. Florence rose, smoothing her apron, while William glanced toward the bassinet where Gerry slept on, undisturbed, as if holding the calm in place for them.

After the meal, William settled at the piano, lifting the fallboard as if greeting an old friend. He let the music move carefully through the house, choosing familiar melodies at first, steady, measured ones, as though anything too bold might tempt interruption.

Florence opened the book and began. “Doctor Dolittle lived in a little house with a large garden...”

William’s fingers answered with a gentle run, light as footsteps. “A man with sense,” he said without looking up. “Anyone who keeps animals and a garden knows where the real conversations happen.”

Bill giggled. “Does he really talk to them?”

“He listens first,” Florence said, smiling. “That’s how it works.”

As she read on, William shifted keys, slipping in a playful flourish when the parrot appeared.

“Polynesia sounds opinionated,” he murmured. “I like her already.”

Dean leaned closer. “Do you think she tells him what to do?”

William nodded solemnly, never missing a note. “Absolutely. All the wisest ones do.”

Laughter spilled out, quick and easy. William improvised then, threads of familiar classical phrases woven with something lighter, almost mischievous, as if the music itself were listening to the story and deciding to join in. Years earlier, he had learned to follow motion on a flickering screen, matching melody to gesture, tempo to surprise, humor to misstep. That instinct remained. The shifted keys when the animals appeared, slipping into a playful flourish that felt as though it had always been waiting for its cue. Florence paused now and then, allowing a cadence to resolve before continuing, her voice and his hands learning each other’s timing.

Even Gerry stirred in his bassinet, then settled again, the sound holding him as surely as arms.

When the last page was turned and the children were tucked into bed, the house grew quiet in a different way. Not empty, but watchful. William closed the piano gently and crossed the room to Florence, drawing her into his arms tenderly. He bent easily to her, his tall frame folding around her, her dark curls brushing his shoulder as she settled against him, the faint sheen of her pearls catching the low light between them.

"You know," he said softly, his voice low so the walls would not carry it, "I watch you with them, and with me, and I fall in love all over again. A good mother. A faithful wife. A beautiful woman. Every moment we share adds to it."

Her breath caught, just enough to still her for a moment.

She lowered her gaze, not out of modesty alone, but because the weight of his words settled somewhere deep, somewhere she did not often let herself look directly.

"William ..." she said quietly, her voice gentler than before.

Her hand found his, her fingers fitting there as though they had always belonged.

"You speak as though it is something I've given you," she continued, lifting her eyes to his at last, a softness there that carried both gratitude and truth. "But it isn't one thing, or even many. It's ... this." She gave the slightest motion of her hand between them—the house, the children, the years that had shaped them both.

A small, knowing smile touched her lips.

"I learned how to be a mother by loving them," she said. "And how to be a wife ... by loving you."

She stepped a little closer, her voice lowering to meet his. "And as for the rest ..." Her gaze warmed, steady and sure. "It is you who sees it. You who makes it something worth keeping."

Her thumb brushed lightly across his hand, a quiet, grounding gesture.

"I do not carry it alone, William," she whispered. "What you love in me ... you have helped to build."

For a moment, she simply looked at him, the fullness of years held in the space between them.

"And I," she added, almost as if it were the most natural truth in the world, "fall in love with you the same way ... again and again, without asking it to be anything more than what it is."

She smiled at that, though her eyes softened with something deeper. There had been a time when love had not felt so certain, when it had arrived not as a promise, but as a question.

She had been younger then, carrying more than she spoke of, moving between worlds that had not asked to understand one another.

There had been years of quiet order, of fields and early mornings, of work that steadied the hands and a family that had taken her in without question. And then, just as quietly, it had been undone, returned to a life she had once belonged to, to a mother whose love was no less real for the distance that had shaped it.

She had learned, somewhere between those two homes, that belonging was not always a place you were given, but something you learned to carry.

By the time she had stepped into the theater, into dim lights and borrowed stories and music that filled the spaces words could not reach, she no longer expected anything to remain.

And then there had been William. Not with grand declarations, but with presence. With music that seemed to understand the unspoken. With a steadiness that did not demand, only remained. She had not trusted it at first.

But love, she had learned, did not always arrive as something sweeping. Sometimes it came gently, returning again and again, until one day, you realized it had never left. Florence rested her head against his chest, his arms steady around her, a shelter she did not question.

"We have enough," he continued. "Our love. Our dedication. It will carry us."

She stood with him there in the dim light, aware that comfort, like music, required tending, and trusting that what they had made together was strong enough to endure whatever asked more of them next.

They were, by nature, gentle people, the kind who believed that kindness, quietly kept, might be enough to steady what the world could not. Because some things were not meant to withstand the world untouched, but to be held through it, again and again, until they became the very thing that lasted.

CHAPTER TWO — MAKING DO

Florence reorganized the pantry the morning after the news of the market crash.

She did not tell herself she was responding to anything in particular. There was simply a sense that the shelves needed attention, that things would fit better if they were shifted, counted, and placed with intention. Order had a way of calming what words could not.

After a while, she set the cloth aside and stepped outdoors with the children, as though answering a need she had not yet acknowledged. Bill and Dean burst into motion the moment their feet hit the grass, racing one another toward the trees, hands slapping bark, testing which branches would hold. They circled back for a breath, then took off again in an uneven game of tag, their laughter brief and sharp, already learning the economy of sound.

Florence sat on the back step with baby Gerry at her breast, his small hand curled against her apron. The garden lay before her, tidy but not finished. Late tomatoes clung stubbornly to the vines. The beans had thinned. She noted what would still come and what would not, the way she noted everything now. For a moment, she allowed herself the quiet pleasure of the view, the illusion of pause.

She was grateful for William's surprising extra hours at the theater, especially now. Fewer men could say the same. At least for the time, the glow of the screen and the hum of the projector offered people a brief distraction from what pressed at their doors.

The evenings had begun stretching without explanation. She had stopped asking for one. Supper would be taken without him. Bedtime too.

Morning would bring his return, tired, but steady. For now,

that was enough. This, she decided, would be the shape of things for now.

Dean lingered near the edge of the yard, crouched low over something only he could see. Bill had climbed the low stone border by the walk and balanced there, arms stretched wide as if mastering a narrow bridge.

Florence steadied the carriage and looked toward them. "Bill," she called gently. "Keep a close eye on your brother, please. I'm going in to settle Gerry for his nap."

"I will," Bill said at once, straightening. "He won't go past the hedge."

Dean did not look up. "I'm not going anywhere," he murmured, turning a leaf over in his hands as though inspecting a secret.

Florence smiled. "Stay where I can see you from the kitchen window."

"We will," Bill said again, already watchful.

She studied them a moment longer — the confident one and the careful one — then turned the carriage toward the house.

She went back inside.

She laid Gerry down in his crib, smoothing the blanket once across his small chest before turning from the quiet of the nursery to the work waiting below.

Florence moved back into the kitchen, drawing the potatoes up from the cool dark of the basement. She set them out on the table, their skins still dusted with earth. For a moment, memory pressed close, long days from another life when she had peeled potatoes by the dozen, hands aching, setting them aside for storage, preparing not just for supper but for seasons ahead. There had been comfort in that work. Order. The steady reassurance of knowing what would last.

She sliced them now without hurry and added them to the pot where the remnants of the roast simmered with onions, the scent rising slowly, familiarly. The bread had finished its second rise. She pressed the dough once more, gently, and slid it into the oven, closing the door with care.

Turning to the pantry, she set the empty containers on the table, the flour tin first, then the sugar canister, then the small glass jars that once held jam and now waited for whatever purpose came next. Each was wiped clean, its edges checked, its lid tested. Florence disliked surprises where food was concerned.

She stepped to the back door and opened it wide.

"Bill. Dean. Time to come in."

A pause. Then the thud of shoes against earth.

"Already?" Bill called.

"Yes, already," she answered. "Wash up."

Dean appeared first, a leaf still clutched in his hand. Bill followed, brushing dirt from his knees.

"Leave the hedge as you found it," she added gently.

"We did," Bill said.

She watched them disappear down the hallway toward the basin, then stepped outside herself.

She pressed her heel into the soil along the back fence, testing it the way she tested lids and seams. The ground gave slightly, then held. It would need turning. Compost. Time.

Some things could be prepared for. Others required patience—and trust—to take root on their own.

She wiped her hands on her apron and went back inside, carrying with her the quiet understanding that the life she was tending, like the garden, would grow only partly by her design, and partly by forces she could not command, only meet with care.

The children hovered in the kitchen, curious but quiet. They had learned, without being told, that this was not a game.

"Can I help?" Bill asked.

Florence handed him a box of buttons—some chipped, some mismatched, none thrown away. "Sort these by size," she said. "The big ones together. The little ones together."

He nodded and carried the box to the corner of the table, the buttons clicking softly as they shifted against one another, aware, Florence thought, that they were being put back into service. Dean was not far behind, also wanting to assist and be a part of his big brother's world.

She worked shelf by shelf. Beans moved to the front. Flour slid back. A jar of peaches, put up the summer before, was placed squarely in the center, its amber contents catching the light. Florence counted silently, committing the numbers to memory. She had always trusted her mind more than lists.

When Bill finished sorting the buttons, he paused for a moment. "You don't have to do all this today," he said gently.

Florence wiped her hands on her apron. "I know."

She did not stop.

He watched for a moment longer, then crossed the room and picked up an empty tin. "This one's still good," he said, almost apologetically.

"I know," she agreed. "It'll hold nails. Or screws."

Or something else, if it had to.

The morning passed quietly. Florence set aside what could be spared and tucked away what could not. Bread heels went into a cloth bag. Bacon grease was poured carefully into a small jar and set near the stove. Nothing was wasted. Nothing was dramatized.

At noon, she ladled soup into bowls she knew would not chip. The children ate quickly, unaware that their lunch was part of a longer calculation. Florence watched them, how easily they trusted the world to provide. She intended to keep it that way as long as she could.

After they finished eating, the children were released back into the yard. Bill and Dean tore down the worn path along the hedges, inventing rules as they went, their voices rising and falling with the wind.

Florence lingered at the table long enough to lift Gerry from his bassinet. He rested easily against her shoulder, warm and milk-heavy, one small fist coiled into the fabric of her dress.

She stood at the back door for a moment, watching the

older boys expend what the meal had given them. Bill leapt the narrow dip near the fence. Dean followed more carefully, adjusting the game as he ran.

Gerry shifted in her arms, then settled.

Florence stepped outside.

She walked the length of the yard slowly, stretching her legs, letting the afternoon settle around her. When the noise thinned into contented quiet, she returned indoors. She laid Gerry in the nearby bassinet, then took her seat by the window and opened her book.

Only a few pages. Enough to remind herself there were still places to visit without leaving home.

That afternoon, she took a cardboard box from the hall closet and filled it with items she could part with. Extra linens. A dress she had not worn in years. Shoes that pinched. She taped the lid shut and slid it beneath the bed, not ready yet to let it leave the house.

Some things were better stored than surrendered.

They gathered again in the sitting room after supper, the light thinning at the windows. Florence took up *Doctor Doolittle* where they had left off, Bill leaning against her knee, Dean stretched out on the rug, listening with his chin in his hands.

"I like it better when Dad plays," Dean said suddenly, not looking up. "The music helps."

Bill answered for her. "He has to work late some nights," he said with the certainty of something already explained. "That's how it is."

Florence nodded once, her thumb holding the page. "Your father will play again," she said evenly. "The piano isn't going anywhere."

She read on, her voice steady, letting the story do its work. When Gerry fussed in his bassinet, she paused, lifting him easily, settling him against her shoulder. The children waited. They always did. When he quieted, she resumed as though nothing had been interrupted—because nothing important had been.

When the chapter ended, she marked the page and closed the book. Bill rose reluctantly, Dean a moment later, the day's weight finally finding them. She walked them down the hall, kisses placed where they always were, the rhythm unchanged. By the time the light was turned low, the house had accepted its night posture, drawn in, attentive, waiting.

She stood a moment in the hallway after their doors were shut.

The day had asked much of her, but it had also given. The boys' easy laughter at supper. Gerry's steady warmth against her shoulder. The small mercies of routine, bread rising as it should, coats hung where they belonged, voices answering when called.

William would not be home until morning. The extra hours had become necessary, and she did not resent them. Still, the quiet felt wider without him in it.

She did not name her gratitude aloud. She carried it inwardly, the way she carried worry, carefully measured, never wasted. What was steady tonight might be strained tomorrow. She knew better than to assume.

She lingered a moment longer in the front room, Gerry warm and heavy against her shoulder, the quiet no longer fragile but earned. The piano stood closed. The book rested where she could find it again. Nothing was missing that could not be returned.

She eased herself into the chair and opened the book once more—just a page or two. The story welcomed her without question. Within its pages, beginnings and endings behaved themselves. Hardships resolved in tidy arcs. She let the words gather her in.

Her eyes began to close.

Gerry stirred, a soft fuss rising from his sleep. Florence smiled faintly and pressed her cheek to his hair before closing the book and marking her place. The world on the page receded. This one remained.

She moved through the house once more before retiring,

checking doors, straightening a chair, touching what needed touching. It was not worry that guided her, but care. The kind that held when noise faded and plans shifted.

This, she understood, was how things endured.
Not through certainty, but through tending.

And tomorrow, she would begin again.

CHAPTER THREE — THE PROJECTIONIST'S UNCERTAINTY

The pay envelope came home thinner than it had the week before.

William set it on the table without comment, sliding it into the same place he always did, just left of Florence's sewing basket. He washed his hands at the sink, dried them carefully, and returned to stand where he could see the children without interrupting them. Nothing in his manner announced the change, but Florence noticed the envelope immediately. She always did.

Later, when the house had quieted, she opened it.

The bills were folded once, then again, pressed flat by habit rather than necessity. Florence counted slowly. She did not rush facts. They had a way of resenting it.

Work, William explained that night, came where it could. Fewer shows. Shorter runs. Sometimes a theater closed for days at a time, waiting to see if people would return. Films still arrived, but audiences were thinner. Men lingered longer at the ticket window, calculating whether the price was worth the dark and the warmth.

"I know it isn't what it was," Florence said finally, breaking the quiet.

William looked up from the table.

"But it matters that you're still there," she continued. "That you're running the projector now. You're steady inside the building itself."

He nodded. "Some of the sound men didn't make the cut. When they shortened the schedule."

Florence pressed her thumb along the fold of the envelope. "I don't forget that."

"Neither do I."

She glanced toward the window, where the streetlight threw a thin square of brightness onto the floor. “People still need somewhere to sit in the dark and breathe for a while. Even now. Especially now.”

He gave a thoughtful smile. “Sometimes I think that’s the only reason the place stays open.”

“Then it’s good work,” she said simply.

Florence listened without interrupting. She did not ask what he thought would happen next. She had learned that predictions were rarely useful and often unkind.

Instead, she folded the envelope and placed it inside the drawer where such things belonged. Bills were stacked beneath it, arranged by urgency rather than size. Some could wait. Some could not. Knowing the difference was a skill Florence had practiced long before anyone named it.

The theater had reduced his hours again that week. Fewer showings. Shorter reels. Too many men waiting in the wings for work that no longer filled a program.

It was through someone he knew from the projection booth, a man who understood wiring and timing, that the new offer had come. A room in need of steady hands. Sound that drifted. Lights that faltered. Evenings mostly. Discreet.

William had said yes.

That evening, as he buttoned his coat, she asked without looking up, “Tell me again what it is you’ll be doing there.”

“Sound, lighting and anything that needs adjusting,” he said. “Control. Making sure the room behaves. Nothing more. Nothing less.”

“And the hours?”

“Late,” he admitted. “But honest. They pay in cash. No promises beyond that.”

Florence met his eyes then, searching for what mattered. “You won’t be drawn into anything else?”

“No,” William said, without hesitation. “I go in, I listen, I fix what needs fixing, and I come home. That’s the whole of it.”

She nodded once. “Then it’s work,” she said. “And we know

how to make room for work."

William showed up at the place below street level, a door without a sign. The hours ran later than Florence preferred but paid better than most. He did not romanticize it. He went because it was work.

The speakeasy called itself Midnight & The Wicked, though nothing about it announced itself aboveground. Inside, the rooms were built to behave; light held low and steady, sound softened where it mattered, doors opening only when they were meant to. William noticed immediately where things faltered.

He adjusted the lighting first, replacing bulbs that burned too hot, angling fixtures so shadows settled instead of scattered. He learned how the air moved through the rooms and corrected it, coaxing smoke and heat upward and away so nothing lingered longer than it should. Hinges were tightened, latches corrected, panels smoothed where a hand might hesitate. The place ran better when it ran quietly.

The venue unfolded in four distinct chambers, each designed not merely as a room, but as an experience.

The Midnight Lounge lay just beyond the entry, low-lit, amber-glowed, with curved banquettes tucked against dark paneled walls. Brass sconces cast soft halos above small round tables where couples leaned close over cut-glass tumblers. A trio played near the corner—upright bass, piano, muted trumpet — their notes curling like smoke. The room did not rush. It persuaded. Conversation settled into velvet. Laughter stayed low. It felt almost conspiratorial, as though one had stepped back into a quieter decade where secrets were exchanged over bourbon and lamplight.

Beyond the lounge pulsed The Wicked.

The transition was intentional, a narrowing hallway, then a sudden widening into height and sound. Here, the ceilings rose and the lighting sharpened. Geometric patterns edged the floor in bold Deco lines. A mirrored bar reflected movement from every angle. When the band took over, the rhythm traveled through the floorboards themselves. Dresses shimmered beneath lights. Shoes struck polished wood with confident insistence. The room did not persuade. It declared.

Further down, set apart by heavier doors and deep crimson drapery, stood The Crimson Theater. Rows of intimate seating faced a raised stage framed in gold-leaf detailing. Velvet curtains gathered thick at either side, ready to part. It was a room built for anticipation, for a singer to command silence, for a comic to fracture it, for a spotlight to isolate a single figure against a darkened crowd. Even empty, it seemed to hold applause within its walls.

And then there was The Vault.

One did not stumble into it by accident. To enter, guests were led down a narrow corridor where the temperature dropped slightly, the air cooler against the skin. At the end stood a real bank vault door—iron, riveted, impossibly heavy. Its wheel required deliberate turning. The mechanism groaned with satisfying resistance before yielding inward.

Inside, the space was unexpectedly intimate. Low ceilings, exposed stone, candlelight reflected in aged metal. Conversations in The Vault carried differently, closer, quieter, almost reverent. It felt less like a room and more like a secret held between those invited to pass through.

The man who had designed it—Artem—watched without interruption.

Later, he showed William the hidden doors and false walls, how movement could be guided without force. A hallway angled just slightly so crowds naturally veered left instead of right. A mirrored panel that disguised a service entrance. A latch concealed within carved molding. The illusion was never about deception, Artem explained. It was about flow.

He moved through the space as though listening to it, palm resting briefly against the wall, eyes measuring distance without ruler or chalk.

"Most men try to command a room," Artem said. "They widen it, brighten it, shout inside it."

He stopped at the threshold between two chambers and adjusted a hinge no wider than a coin.

"But rooms respond better to suggestion."

The door settled into place with a softened click.

"You never push people," he said. "You let the space decide for them."

William considered that.

Steel behaved similarly. Under pressure, it resisted. Guided properly, it strengthened. Engines failed when forced beyond tolerance; they endured when calibrated with patience. Even crowds, he had noticed, preferred invitation to insistence.

William did not know then how often he would return to that sentence, how it would surface years later in unexpected places: in a crowded exhibition hall where curved displays guided the public without command... in factory discussions where efficiency mattered more than spectacle ... even in his own home, where children moved by example, rather than decree.

At the time, he only nodded.

"And if the space is wrong?" he asked quietly.

Artem's expression held the faintest hint of a smile. "Then you redesign it."

William studied the hinges, the counterweights, the small calibrations that allowed heavy doors to close with a whisper instead of a slam.

He offered a suggestion or two in return, nothing showy, just small adjustments that made the mechanisms behave as intended. A shift in balance here. A reinforcement there. A way to prevent strain before it formed.

Artem considered, then nodded once.

Genius, William had learned, was usually practical at heart.

He kept to the edges, working late, speaking little. When the rooms filled, his attention stayed on thresholds and timing, when to open, when to wait, when to close again. He understood that the success of a night did not lie in spectacle alone, but in the unseen choreography beneath it.

At the end of the evening, when music thinned and chairs returned to their places, he wiped his hands clean, folded the cash carefully, and brought home what mattered.

William had not expected the music to follow him home.

The speakeasy carried it whether he listened or not—pianos bright and insistent, rhythms tumbling forward faster than thought. It was not the sort of music he and Florence had known together, before the children. Too quick. Too playful. Too unconcerned with reverence. And yet, he found himself paying attention.

At home, after the children were asleep, he sat at the piano and worked it out slowly, piece by piece. He learned "Dizzy Fingers," then "Kitten on the Keys," popular tunes by Zez Confrey, built less on emotion than on precision. The music required discipline. Timing. Control. William respected that.

Florence listened from the doorway at first, then from the chair beside the lamp.

"That's not Chopin," she said lightly.

"No," he answered, without looking up. "It isn't meant to be."

"It sounds … busy."

"It is." A smile touched the corner of his mouth. "Keeps the hands honest."

She did not ask where the melodies came from. She heard instead how carefully he played, how nothing was rushed, how even the quickest passages were held in check.

"Is this for the new work?" she asked at last.

"For whatever room I'm in," he said. "People like something lively."

"And you?"

"I like knowing where every note lands."

The music was lively, almost reckless in its speed, but it was not careless.

It became something they shared quietly. Another way of bringing order to what might otherwise have remained unsettled.

When William finished, he closed the piano gently.

"You'll play it there?" she asked.

"If they need it."

Florence nodded. "Then play it well."

He met her eyes then. "I always do."

She rose, straightened the lamp, and together they turned out the light.

Florence did not ask for details. She saw the envelope placed beside the others and understood what it meant, not excess, not indulgence, but margin. Enough to keep the house steady a little longer. Whatever the world called the place, to her it was simply another container, engineered, temporary, and doing exactly what it was meant to do.

It did not take long for word to travel.

William was approached again—not by someone he knew, but by someone who knew of him. The place was Club 21, the address given quietly, the expectation unspoken. The name attached carried weight in the city—Max "Boo Boo" Hoff—the kind of man whose reputation entered a room before he did.

William listened. He asked careful questions. What was needed. How long. Who else would be involved.

The answers were imprecise. The assurances generous. Too generous.

He understood then that this was asking more of him with a greater risk to the family.

He had lived in Philadelphia as a younger, single man, long enough to recognize how proximity hardened into association. A man's name did not need to be spoken often, only once, in the wrong room. After that, it traveled on its own.

There were systems in the city that functioned efficiently, even elegantly, but they were governed by loyalties that did not loosen. Work given easily could be called upon later, in ways less visible and far less optional.

William did not fear the men involved. He feared the narrowing of choice.

He had no intention of being pulled into a world he did not build, answering to rules he did not set, or risking harm, legal or otherwise, that could ripple beyond himself. Florence deserved steadiness. The boys deserved a father whose name opened doors without quietly closing others.

He declined without drama.

The man across from him did not argue. He only nodded, as though filing the decision away.

William rose, settled his coat, and stepped back into the night air. The door closed behind him with an ordinary click. Inside, laughter resumed.

He did not look back. He did not need to.

In places like that, entrances were noticed. So were exits.

But there was work he would take, and work he would not. William had learned that systems mattered, but so did who controlled them. And he would not place his future, or his family, inside one that thrived on leverage.

At home, the children moved through the house unaware. Shoes were kicked off by the door. Books and paper spread across the table. Laughter came easily. Florence encouraged it. She believed that worry, like food, should be portioned carefully.

William found himself tending to the house more than usual. Not out of restlessness, exactly, but habit sharpened by uncertainty. When work wavered, his hands sought what could be made steady.

A stair tread that shifted slightly was secured before it loosened further. The pantry hinge was adjusted so it would no longer swing too wide. A window that rattled when the wind came off the river was coaxed back into alignment until it closed cleanly, the latch fitting as it should. None of it announced itself. He preferred it that way.

Florence noticed, of course. She always did. But she did not remark on the changes. She moved through the house and found it holding. That was enough.

She had her own ways of answering uncertainty. She took older dresses from the back of the wardrobe, fabric still good, seams simply tired, and set to work at the table near the window. A hem lifted. A bodice reshaped. Buttons moved and sleeves narrowed until something familiar emerged renewed, not disguised but improved. The result was feminine and assured, as though the cloth itself had been waiting for permission to become something else.

William noticed, though he said nothing at first. He watched her fasten a pin, step back, then return to her work with the same measured care she brought to everything. "That's new," he said finally.

"It's not," she replied, smiling. "It's just learned to behave better."

She mended the children's clothes in the evenings, reinforcing knees, letting out cuffs, turning collars so they would last another season. Nothing was wasted if it still had use. There was satisfaction in that, in drawing more life from what they already owned.

Between them, the house adjusted. He tightened. She reshaped. What could be repaired was repaired. What could be made to last, did. And without naming it, they were already doing what they would continue to do, meeting change not with fear, but with skill.

One evening, William folded her coat where she had left it over the back of a chair, smoothing the sleeve she always caught on the doorframe. He brushed a trace of soil from the hem of her skirt without comment. Once, noticing the thinning at the elbow of her sweater, he set it aside where she would find it in the morning, ready for her careful hands.

They did not speak of these exchanges. Each understood the other's work. Care, they had learned, did not require naming to be real.

William lingered one evening, repairing a loose hinge on the back door that had worked just fine the day before. Florence recognized the impulse.

"You'll wear the screwdriver down before the hinge," she said gently.

He smiled at that, a brief flash of relief. "Just making sure it holds."

"It does," she said. "It has."

Over the following weeks, some envelopes were lighter. Some heavier. None were predictable. Florence responded by tightening the margins the way she had learned to tighten jars, firmly, without cracking the glass.

William watched her ladle the soup, careful to give each bowl the same portion.

"You always make it look like enough," he said.

Florence smiled faintly. "It is enough."

"It doesn't always feel that way."

"It doesn't have to," she replied. "On the farm, we learned that food stretches when it's treated properly. Waste is what makes scarcity loud."

He studied her hands, steady, practiced. "You never seem worried."

"I was trained," she said. "Long before this."

Meat stretched into soup. Soup into stew. Leftovers reappeared with new names. She altered recipes quietly, confident that nourishment depended more on care than quantity. The children did not notice. William did, and he said nothing.

When money tightened, Florence planted instead. Lettuce went in close together. Beans were trained upward along string William salvaged from a crate. She believed growth, like savings, responded to attention.

The Amish farm, where she had lived most of her childhood, had taught her that nothing was wasted, not flour, not time, not sorrow. Work was done before it was needed. Wood stacked before winter. Jars filled before frost. You prepared while the sun was still warm.

At night, Florence lay awake long enough to listen to the house settle. Pipes cooled. Wood shifted. The home held, even as pressures changed within it. She took comfort in that.

There had been years she did not understand while living them, disciplines that felt excessive, watchfulness that felt severe. Only now did she see their shape. She had been formed in steadiness long before steadiness was required of her.

For such days as these, perhaps.

She did not imagine herself chosen. Only positioned. Placed where she could tend what was given her without spectacle.

She understood now what the pantry had taught her the day before: security was not the absence of uncertainty. It was the ability to meet it without letting it spread. Some things, she knew, would arrive whether she invited them or not.

The letter arrived folded twice, its paper thicker than most, the address written in a hand Florence would have recognized anywhere.

She did not open it right away. She set it beside the breadbox, washed her hands, then returned and broke the seal carefully.

Her foster mother, Sara Blank, known as *Mamm*, wrote of ordinary things, weather, the early frost, a calf born strong and loud before dawn. She asked after the children. She reminded Florence that the spare room was still there, just as it always had been.

Florence read it once, then again.

When she finished, she reached into the cupboard above the stove and drew out the small handwritten recipe book Mamm had given her after she married William, nearly a decade ago. Its pages were softened by use, corners curled, margins darkened by spills and drips that marked meals remembered more than measured.

She flipped through it the way one greeted an old friend,

pausing at recipes that had become fixtures in her own kitchen, food now tied to her children's voices and William's chair at the table.

Her fingers rested on a page stained faintly with broth.

Suddenly she was small again—boots damp from snow, cheeks burning from cold. The kitchen door opening. Heat rushing forward. Mamm Sara standing at the stove, apron dusted with flour, steam rising around her like a blessing. The smell of onions in butter. Bread already set to rise. No questions asked before a bowl was pressed into her hands.

She had known two worlds.

The first, brief and broken, city noise, sharp edges, voices that did not stay.

The second, quieter. Ordered. A farm where work began before dawn and ended when it was done. Where she had been taken in at five and grown through her tallest years beneath a different roof. Where silence was not emptiness, but discipline.

For a moment, she was back there. For a moment, she wanted to be.

She lifted the book briefly to her face, as if scent might rise from the pages, the imagined warmth of broth, dough bubbling patiently, onions softening in butter.

Those were the years that shaped her hands. Five to seventeen. The years when steadiness was not discussed, only practiced. She drew on them now without effort, as though they had been stored for a season she had not yet understood.

That night, she slid the letter back into its envelope and placed it beneath the others, for another time when she could return to it.

Some places, she knew, remained steady no matter how the world shifted.

William's envelope would arrive again next week. She did not know what it would contain.

But she knew where it would go.

And she knew, now, where she might need to go herself.

CHAPTER FOUR — THE ROAD TO LANCASTER

The road to Lancaster always slowed Florence down.

Not because of traffic, but because of the way the land opened, fields stretching wide enough to loosen a breath she hadn't realized she was holding. The city released its grip mile by mile. Brick gave way to hedgerows. Noise thinned. Even the air seemed to settle differently, as if it had learned patience from the soil itself.

Florence packed carefully. A picnic basket with sandwiches wrapped in wax paper. A jar of pickles sealed tight. Bread tucked into a cloth to keep it from drying out. She believed that traveling well depended less on what you brought than how thoughtfully you contained it.

The children leaned against the car doors, counting cows, then fences, then red barns that appeared just long enough to be named before slipping behind them again. William drove steadily, his hands relaxed on the wheel in a way Florence rarely saw in town. Here, even movement felt unhurried.

"Did you come this way when you were little?" Dean asked, squinting at a windmill as it turned slowly against the sky.

Florence smiled faintly. "Not quite this way."

"How then?" Bill pressed.

"By train," she said. "I remember the sound more than the sight. Wheels against the track. Smoke drifting past the window. Everything moving too fast to hold onto."

"You came alone?" Bill asked from the back.

"For the last part," she answered gently. "There was a woman who walked me from the station. I had a small sack. It felt heavier than it was."

The children fell quiet for a moment, imagining it.

"Was it scary?" Dean asked.

She considered the question. “It was certain,” she said at last. “And I was small.”

She turned her gaze toward the fields moving past them now—ordered rows, fences set straight, barns standing where they had always stood.

“I did not know then,” she continued softly, “that I would ever return by choice.”

The automobile carried them forward without smoke or soot, without the clatter that once marked the edge of her childhood. No one was taking her now. No one was deciding for her.

Bill leaned forward between the seats. “I like coming this way,” he declared.

“So do I,” she replied.

The fields did not rush past her anymore.

They opened.

After a long stretch of road, William lifted one hand from the wheel and let it rest loosely between them, as though the car itself knew the way. Florence noticed at once. She reached across the narrow space and laid her hand over his, her thumb fitting easily where it had learned to belong. Their eyes met, just briefly, but it was enough. A quiet smile passed between them, shared and certain, as if they were already there.

“Is this the farm?” Bill asked, already half-turned in his seat.

“Not yet,” William said, giving Florence’s hand a gentle squeeze. “But we’re close.”

Dean pressed his nose to the glass. “I see the red barn again.”

“That means we turn soon,” William said.

A moment later Bill wrinkled his nose. “What’s that smell?”

Dean pulled back from the window. “It smells like ... something died.”

William’s mouth twitched. “Nothing’s died.”

“It smells worse,” Bill insisted.

Florence laughed softly. "That's manure."

"For what?" Dean asked.

"For the fields," she said. "It helps things grow."

Bill leaned toward his brother. "You smell like that after baseball."

"I do not."

"You do too."

From the back seat, Gerry fussed.

Florence smiled, her gaze still on the fields.

William returned both hands to the wheel as the road curved, carrying them the rest of the way.

When they arrived, the farm received them without ceremony.

Amos Blank stood near the barn, his posture easy, as if the land itself had shaped him that way. He greeted William with a firm handshake, then bent to Bill and Dean, his eyes warm and curious.

"Come," he said, already turning. "There's plenty to see."

The boys followed at once. William went with them, listening as Amos pointed out the cows, the condition of the stalls, the way the barn held heat through winter.

Bill kicked at a loose clump of hay, sending it skittering across the packed earth. "It smells different in here," he said.

"That's the animals," Amos told him. "And the work."

Dean reached for the gate latch, lifting and dropping it again just to hear the metal knock. It rang once, clean and hollow, before settling back into place. "This one's heavy."

"It's meant to be," Amos said. "Keeps things where they belong."

The boys trailed behind, boots scuffing, then stopped short when a cow shifted in its stall. The sound of it—slow breath, the scrape of hoof—held them still. They pressed closer to William and pointed. "That one moved."

William rested a hand on Dean's shoulder. "They all do," he said. "Even when you're not watching."

Amos chuckled. "Especially then."

They walked the length of the barn together. Hay dust lifted with each step. Boards creaked. Amos spoke of soil and weather, of fixing what loosened before it failed. William asked questions, practical ones—what held best through frost, how long repairs lasted when done right. The two men moved easily side by side, bound by work that respected order and restraint.

Florence paused at the back porch.

The screen door opened and closed behind her, and she stepped into the kitchen she had carried with her all these years without knowing it. Bread baked in the oven. A roast rested, patient and fragrant. On the counter, a shoofly pie cooled—its dark, glossy center holding beneath a thick crumb topping, sugar and butter pressed just enough to crack at the edges, the wet-bottom molasses rich and familiar now, the kind Florence had learned to love slowly, until it no longer tasted like something new, but like something claimed. The long table stood ready.

Mamm Sara looked up, her face softening the moment she saw Florence. She came forward without hesitation, taking Gerry into her arms as though this had always been the plan.

"I never thought," she said quietly, settling him against her shoulder, "that I would hold your child."

Florence watched, her throat tightening. Mamm Sara had raised her from the age of five, twelve years of steady love and quiet security. This, too, belonged.

"It's as it should be," Florence said.

They sat together at the table, time folding in on itself. Mamm Sara poured coffee, rich and dark, and set out warm sugar cookies she had baked earlier, their tops lightly cracked. Florence breathed in the familiar scents—bread, roast, coffee—and felt the deep rightness of it.

They spoke easily. Of the children. Of the city. Of work. Laughter came gently, unforced. It was as if no years had passed at all.

Gerry shrieked suddenly, sharp with hunger, and both

women laughed.

The screen door opened again, then closed, followed by the pitter-patter of bare feet across the floor. Bill and Dean burst in, flushed and breathless, their stories tumbling over one another.

"They showed us the calves," Bill said.

"And the garden," Dean added. "Grandpa Amos says it's almost time to turn the beds."

The meal came together without instruction. Hands moved where they were needed. A brief, quiet prayer was spoken, and then they ate, plain food, well prepared, shared without hurry.

Bill took his first bite and looked up, surprised. "This tastes like yours," he said, already reaching for another piece.

Florence smiled, the kind that did not ask for praise. "It's the same idea," she said. "Good ingredients. Time."

Dean nodded seriously. "It's better when it's hot," he added, as if this were something worth remembering.

The shoofly pie was cut last. The knife sank easily through the crumb topping, the center yielding dark and soft beneath. When the slices were lifted, the molasses clung, slow and generous.

"That's the best part," Dean said. "The gooey."

Gerry grinned, sticky-fingered and pleased. William watched them, content to let the moment hold.

Florence tasted it too, familiar now in a way that surprised her. She understood then that food carried more than hunger. It carried place. It carried care.

Afterward, with hearts full and voices softened, William glanced at the light outside. "We should be heading back."

The children ran once more to the old oak at the edge of the yard, racing each other as Florence once had, touching its trunk as if to take something with them.

Florence lingered behind.

Beyond the fence line, across the low stretch of field, she could just make out the Weaver house—white siding dulled by sun, smoke rising faintly from its chimney. For a moment she saw not the house, but a younger version of herself walking that distance with a tin of saved seeds in hand, Mary Weaver beside her, sleeves rolled, laughter carried by wind. They had traded more than cuttings—calendula for beans, thyme for late asters—passing small paper envelopes back and forth as though exchanging futures.

Mary had pressed a handful of zinnia seeds into her palm the summer before Florence married. *So you'll always have something bright,* she had said.

Florence had planted them the first spring in Haverford.

Mamm Sara followed her gaze without asking why. "Mary's doing well," she said. "Seven children now. They love her flowers as much as she does. Herbs too."

Florence smiled. "I'm glad."

The wind moved lightly across the field, bending what had taken root.

"Bill," William called gently. "Dean. Time."

The boys gave the oak one last touch before running back.

Florence turned from the field and followed her family to the car.

Amos and Sara brought out what they had prepared. Wheat sacks, stitched and sturdy, filled with wrapped cuts of meat. Two wooden crates packed tight with canned goods from the garden—beans, peaches, tomatoes sealed against winter. Florence did not argue. She accepted them as they were meant to be received, with both hands and a quiet nod.

She had learned long ago that refusing generosity was another form of pride. On the farm, giving and receiving were not transactions. They were continuations. What one household spared today, another might supply tomorrow.

There had been seasons when she had stood on the other side of such offerings, small, uncertain, needing what was pressed into her hands before she knew how to ask. She understood now that survival was rarely solitary. It moved through people, quietly, from one table to another.

These were difficult times, yes. But difficulty had never excused withholding. If anything, it clarified what mattered.

On the drive home, the children fell asleep quickly, the day having taken all they could give.

William drove for a time in silence, the weight of the sacks settling the back of the car lower than usual. Then he spoke.

"Amos and I talked," he said. "About the news."

Florence turned slightly, listening.

"There's trouble in Germany. A man rising fast. Dangerous ideas." He paused. "Some Anabaptist communities there —Bruderhof, others—they're already under pressure. Pacifism doesn't leave much room when power wants obedience."

Florence watched the road unfurl ahead of them. "Faith always costs something," she said.

"Yes," William replied. "Amos worries for them. For what happens when conscience won't bend."

She rested her hand briefly against his arm. "It matters that he sees it," she said. "That he names it."

The road carried them home.

The city did not press in immediately. The calm traveled with them, settling into the house. William carried in the sacks two at a time, setting them gently by the pantry wall. Florence unpacked what they had been given, her movements unhurried, jars returned to shelves, meat wrapped and stored, flour sacks folded down and saved. Nothing was wasted. Nothing rushed.

Later, after the children had been washed and settled and the house quieted, Florence set the kettle on once more. She carried two cups into the front room where William waited, his shoes already set neatly by the door.

They sat without speaking at first, the day still warm between them.

"The boys ran that field like it belonged to them," William said at last.

"They did," Florence smiled. "Bill thinks he beat you to the oak."

"I let him."

She laughed softly.

He glanced toward her. "You were quiet out there. By the fence."

Florence wrapped both hands around her cup. "I was thinking of Mary Weaver."

"The one with the flowers?"

"Yes. Mamm says she has seven children now. Still planting. Still saving seeds."

William nodded. "Some people know how to keep things growing."

Florence looked into her tea. "She once told me to plant something bright wherever I land."

He reached for her hand then. "You did."

They sat a little longer, recalling small things—Dean's careful steps through the fields, Gerry's insistence on being held, the way Mamm Sara's kitchen still held the same warmth it always had. The ordinary details felt larger somehow, as though they had carried something home besides leftovers.

Later, in the quiet stillness, she sat at the small desk by the window and took out her paper. The lamp cast a small circle of light, enough for ink and thought. She wrote carefully, thanking Amos and Sara, not only for the food, but for the day, for the steadiness, for what had been shown without being said.

She thanked them for the years that had shaped her hands. For teaching her that work begun early lightened the afternoon. For showing her that family was not declared in grand gestures, but built in repetition, meals shared, tools returned to their place, prayers spoken whether times were lean or full.

She wrote of the children, how they were learning the difference between noise and quiet, between hurry and purpose. She told them she was grateful her children knew them—knew the cadence of their speech, the order of their days, the dignity of labor done without applause.

Hard work, she wrote, was not hardship when it was shared. It was belonging.

She paused before closing, considering what could not quite be written—that the love she had been given there had not ended when she left. It had followed her. It had shaped her marriage, her pantry, her garden rows planted close together against want. It had made the largest difference in the smallest decisions.

She folded the letter with steady hands and slid it into the envelope. For a moment she rested her palm flat against it, as though sealing more than paper. Then she pressed it closed.

The gesture felt different now. A joining of what had shaped her and what was still forming.

She dated the note.

She understood then that steadiness could be learned.

Some places taught you how to endure. Others taught you how to trust.

Florence intended to remember both.

CHAPTER FIVE— WHAT IS NOT SPOKEN

Florence learned early that silence could be shaped.

It was not the same as secrecy. Secrecy hid. Silence protected. There was a difference, and she paid attention to it the way she paid attention to heat on the stove or water nearing a boil. Left unattended, any of it could do harm.

By the end of 1933, the house had learned new rhythms.

Bill was eight now, already tall enough to reach the high shelf if he stretched. Dean followed close behind at six, quick to observe, slower to speak. Gerry, four, still moved through the world as though it were something to be tested by touch. Baby Ron—just past a year—had learned the shape of Florence's days before the others left for school, his weight familiar against her hip as coats were buttoned and lunches set out.

"Hats," Florence called, as the door banged once and then swung back open.

"I've got mine," Bill said, already halfway down the steps.

Dean stopped short and patted his head. "I don't."

Gerry darted past him, boots half-laced. "I forgot my apple."

"You didn't have one yet," Florence said, turning back to the counter. "And slow down, someone's going to trip."

The door opened again. Then closed. Then opened once more.

"My lunch," Bill said, breathless, reaching for the tin.

She handed it over. "And this time, take it with you."

"Yes, ma'am," he said, grinning, and was gone.

The noise thinned as quickly as it had gathered—footsteps fading, voices calling back promises they would forget by noon. Florence stood for a moment, listening until the house settled into its daytime shape.

Ron shifted against her shoulder, heavy with the comfort of routine. She carried him back to the front room and lowered herself into the chair by the window. The light there was gentle, already familiar to him. She rocked once, twice, and began to sing, softly, almost to herself. An old lullaby, barely more than a hum, the kind her Mamm Sara had used when words were too much.

Ron's fingers clung into the fabric of her dress. His breathing slowed.

Florence rested her cheek against his hair and stayed until the morning held. When she finally laid him down, she did so carefully, as if sleep itself were something that could be disturbed by hurry. The house settled again, holding its quiet.

It was in that quiet, when nothing asked of her, that her thoughts moved elsewhere.

The unsent letters remained in a shallow box beneath the bed. They were folded neatly, addressed carefully, sealed but never stamped. Names written once, then not again. Florence did not reread them often. She did not need to. The weight of what they contained was familiar enough.

Atop the stack rested the seed envelope, kept with the same care she gave the letters—dry, dark, undisturbed. Some things were not meant to be handled often. They required patience more than reassurance.

The children did not know the box existed. They knew instead the rhythms of the house, the way mornings began, the order in which coats were hung, the sound of the pantry door closing, firm but not loud. They knew that questions were welcome, but worry was not theirs to carry.

Florence believed children deserved clarity, not burden.

William understood this instinctively. When he came home with news that unsettled him, he measured his words before offering them.

"Hours might be shorter after the holidays," he said one evening, loosening his tie. Not gone. Just shorter.

Florence nodded. "Then we'll adjust."

That was all.

She decided what belonged inside the walls of the house and what did not.

Some evenings, after the children were in bed, Florence sat at the table with a letter unfolded before her. She held the paper steady, read a line or two, then refolded it.

If circumstances change—if work is interrupted or illness intervenes—I am asking only for clarity. I am their mother. I am present. There is food, and there is order, and there is no cause for removal. My children are not neglected. They are not abandoned. They are held.

The words rose uninvited some nights, memory pressing close.

She was five when her own mother had asked for help.

Not because of neglect. Not because of absence of love. But because her father had left, and in 1910 there were few protections for a woman alone with children and no wage of her own.

Charitable societies promised temporary relief. County boards spoke of provisions and oversight. Churches offered lists and ledgers and forms to be filled.

Assistance, they said.

What came instead was separation. Children placed where there was room. Decisions made in offices far from kitchens that still smelled of bread.

Florence did not blame her mother. She never had. She understood now how quickly a woman could be cornered by circumstance, how narrow the margin between keeping and losing could become. But the memory of it, the official language, the tidy signatures, the irreversible parting, had lodged itself deep.

She would not allow that to happen again. Never to her children.

Outside the house, the world spoke loudly. Men argued on street corners. Newspapers announced what they could not yet explain. Rumors traveled faster than facts. Florence absorbed only what was useful. The rest she left where it fell.

Some truths demanded voice.

Others demanded patience.

Florence had learned to tell the difference.

And in a world growing louder by the day, she chose, again and again, to keep what mattered safe by knowing when not to speak.

Ron stirred against her shoulder as she turned out the light, his small hand catching briefly in the fabric of her sleeve, already learning how to hold on.

Outside, December had laid its first clean blanket across the yard. By morning the children pressed their faces to the window, breath clouding the glass, calling out to one another before boots were even tied.

The snow had come early that year.

Dean declared the yard a battlefield before breakfast, packing his first snowball with grave intention. "Stand back," he warned, though he was already laughing.

Gerry insisted the fort required proper walls. Bill took command of construction. Ron toddled through drifts nearly to his knees, falling more than walking, rising again with mittened determination.

William stepped outside long enough to be ambushed, surrendering with theatrical dignity as snow struck his coat. "I see I am outnumbered," he called.

Florence stood at the doorway at first, arms folded against the cold, memorizing the sound of it—shrieks, argument, alliance, forgiveness—all resolved within minutes and begun again.

"Mother!" Bill called. "You're on their side!"

"I'm on no one's side," she answered, chuckling. "Except perhaps the side of order."

That earned her a snowball, loosely thrown and easily dodged.

For a moment she hesitated, some old instinct urging her to remain the watcher, the keeper of thresholds. Then she stepped down from the porch.

The cold surprised her. It bit through the thin sole of her shoe. Snow gave way beneath her weight with a sound she had not heard in years—the soft collapse of something newly fallen.

Dean thrust the wooden sled upright, its runners catching light. "We're taking it to the hill!" he declared.

The boys dragged it past the great oak at the edge of the yard, its branches bare and reaching, dark against the pale sky. Snow clung to its limbs, outlining strength rather than hiding it. The sled left twin lines behind them, two steady tracks pressed into fresh ground.

Florence paused there, just for a breath.

Once, she had stood beneath another oak, watching a world shift beyond her choosing. Now she watched her sons race downhill, their shouts rising bright into winter air.

Dean handed her a small, imperfect snowball. "You must choose a target."

She did.

William never saw it coming.

The children roared as it struck his shoulder. He stared at her in exaggerated disbelief. "Mrs. Adams," he said gravely, "I did not expect treachery."

Florence felt the laughter rise unguarded. Not careful. Not measured. Simply present.

"Christmas is coming," Gerry announced suddenly, as though this explained everything.

"Yes," she said, brushing snow from her gloves. "It is."

Lists had been discussed in whispers for weeks. Nothing extravagant. Another sled to share. New mittens. A book with animals that spoke and journeys that ended safely. Florence had folded brown paper carefully in the drawer, saving string from parcels, setting aside coins the way other women might tuck away lace.

Christmas would not be grand.

But it would be kept.

And when she gathered Ron back into her arms, snow clinging to his coat, she understood something she had not known at the ages of her children: joy, too, could be chosen because inside these walls, and beneath this winter sky, she had made it so.

Survival was rarely dramatic, she knew. It arrived instead through steadiness, through meals prepared, words weighed, fears held in check. By the end of 1933, nothing in her life felt resolved, but much felt secured. The house still stood. The children were fed and growing. Work continued, if unevenly. What had once been taken from her would not be taken again. She had learned how to hold a family together not by force or noise, but by attention, by restraint, by the careful shaping of what was spoken and what was not. The world beyond the door remained uncertain, but inside, something durable had been made—and it would carry them forward into whatever came next.

Christmas came quietly that year. Snow lay clean and shallow along the walk and gathered in the hedges, softening the edges of the street. Small hands flattened against the pane as they peered out, their warm breath fogging the edges.

"It stayed," Bill said, hopeful.

"It always does when it's cold enough," William replied, pulling on his sweater.

Dean was already tugging at his boots. "Can we go out now?"

"After breakfast," Florence said. "And after hats."

Gerry circled the decorated tree, touching each paper chain as if counting them twice. "Did we make this one?" he asked.

"You did," Florence said. "All of it."

The tree was small, trimmed with what they already owned, paper chains the boys had made at the table, a string of dried orange slices tied with twine, their scent still faintly sweet. Florence set out a bowl of apples and nuts, their colors bright against the worn wood. She roasted a turkey and would stretch it into soup the following day. Bread was baked. The house was warm.

"It smells like Christmas," Dean said solemnly, standing near the stove.

Florence smiled. "It smells like supper."

Breakfast was simple and loud in the way only Christmas breakfast could be, toast torn too quickly, jam passed twice, chairs shifting before plates were fully cleared.

"Boots," Florence reminded them, though they were already halfway to the door.

The yard received them in bright, brittle light. Snow packed firm beneath their heels. The sled made its first triumphant run before William had even fastened his coat. Laughter carried clean across the white lawn, startling a pair of sparrows from the oak.

They ran until their breath came in visible bursts, until mittens grew damp and cheeks burned red with cold. Dean insisted on one final race to the fence. Bill declared himself undefeated. Gerry fell twice and rose both times without complaint.

"Inside," their mother finally called, though she was smiling as she said it. "Warm yourselves before you freeze solid."

They returned in staggered procession, boots thudding against the mat, scarves unwound, fingers held toward the stove. The house closed around them again, holding the warmth they had left behind.

William rubbed his hands together briskly. "I believe there is unfinished business beneath that tree."

Florence smoothed her apron, glancing once at the small pile of carefully wrapped parcels. "Then let us proceed properly," she said.

They opened their gifts slowly, as Florence had insisted, one at a time so nothing was missed. A book for Bill, who opened it carefully and read the first line aloud before looking up. A small wooden truck for Dean, who rolled it across the floor and back again, testing its sound. A scarf Florence had knitted for Gerry, who wrapped it once around his neck and then abandoned it for the ribbon, which he snapped between his fingers like a prize.

Baby Ron clapped at the paper and laughed, delighted by the sound of it tearing. He banged two scraps together, certain this was the best part of all.

The boys barely heard her at first. Paper still rustled. Ribbon snapped. Dean made the wooden truck climb the leg of the sofa as though it were a mountain pass.

But the scent reached them all the same, rich and steady, rising from the kitchen in patient waves. Butter warming. Herbs releasing their fragrance. The quiet promise of something tended carefully for hours.

William rose first. "Your mother has called us to the table," he said lightly, lifting Ron from the floor before the baby could taste another scrap of wrapping.

The gifts were gathered, as Florence tied ribbons into a small pile to save. The book was set aside carefully. The truck was carried to the table to be admired again later.

They washed hands at the basin, one after another, water cooling quickly in winter air. Chairs scraped gently into place. The room settled.

After the meal, the plates sat emptied in honest satisfaction. The turkey, roasted and seasoned the way Mamm Sara had shown her during their recent visit to the farm, had filled the house with a familiar fragrance long before it reached the table. Florence had followed the instructions carefully: butter beneath the skin, herbs tucked inside, slow turning for even browning.

The boys declared it the finest they had ever tasted.

"It's the farm way," Florence said, smiling.

They worked together afterward without complaint. Dean carried plates. Gerry gathered silver. Bill insisted on drying, though his towel left faint streaks behind. Even Ron toddled between them with solemn purpose, delivering nothing in particular.

Order restored itself in small motions.

When the kitchen was set right again, they moved into the front room, the tree steady in its stand, its modest ornaments catching lamplight. William settled at the piano bench, testing a chord as though asking permission of the room.

"What shall it be?" he asked.

"'Silent Night,'" Gerry answered at once.

"No, the marching one!" Dean objected.

"One at a time," Florence said, settling into her chair.

William obliged them all. Hymns first. Then a lively tune that sent the boys tapping heels against the rug. A bit of something playful from his theater days, slipped in just to make them laugh. The room filled not with grandeur but with sound layered upon sound, familiar, requested, known.

Florence watched the boys stretched on the floor, heads tipped back toward the ceiling as if the music might gather there. The tree held its place. The fire kept its quiet work. No one was counting what was missing. No one was being measured or recorded. No decisions were being made beyond the choosing of the next song.

She felt the difference without naming it.

Outside, the oak stood outlined in white, its branches holding snow the way hands hold memory.

Later, when the room had quieted and the snow beyond the window had begun to glow blue with late afternoon light, Ron fell asleep against his father's chest. William did not move.

Florence stood back for a moment, taking in the room, the boys on the floor, the tree holding, the simple order of things. Celebration, she understood, was not about what arrived. It was about what remained.

William looked up at her, his voice low so as not to wake the baby.

It's enough," he said.

Florence nodded. She had never believed otherwise.

After Christmas, Florence noticed how the newspapers sounded different. Less braced. Less careful. As though the year, having given what it would, had finally exhaled.

They kept returning to the same date—December fifth—printed plainly, almost insistently, as if a day alone could steady a country. Prohibition was over.

She remembered that evening clearly.

William had come home with a looseness in his shoulders she recognized at once, the kind that arrived only when something long carried had finally been set down.

"It's done," he had said. "Really done."

She had set another place at the table without comment. Change, Florence knew, did not require celebration to be real.

The end of Prohibition had reached her house in small signs, in steadier pay envelopes, in conversations no longer dropped to a whisper, in the sense that the danger had eased, even if its memory had not.

William was no longer needed where doors stayed locked and music played low behind drawn curtains. The men who had once required discretion now required licenses. What had been hidden stepped into storefront windows. Work shifted. Hours changed. The city exhaled unevenly.

He did not speak much about that season closing. Florence did not ask. Some chapters were best folded rather than reread.

But she noticed new things.

He lingered longer at the small workbench near the kitchen stove. He brought home discarded engine parts once meant for repair and instead took them apart simply to understand them. Springs. Casings. Cylinders. He turned metal over in his hands the way other men might turn a coin, measuring weight, testing balance.

"It's the motion of it," he said one evening, almost to himself. "Up and down. Contained power. If it could run cleaner ... steadier ..."

Florence did not fully understand what he meant. She did

not need to. She had learned by then that when William grew quiet in this particular way, something was forming. All part of the design process.

She did not explain any of this to the children. They did not need to know what had ended, only that supper arrived on time. That voices stayed calm. That the house remained a place where the outside world was filtered before it crossed the threshold.

At night, she lay awake long enough to take inventory.

Had anyone gone hungry? No. Had fear been allowed to roam unchecked? No.

Beside her, William's hands, once occupied by keeping other men's secrets, now rested empty for a moment, as if waiting to build something worthy of daylight.

She rested one hand over her abdomen without thinking, the habit of motherhood already shaping what came next. There would be another child. She felt that certainty settle quietly, the way other truths had, without announcement or doubt.

When she finally slept, it was without dread.

PART II — ROOTS AND RECKONINGS (1933–1938)

CHAPTER SIX — THE WORK OF HANDS

William learned early that ideas required shelter. Not every notion deserved immediate exposure. Some needed to be handled, tested, and returned to their place until they proved they could survive more than hope. His work lived first in drawers, sketches folded and refolded, measurements penciled lightly enough to be erased, revisions stacked rather than discarded.

Florence understood this without explanation. Timing mattered. She had lived long enough to know that forcing a thing forward could damage it beyond repair.

When he converted one bay of the garage into a drafting space, she did not mark the change as an event. It was simply an adjustment to the way their lives already worked. A table arrived. Then shelves. Toolboxes were arranged, rearranged, and finally left alone.

She watched him one evening as he stood over the table, sleeves rolled, pencil resting behind his ear.

"You're not just fixing engines anymore," she said.

"No," William answered after a moment. "I'm trying to understand them."

She nodded. "That's different."

"It feels necessary," he said. "If work thins again ... I don't want to be waiting for it to come back."

Florence leaned against the doorframe. "There are courses," she said casually. "Mail-away ones. I saw an advertisement in the paper. Chicago. Engineering."

He glanced up. "That's a long way off."

"The lessons aren't," she replied. "They come to you. You work when you can. You keep what you learn."

He considered this, the way he considered everything—by turning it over slowly. "It would mean evenings. After the boys are down."

"We already live that way."

William nodded once. Not agreement yet—recognition.

Florence felt it then, the way she felt other things before they arrived. The seed had already been planted. What followed would take time and tending, but it would be welcome. Some work began long before it showed itself.

And sometimes, she thought, it arrived all at once.

The house had shifted its rhythm in recent days. Voices lowered themselves without being asked. Footsteps slowed near the bedroom door. Even the older boys, usually restless as wind, seemed to move with a new awareness.

In her arms, wrapped tight in soft cotton, lay their fifth son, Dale.

His weight was small but certain, a warmth against her that felt both fragile and enduring. His breaths came in uneven sighs, each one a quiet insistence on staying. A new pulse within the walls of the house.

William stood beside the bed, not speaking at first. He had always met new life with a kind of reverence, as though entering a workshop already in motion.

"Five," he said finally, almost to himself.

Florence smiled faintly. "Five."

He traced one careful finger along the curve of the baby's hand. Dale's fingers closed around it instinctively, firm, unyielding, unaware of the strength he already possessed.

"Strong grip," William murmured.

"Strong will," Florence replied, her voice soft but certain.

Outside the bedroom, the boys whispered in uneven turns, waiting for permission to enter. The house felt fuller, expanded in a way that made room for what had not yet been imagined.

Florence looked down at the sleeping child and felt again that quiet knowing. Seeds did not ask permission before growing. They simply took root and reached toward whatever light was offered.

"He's found his place already," she murmured, her voice scarcely more than breath.

William, seated close beside her, leaned in, his gaze moving from the child to her face. "So have you," he said gently.

She gave the smallest shake of her head, a soft smile following. "No ... I'm still learning where the light falls."

His hand settled over hers, careful not to disturb the baby. "You've been finding it all along."

From the doorway came a quiet shuffle, shoes against wood, the restrained patience of children trying very hard to be still.

Florence glanced up. "They're waiting."

William turned slightly, his expression warming. "Come on, then," he said softly, beckoning. "He won't run off."

A small cluster gathered near the bed, their curiosity held in check by something like reverence.

"Is he ours?" Gerry whispered, as though the question itself might wake him.

Florence's eyes softened. "Yes," she said. "He is."

William looked down at the baby again, then back to Florence, something unspoken passing between them, gratitude, perhaps, or wonder that had not yet found its words.

"He'll grow fast," he said quietly.

Florence returned her gaze to the baby, her hand resting lightly against his back. "They always do."

William watched as Bill traced his finger along the baby's hand, and the tiny fingers closed around him, instinctive and sure. Then, to his surprise, Dale's eyes opened, as if the world had just come into view, and Bill was the first thing in it.

"Did you see?" Bill whispered, hardly daring to move. "He looked at me."

William watched the small fist remain closed, studying it with the same quiet focus he gave to broken radios and stubborn engines. He was drawn not merely to movement, but to what made movement possible.

His fascination with automobiles had deepened over time. Speed drew his attention first, but it was never what held it. What captivated him were the inner workings, the way power was made to behave, the fragile balance between force and restraint.

In time, that curiosity would lead him toward a partnership neither he nor Florence could yet name, built on shared precision and trust.

The piston design began as an answer to a racing problem. Engines failed not from speed, but from heat, metal giving way under sustained punishment. William worked backward from the failure, rethinking tolerances, shaving weight where it mattered, strengthening what endured stress. He adjusted ring placement. Reshaped the crown. Nothing was tested in haste.

Evenings found him at the table long after the boys were asleep, paper spread carefully, measurements penciled in and erased again. Florence passed behind him, refilling his coffee, never asking how close he was. She understood the difference between effort and arrival.

The sketches stayed in their drawer until the work could answer for itself.

When the time came to take the ideas beyond the house, it did not feel like departure so much as continuation.

The track was already alive when he arrived, engines coughing awake, men shouting over one another, the smell of oil and scorched rubber clinging to the morning air. A few of the smaller race cars looked almost apologetic among the larger machines, bodies dusted with dirt, engines quiet.

William did not linger. Race days were not for persuasion; they were for action. His design idea would wait for another time.

When the flag dropped, the field surged forward. The smaller race cars fell behind early, swallowed by noise and motion. Then the laps began to sort themselves out. Engines strained. One faltered. Another coughed smoke and fell back. Heat rose. RPMs climbed.

The smaller race cars held.

Lap after lap, the engine of one stayed steady where others wavered. No knock. No stutter. It did not lead, but it endured. By the final stretch, the driver pushed harder than planned. The engine answered calmly, crossing the line intact.

Later, as the motor ticked while cooling, a man William did not know leaned in, studying the block.

"That engine should've given up," he said.

William wiped his hands on a rag. "It was built not to."

The man straightened. "You design that piston?"

"I adjusted it," William said.

The man nodded. "Keep at it."

Back in the garage days later, William returned the sketches to their drawer. They no longer felt speculative. They felt earned.

The envelope arrived on an ordinary afternoon.

It was heavier than expected, its paper thick, the return address printed cleanly across the corner. Chicago. William set it on the table and did not open it right away. He washed his hands first, dried them carefully, then returned and slid a finger beneath the flap.

Inside were pages held together with a small brass fastener. Diagrams. Paragraphs dense with instruction. No greeting, no encouragement. Just the work.

Florence watched from the stove, a soft wavy curl slipping loose and resting against her cheek, warmed by the glow of the burner. She brushed it back, her gaze fixed on him.

"That's it?"

William nodded. "Lesson one."

She crossed the room, the hem of her dress whispering against the floor, and leaned beside him, one hand resting lightly on the table. A faint trace of flour still marked her fingers. She glanced at the top page. Terms she recognized only partly. Ratios. Loads. Heat transfer. Nothing decorative. Nothing wasted.

"They don't assume you know much," she said.

"They assume you'll learn," he replied, lifting his eyes just long enough to meet hers, a knowing glance, softened by a small, familiar smile meant only for her.

He returned to the page, pencil already in hand, copying a figure into his notebook before reading on. Florence lingered a moment longer than necessary, watching the way his brow drew slightly in focus, the steady surety of his hand. There was something in it she had come to trust, something that steadied her in return.

"Will it help?"

"It already is," he said, not looking up, though his voice carried a quiet warmth that reached her all the same.

She let her fingers rest briefly at the back of his shoulder, a touch so light it might have been missed, then withdrew.

She smiled and returned to the stove, stirring slowly, her movements unhurried now. The house held its usual sounds, the tick of the clock, a child shifting in the next room, but beneath it, something gentler moved between them, unspoken and certain.

The ordinary continued, steady as breath, while something deeper, rooted in trust, in knowing, quietly grew.

"Tomorrow," William said.

Florence nodded. "That's how it starts."

Two evenings later, after the children had finished their lessons and the house had quieted, Florence noticed the kitchen table was clear.

The lamp still burned, but William was not there.

She found him in the garage workshop, the narrow space warmed by a single hanging bulb and the faint scent of oil and metal. The workbench was crowded now, diagrams weighted with bolts, a small assembly of parts laid out in careful order. Outside, winter pressed against the doors. Inside, something was taking shape.

An envelope lay open near his elbow.

"The piston?" she asked gently from the doorway.

"Yes."

He did not look up at first. He adjusted the measurement, then finally set the caliper down. "It's not finished."

"It doesn't have to be," she said, smiling and stepping closer. "It just has to keep becoming what it's meant for."

He gave a small breath that might have been a laugh.

"Engines change," he said. "But the principles don't. Motion. Compression. Timing. Someday they'll need something smaller. Lighter. Reliable. Something that wastes less."

Florence rested her hand briefly against the edge of the bench, careful not to disturb the order he had made.

"Someday," she said softly, "tends to arrive faster than we expect."

That made him pause.

He folded the paper once, not away, but carefully, and slid it back into the envelope as if returning it to a future he intended to meet.

When he turned out the hanging bulb, the garage did not feel abandoned. It felt paused.

Drawers closed. Tools quiet. Work held safely until it was time again.

He followed her inside.

At the doorway, he closed the distance between them, his hand resting lightly at her back. Not hurried, not asking, only there.

Florence slowed, just enough to lean into it.

"For all your careful plans," she said quietly, "you never rush the important parts."

A faint smile touched his voice. "I've learned where not to."

Upstairs, the house had already begun its quieting, doors closed, lamps dimmed, the last sounds of the day settling into stillness.

When they lay down, he reached for her in the dark, not to take hold, but to be certain of her nearness.

She answered without speaking, turning toward him as she always did.

The fourth lesson arrived thinner than the others, but it took longer.

William sat at the table with the pages spread before him, pencil unmoving. The diagrams made sense in isolation. Together, they resisted. Heat curves intersected where he hadn't expected them to. Stress points appeared where his intuition said they shouldn't.

He turned the page back, then forward again.

"That's not right," he said quietly.

Florence looked up from where she was mending a cuff. "What isn't?"

"The math," he replied. "Or my reading of it."

She did not offer reassurance. She watched instead as he erased a line, redrew it, then pressed the pencil down harder than necessary.

"You've been at that one awhile," she said.

"It shouldn't be this stubborn," he answered. "I've built things more complicated than this."

Florence folded the shirt and set it aside. "Books don't know you," she said. "They don't adjust."

William exhaled, a short sound of impatience. He pushed his chair back and stood, pacing once, then stopping at the window.

"I don't like not understanding," he said.

"I believe that's how learning works," she replied. "It removes what you're good at using."

He returned to the table, reading again, slower this time.

Florence rose without comment and moved through the house. She set the kettle on, not to boil, just to be ready. She lifted Dale from his blanket before he could fuss and carried him into the back room, closing the door softly behind her. When Bill and Dean drifted in with questions, she answered them in whispers and sent them back out with their coats.

"Not now," she said gently. "Your father's working."

When she returned, the table was unchanged. William had not moved, but something in him had settled.

"The problem isn't the equation," he said at last. "It's the assumption."

Florence smiled faintly. "That happens too."

After supper, while she wiped the counters and tucked the leftovers away, William gathered the children into the front room. They followed him eagerly, piling close as he sat at the piano. He began with "Kitten on the Keys," the bright, skittering notes sending the children into fits of laughter. The boys dropped to the floor at once, arching backs and batting at invisible strings, meowing dramatically as William leaned into the play.

Florence smiled when the tune drifted into the kitchen. She finished quickly, drying her hands as she went, and joined them just as the last playful notes faded. She settled into her chair with a book on her lap, ready to read, when William's hands shifted. The room quieted as the opening strains of "Moonlight Sonata" filled the space, slower, steadier, drawing the evening inward.

The boys stilled, leaning against one another, the earlier laughter giving way to calm. Florence did not read. She simply listened, watching the way the music softened the room, how it carried William back toward himself.

He let his hands rest on the keys a moment longer, the last note settling into the corners of the room. Florence caught his eye, smiled once, and gathered the children.

She ushered them upstairs, heard their prayers, smoothed blankets, and pressed her lips to foreheads warm from sleepiness. William remained below, the faint scratch of pencil against paper drifting upward as he worked another hour without speaking.

When Florence returned, she carried two cups of tea.

She set one beside him. "That's enough for today."

He glanced up at her, the lamp casting a soft line across his brow. "Is it?"

"It is," she said gently. "The work will still be there tomorrow. They will still need you steady."

"And you?" he asked quietly.

She smiled at that. "I have needed you steady for years."

He leaned back slightly, studying her in the way he did when something unspoken had passed between them.

"I used to think," he said, "that providing meant outrunning whatever might come for us."

"And now?"

"Now I think it means staying." His fingers brushed the edge of the lesson pages. "Building something that doesn't disappear when the lights go out."

Florence settled across from him, folding one leg beneath her, the cup warm between her hands.

"You've always stayed," she said. "Even when the world was louder than it should have been."

He shook his head faintly. "Not always gracefully."

"Grace is overrated," she replied. "Consistency is better."

That drew the smallest smile from him.

They drank without hurry, wrapped in the soft hum of the house settling for the night — pipes ticking, floorboards easing, children turning in sleep. It was a private stillness, the kind earned through years of work, children, uncertainty weathered and set aside.

When the cups were empty, William reached for her hand.

"Ready?" he asked.

She squeezed once. "Always."

Together they rose, leaving the room as it was, lamp dimmed, papers stacked, piano closed, ready for morning.

CHAPTER SEVEN — THE PARTNER

William did not choose a partner lightly. Ideas could be stored in drawers; people required stronger containers. Trust, once mishandled, was difficult to retrieve intact.

He met Isaac Rosenfeld through careful introductions—names offered once, never repeated. Isaac was precise in speech and deliberate in movement, a man accustomed to weighing not only opportunity but consequence. He understood how quickly attention could shift, how success could invite scrutiny long before it brought security.

Their meetings were modest. Coffee cooled untouched. Sketches were shared selectively, turned just enough to be understood. Isaac asked questions William did not expect. Not how fast something could go, but how long it could last.

"What happens," Isaac asked once, "when materials are scarce?"

William considered. "You adjust."

"And when fuel is inconsistent?"

"You build for tolerance."

Isaac nodded. "And when reliability matters more than performance?"

"Then you stop chasing praise," William said, "and build something that finishes."

Contracts followed slowly. Drafts were written, folded, set aside. Certain clauses were softened. Others left deliberately narrow. The final folder rested on William's desk, heavier than it should have been, considering it held no signed pages at all.

January of 1935 arrived sharp and iron-cold, the Schuylkill rimmed with frost and the city's breath visible in the early morning air. The Depression had not loosened its grip, but neither had it extinguished the Greater Philadelphia area's appetite for spectacle.

The Philadelphia Auto Show that year opened with drama. Streamlined fenders curved like sculpture. Headlamps gleamed beneath polished visors. Grilles rose tall and deliberate, inspired by the sleek pull of trains and the promise of speed. Even in the depths of winter—and deeper still in the shadow of the Depression—the exhibition pulsed with Art Deco confidence. Chrome lines were sharp, geometric. Signage arched in metallic lettering. Showgirls in arranged gowns stood beside luxury sedans as orchestra music filtered through the rafters.

For a moment, William forgot the thin profit margins, the careful accounting, the slow climb of their young engineering venture.

He paused just inside the entrance.

"Would you look at that," he murmured.

Isaac Rosenfeld adjusted his gloves, eyes already scanning with purpose. "They're not just selling cars," he said. "They're selling the future."

They approached a Ford display where a representative extended his hand.

"Adams & Rosenfeld Engineering," Isaac said evenly.

The man's grip tightened a fraction at the surname, his smile cooling just slightly. "Adams," he replied, eyes flicking briefly past Isaac before returning. "And ... Mr. Rosenfeld."

Isaac did not shift. His voice remained steady. "We've developed a piston modification that reduces heat stress under prolonged load. Particularly valuable in commercial fleets."

The representative hesitated only a breath before business reclaimed him. "Efficiency's what everyone's after."

"Yes," Isaac replied. "Efficiency is what keeps a company standing."

William spoke next, deliberately linking their work. "We've tested the durability under extreme compression. We'd welcome a technical review."

It was subtle, the moment. Nearly invisible. But William felt it—and so did Isaac. They moved forward together, not past it.

The crowd thickened as the afternoon wore on. Families pressed close to view luxury sedans they could not afford. Boys traced fingers along the curve of a fender. Women peered inside practical family vehicles, measuring space and possibility. William stepped aside to allow a family through—father guiding, mother steadying a small boy eager to touch the chrome.

That was when he saw him.

Across the polished floor, near a display of architectural renderings for a future showroom design, stood Artem.

The same composed posture. The same stillness amid motion.

For a moment, neither man moved. Then Artem inclined his head slightly, not surprise, not performance. Recognition.

William returned the nod.

No words were exchanged. None were needed. The orchestra intensified overhead. The crowd pressed and shifted. Yet both men stood untouched by its urgency.

Isaac followed William's line of sight. "Friend of yours?"

"Designer," William replied quietly. "He understands thresholds."

Artem gestured toward the curved exhibit walls, subtle angles guiding visitors from one manufacturer's display to the next without bottleneck or confusion. The arrangement felt effortless. It was anything but.

William watched how the crowd flowed. No one seemed directed, yet everyone moved where intended.

"You never push people," Artem had once said. "You let the space decide for them."

William felt the truth of it again here, not only in rooms, but in industry. In partnership. In fatherhood. In a nation clawing forward through hardship.

A salesman nearby raised his voice to draw attention to a feature. The pitch fell flat.

The crowd, William noticed, preferred invitation to insistence.

Artem's gaze returned to him briefly. A shared understanding passed between them, that design, whether of steel or of walls, required restraint as much as innovation.

Then the moment dissolved.

A group stepped between them. When the space cleared, Artem had moved on, absorbed into the architecture he admired.

William turned back to Isaac. "This is the future," he said.

Isaac studied the sweeping arrangement of exhibits, the orchestrated movement. "Yes," he replied. "And the wise ones will build it without forcing it."

William thought of Florence at home, of children growing, of bills folded neatly in a drawer. He thought of the way she believed in steadiness. Innovation, he realized, was another form of steadiness. It was refusing to remain where hardship insisted you stay.

Above the men, the vast ceiling of Convention Hall arched like the hull of an enormous ship. For a fleeting second, William imagined the building itself as a vessel carrying the city forward. Cars were no longer novelties. They were symbols—of freedom, of movement, of leaving behind what had once held you still.

At one exhibit, a display board illustrated engine components under magnified diagrams—pistons cut away to reveal internal movement.

William lingered. "Stronger alloys," he murmured. "Lighter weight."

Isaac studied the illustration longer than necessary. "If Europe continues its unrest," he said quietly, almost to himself, "industry will not remain civilian forever."

William looked at him. "You think it will come to that?"

Isaac's jaw set just slightly. "History rarely moves backward."

For a fleeting moment, the bright hall seemed less theatrical. The polished chrome reflected something sharper, a future not yet named.

They made their introductions carefully, business cards exchanged, hands clasped firmly. Manufacturers were listening now to men who could improve efficiency without extravagance. The Depression had thinned confidence, but it had sharpened ingenuity.

By late afternoon, Isaac gathered a stack of pamphlets and technical sheets. William tucked one aside, a glossy brochure featuring a streamlined sedan illustrated in bold Deco lines.

"For the boys?" Isaac asked, noticing.

"Yes," William replied with a smile. "They will like the drawings."

"And Ron will chew the corners," Isaac said.

William laughed. "Probably. Anything to get it away from his little brother, Dale."

When they stepped back into the cold evening air, their pockets held more than pamphlets. They carried names. Meetings to follow. Possibilities.

The wind bit at William's collar, but his stride had lengthened.

"Well?" Isaac asked.

William looked once more at the illuminated facade of Convention Hall behind them.

"They're building the next decade in there," he said.

Isaac nodded. "Then we'd best make sure our work is part of it."

They walked toward the train station, breath rising in pale clouds, the city lights flickering against the frozen streets, two partners moving through winter with the firm belief that spring would come.

Florence had just set the kettle when the door opened and winter followed William inside.

"You're late," she said gently, helping him from his coat.

"Worth it," he replied.

He gathered the children into the front room, producing the brochure like a magician revealing a prize.

Bill and Dean dropped to their knees at once. Gerry leaned in close. Ron tried to turn the pages faster than the others allowed.

Dale toddled determinedly into the circle, unsteady but resolute, one hand still clutching the wooden block he had refused to part with all evening. He lowered himself with great seriousness beside his brothers, though he immediately leaned too far and tipped gently into Bill's shoulder.

"I see," Bill announced importantly, though he clearly did not.

Dale reached out and patted the glossy page with his open palm, then looked up at his dad as if awaiting confirmation that he, too, understood something vital about pistons and chrome.

"That's right," William said solemnly. "You're inspecting the workmanship."

Dale beamed at being included, then attempted to grab the corner of the brochure and chew it.

"Careful," Florence laughed softly, rescuing the page. "Engineers do not eat their designs."

Gerry shifted slightly to make room, and Ron reluctantly slowed his page turning. Dale settled back onto his diapered bottom, swaying a little as he studied the pictures upside down.

He did not know about horsepower or aerodynamics. He knew only that his brothers were intent, his father was speaking, and something important was being shared.

That was enough.

William glanced around the circle, boys shoulder to shoulder, one barely steady on his feet, and for a brief moment, the future did not feel abstract. It felt seated directly in front of him.

"It looks like it's moving even standing still," she said.

"That's the idea," he answered.

Laughter filled the room.

Florence watched from her chair, noting the way William

explained airflow and compression as though speaking of something alive. The children listened with a reverence usually reserved for bedtime stories.

Later, when the house quieted and the brochure lay folded carefully on the side table, Florence found William standing by the window.

"You see something in it," she said softly.

"I see what comes next," he replied.

She slipped her hand into his.

Neither of them could yet know how completely those engines would matter, how factories would one day shift from elegance to endurance, how pistons and steel would be counted not in sales but in service. But something had shifted that evening. Not hope exactly.

Direction.

Outside the realm of work and family, the newspapers grew louder.

Florence read them each morning, folding the pages back to front. Germany appeared more often now, new laws, new rallies, language that spoke of unity while naming who did not belong. She read carefully, alert to what was said plainly and what was implied.

At supper one evening, William mentioned it quietly. "Isaac says his cousin's shop in Frankfurt closed last month. No explanation given."

Florence looked up. "And people?"

"They're leaving if they can," he said. "Waiting if they can't."

She folded her napkin. "Waiting is its own risk."

Across the table, Bill had stopped chewing. "What does that mean?" he asked.

Dean leaned forward. "Why would someone close his shop if he didn't want to?"

William set down his fork. He glanced once at Florence before answering.

"Sometimes," he said evenly, "rules change. And not everyone is given the same protection under those rules."

Bill frowned. "But if it's his shop, can't he just keep it?"

Florence spoke gently. "Ownership only matters when the law agrees with you."

Dean considered this. "So they're making new laws?"

"Yes," William said. "And some of those laws are not fair."

Gerry, quiet until now, looked between them. "Will that happen here?"

The room stilled for a breath.

Florence reached for the bread basket, passing it as she answered. "This country was built differently. We have laws, too. And courts. And elections. When something isn't right, there are ways to speak against it."

William nodded. "And we pay attention. That's important."

Bill absorbed this. "So Isaac's cousin ... he didn't do anything wrong?"

"No," William said. "From what I understand, he did everything right."

Dean's brow tightened. "Then why—"

"Because sometimes," Florence interrupted softly, "when people are scared, they pick someone who says they'll be strong and fix everything. But being strong doesn't always mean being kind."

The boys were quiet.

After a moment, Bill said, "If they're leaving, where do they go?"

"Where they have family," William answered. "Where they can begin again."

Dean looked down at his plate. "That sounds hard."

Florence met his eyes. "It is. But people are more capable than they know."

Gerry, satisfied, returned to his potatoes. Ron pushed his broccoli aside and Dale banged his spoon against the tray of his highchair, unconcerned with international affairs.

The meal resumed its rhythm. Plates were passed. Water poured. The stove kept its steady hum.

Florence had not raised her voice or dramatized what she knew. But she felt the weight of it, the early tremor beneath the surface of the world.

The boys moved on to smaller concerns—whose turn it was to dry dishes, whether snow might come again before week's end. Dale banged his spoon against his tray with satisfied insistence.

Florence listened, but her mind lingered.

She had learned, long ago, how swiftly official words could alter the course of ordinary lives. How decisions made in distant rooms, measured, documented, stamped, could arrive at a kitchen table without warning.

It never began with shouting. It began with language. With assurances. With the careful redrawing of who was protected and who was not.

She rose to clear the plates, steady in her movements. The boys would not carry the weight of what they could not yet shape. That was work for grown hands.

But they would be taught to notice. To listen when language shifted. To measure promises against what they produced.

William caught her eye as he stacked the last dish. No alarm passed between them, only understanding.

The world beyond their door might be unsteady. Inside, vigilance would be quiet. And constant.

Isaac did not speak much of it himself. When he did, it was measured.

"They call it order," he said, eyes on the drafting table. "But order that requires exclusion is never finished. It always needs more."

Isaac's presence in their evenings came easily, without announcement. He and William worked well together, not because they were alike, but because they listened for the same things. Florence noticed it first in the pauses between them, the way a thought could be handed off without being finished aloud.

By early spring, their weeks had found a new rhythm.

On Thursday afternoons, Aunt Mae arrived from the city on the Philadelphia and Western Railroad, known simply as the P&W, stepping down from the Strafford car with her hat pinned firmly and her small leather case tucked beneath one arm.

She was William's aunt, his steady harbor in earlier years, who, with her husband, Uncle Luther, and his modest Philadelphia grocery store, had opened their home to him while he studied at the conservatory, long before Florence entered his life.

A small, petite lady, she carried herself upright, with a quiet, teacherly air that left little room for disorder. She and Luther had no children of their own, and there was in her a gentle, unspoken wish to pass music forward, to place it carefully into willing hands.

The boys knew the schedule as surely as the church bells. They watched for her from the front window, counting the minutes from the train's expected arrival.

"Is she coming today?" Dean would ask, though he already knew the answer.

"She has not missed yet," Florence would reply.

Aunt Mae brought with her the faint scent of coal smoke and city air, along with sheet music folded neatly into her case. She believed in posture and patience. Fingers curved, wrists lifted, no pounding. Even Ron learned to sit quietly when she tapped the metronome into motion.

William hovered at first, offering small corrections or turning pages, but soon surrendered the bench entirely. The house shifted during those lessons—less noise, more intention. Even the oak outside seemed to listen.

Mae stayed the night most weeks, claiming the small guest room without ceremony. "Children need music," she would say, removing her gloves. "And parents need an evening."

Florence did not argue.

On those nights, after lessons were finished and the boys tucked beneath quilts, William and Florence would step out together, sometimes only as far as the corner coffee shop, sometimes into the city itself, walking beneath lamplight as though rediscovering something that had never quite been lost.

Isaac joined them on occasion.

Some nights, the three of them went out together, once to a boxing match, the crowd loud and restless, William intent, Isaac tracking the rhythm of the rounds. Other evenings, they stayed in, chairs drawn closer to the radio as the bouts came crackling through the speakers. Florence did not care for the violence itself, but she understood the discipline of it, the measured rounds, the rules enforced, the bell that ended what force began.

"That bell," William said once, leaning back as the announcer's voice faded, "it's the only thing that keeps it honest."

Isaac nodded. "It's the stopping that matters. Anyone can throw a punch." He glanced toward Florence, looking thoughtful. "Knowing when not to, that's the work."

Florence smiled slightly. "That sounds less like boxing and more like partnership."

Isaac laughed under his breath. "Most things are, if you're paying attention."

William reached for his coffee. "You learn fast who respects the limits," he said. "And who doesn't."

Florence watched them then, not just the words, but the ease between them. The respect was mutual, unspoken, reinforced in small ways: a shared look when something rang true, a quiet correction accepted without offense, a willingness to stop when the moment called for it. She understood why the work held. It wasn't force that bound them, it was restraint.

One evening, Florence suggested to William they go out alone. Their kind neighbor, Dottie, stepped in to care for the children since Aunt Mae was not available. "Coffee," she said. "And cake."

They stood shoulder to shoulder at Horn & Hardart, the automat where they had once shared their first awkward time together, twelve years ago. Coins were placed carefully into the slots, porcelain cups sliding forward with a soft click. Florence liked the honesty of it. You paid. You received. Nothing hidden.

For a moment, she remembered the way he had stood just slightly too straight that first evening, hat in hand, unsure whether to speak or listen. The coffee had tasted the same then, strong, uncomplicated, but everything else had felt entirely new.

Now their shoulders touched without hesitation. The clicks and slides of the machine sounded unchanged, but they were not the same two people who had first stood here.

William watched the mechanism with interest, the precision of it, the way order was built into even the smallest exchange.

"Clear rules," he said. "That's why it works."

"And everyone knows them," Florence replied. "No one's guessing."

They carried their cups to a small marble-topped table near the window. The evening crowd moved in steady rhythm around them, coats buttoned, hats lowered, conversations low and ordinary.

William returned with a single slice of custard pie, the top lightly browned, the center still soft.

"One fork?" she asked.

"We've managed before," he said.

They sat close, shoulders nearly touching, steam rising from their coffee as Florence pressed the fork gently into the pie and lifted the first bite. She tasted vanilla and warmth, something steady and familiar.

William took the next bite, thoughtful.

"No hidden doors," Florence said quietly, glancing around the bright room. "No back entrances."

"No names questioned," he added.

The fork paused between them.

She met his eyes.

"That's what it should be," she said. "Simple. Honest."

William nodded once. "That's what we're trying to build."

She smiled faintly at that, not because it was ambitious, but because it was true.

Outside, the city moved in uneven currents, suspicion here, certainty there, spectacle and warning flickering across screens. But inside this small, well-lit room, coins bought coffee, coffee came forward, and a slice of pie could be shared without calculation.

Florence rested her hand briefly over his. "Then we begin small," she said. "And we keep it clean."

William covered her hand with his.

They finished the pie slowly, as if there were no need to hurry what was already enough.

Afterward, they walked to the theater. Before the feature, a newsreel flickered onto the screen, marching crowds, raised arms, flags carried high. The theater fell unusually still. Then another reel followed, quieter but firm, warning of what such movements demanded once the applause faded, of the cost that followed spectacle.

William watched without speaking, his jaw set, eyes steady.

Finally, the feature film began, and a settling was felt within the walls of the dark space.

Once outside, Florence spoke up. "They're telling the story as if it's already decided."

"Yes," William replied. "And calling it inevitability."

"Nothing is inevitable," she said. "Only unchallenged."

William looked at her then, really looked. "That's what frightens them most," he said. "When someone refuses to accept the ending they're being handed."

They walked a few steps more before he added, quietly, "Isaac refused something awhile back at the auto gathering."

Florence turned toward him. "At the convention?"

He nodded.

"When he introduced himself to the manufacturer's agent, the man smiled at first. Firm handshake. Interested." William's voice remained even. "Then Isaac gave his full name."

Florence said nothing, waiting.

"The smile changed. Not gone. Just ... altered. The questions became different. Who had financed him. Who stood behind him. Whether he had 'proper affiliations.'"

The streetlight caught the tight line of William's mouth.

"As if engineering required pedigree," she said softly.

"As if intelligence needed sponsorship," he replied. "He answered every question plainly. Better than plainly. The man listened, but he no longer heard him."

"And the others?" she asked.

"Some watched. Some pretended not to."

They walked past a storefront window reflecting their movement.

"It was subtle," William continued. "No insult spoken. No door slammed. Just suspicion laid gently across the table like it belonged there."

Florence's expression did not harden; it steadied.

"That's how it begins," she said. "Polite. Reasonable. Measured."

William exhaled slowly. "Isaac didn't flinch. He finished the conversation. Thanked him. Walked away."

"And afterward?"

"He said, 'They fear what they cannot place in a box.' Then he went back to studying the engine models."

Florence absorbed that.

"Will it hurt his work?"

"It may," William said. "But it will not change it."

They walked on in silence, the streetlights stretching their shadows ahead of them, two figures moving forward, alert now, carrying what they had seen with them.

Florence slipped her hand into his.

"Then we build," she said.

"Yes," William answered. "We build."

Knowing it would ask something of them in time.

Once home, Florence thanked Dottie for watching the children. The house was quiet, the kind of quiet that listened back. Before turning in, she and William moved from room to room, pausing at each bedside, small chests rising and falling, dreams intact for now. Neither said what they were thinking, but both understood that what they had seen together would not remain outside the door.

At Dale's room, Florence drew the blanket higher. William rested his hand briefly along the doorframe, watching.

"They sleep as though nothing's changed," he said softly.

"For them, it hasn't," Florence replied, though her voice held something steadier than certainty.

He glanced at her then, not to question it, only to share the knowing.

In the last room, they lingered a moment longer than needed. Florence's hand rested lightly at the edge of the bed before she let it fall.

"They'll need us steady," she said.

"They have us," William answered.

She looked at him then, really looked, and gave the smallest nod.

In the hallway, the light had been left low. William reached past her to turn it down further, then let his hand settle, gentle and unhurried, at her shoulder.

"For tonight," he said quietly.

Florence leaned into the touch, just enough. "For tonight."

He stepped back to let her pass through the bedroom doorway first. She did, and when he followed and closed the door behind them, the house felt held.

That winter had been a long one. Snow fell early and lingered late, gathering in gray ridges along the streets and pressing against the foundation of the house as though reluctant to release its hold. The boys had worn paths through the yard in boots too small by February, their laughter thinner in the brittle air. Even indoors, the cold seemed to settle into the walls.

By March, Florence had begun to wonder if the thaw would ever truly come. Spring did not arrive boldly that year. It crept. It hesitated. It waited its turn.

And then, one evening just after supper, there was a knock at the door.

The boys were still lingering at the table and Dale had begun to grow restless in Florence's lap.

William opened the door to find Isaac standing on the step, hat in hand, a narrow parcel wrapped in white cloth balanced carefully against his coat.

"I won't stay," he said. "It is Passover this week. I thought ..." He hesitated only slightly. "I thought I might share a little of it."

Florence moved forward at once. "Please, come in."

Isaac removed his hat and stepped inside, bringing with him the cool air of early spring. From the cloth he revealed a small plate—plain, not ornate. Upon it lay three pieces of flatbread, pale and rigid, and a small glass dish of something dark and finely chopped.

"Matzah," he said, almost apologetically. "And charoset."

The boys had gathered by then. Bill reached out, but Florence steadied his wrist gently. "We wait," she murmured.

Isaac's expression softened at that. "It is the bread of haste," he explained simply. "Made without time to rise."

He did not elaborate further. He did not need to.

Florence invited him to sit. The children watched as Isaac broke one piece cleanly in half. The sound was dry and definite in the quiet kitchen. He handed portions first to the boys, then to William, then to Florence.

"It reminds us," he said, not instructing, only stating, "that freedom can arrive suddenly. And that we must remember it."

The charoset was sweet against the stark plainness of the bread. Its dark-colored mixture of finely chopped fruits and nuts was eaten at Passover, symbolic of the mud used to make adobe bricks during the Israelites' enslavement in ancient Egypt. Gerry made a small face at the dryness; Dean chewed thoughtfully; Ron asked if people truly left in a hurry.

Isaac nodded. "Yes."

Dale, determined not to be left out, gnawed his softened piece with solemn intensity, crumbs collecting on his collar.

William leaned back slightly in his chair. "Thank you," he said, not for the food, but for something else.

Isaac rose soon after. He would not intrude upon their evening. At the door, he paused only long enough to add, "It is a story told each year. So it will not be forgotten."

After he left, Florence gathered the small remaining fragments of matzah and wrapped them carefully again in the cloth.

She did not know all the words Isaac might have spoken had he stayed longer.

But she understood the instinct to keep a story alive by placing it into the hands of children.

Later that night, as she turned out the kitchen light, she thought of bread that did not rise.

And of faith that did.

In the days that followed, the house returned to its usual rhythms—schoolbooks spread across the table, laundry folded warm from the line, drafts and measurements accumulating in the garage. The first inquiry arrived not long after, as if the question itself had been listening. The letter was carefully worded, curious without urgency, complimentary without commitment. It referenced performance under sustained stress and applications beyond competition environments. No department was named, but the implication was clear enough: their work was being noticed, and might be taken up for purposes they would not be allowed to question.

But Florence noticed the letter where it lay, open but unanswered. She said nothing.

That evening, the men sat in the garage, the drafting table

between them. Isaac read the letter once, then folded it along its original crease.

"They're not asking yet," he said. "They're measuring."

"Me?" William asked.

"The work," Isaac replied. "And what it might be turned into."

William leaned back. "It's a racing piston."

"Today," Isaac said quietly. "They'll start with small adaptations. Then urgency. Then requests that sound reasonable until they aren't."

The word lingered between them.

Urgency.

Florence, passing through with a basket of mending, paused just inside the doorway. She thought of flatbread broken cleanly in half. Of leaving in haste. Of stories told so that fear would not rewrite them.

Isaac tapped the desk once. "You don't have to refuse. Just don't hurry. Let them put it plainly on paper."

Florence entered then, straightening a stack of sketches, closing a drawer left ajar. From a shallow tray of unassigned parts, she lifted an empty envelope and placed it beside the contract folder.

"For whatever doesn't belong together," she said.

Isaac smiled at that, not broadly, but with recognition.

He stayed a moment longer than usual.

William had begun returning tools to their places when he noticed Isaac still seated, hands folded loosely, gaze resting on the closed desk.

"You all right?" William asked.

Isaac nodded. Then paused. "My sister writes less often now."

William waited.

"She says it's easier that way," Isaac continued. "Safer. Fewer details."

Florence, moving past the doorway, slowed without stopping.

"They think silence protects," Isaac said. "Sometimes it does. Sometimes it only delays the question."

Florence met his eyes then. "Silence has its uses," she said. "But it should never belong to fear."

Isaac smiled faintly. "You understand that."

She nodded once. "I had to learn it young."

Isaac rose, buttoning his coat. "If the work ever puts you in a position you can't step back from," he said to William, "promise me you'll say so plainly."

William answered without hesitation. "I will."

Isaac opened the door, then turned back. "That's why this works," he said. "Not the design. The pause."

When he left, Florence closed the door carefully behind him. "He carries more than he shows," she said.

William nodded. "He always has."

"And that's why," she replied, "he chooses his containers well."

Later, alone, William opened the folder again. He slid certain pages into the envelope and locked the desk. The folder remained empty by design, holding possibility, not obligation.

Outside, the world continued to announce itself loudly.

Inside, the work stayed contained. For now, that was enough.

Easter morning arrived pale and cool, the light filtering softly through the curtains before the children stirred.

Florence had risen early. The eggs had been boiled the night before, their shells now tinted in muted shades—pale blue, soft yellow, a faint rose coaxed from diluted dye and patience. Nothing extravagant. Just enough color to mark the day.

She arranged them in simple woven baskets lined with newspaper and a square of white cloth. Outside, the grass still held the damp of dawn.

By the time the boys tumbled downstairs, collars half-fastened and hair slicked hurriedly into place, William was already standing at the back door, surveying the yard as though inspecting sacred ground.

"No running until I say," he warned, though a smile betrayed him.

Dale clutched the railing and bounced in place, determined to keep up with brothers twice his speed.

Florence stepped onto the porch. The air smelled faintly of turned earth and early tulips pressing through the beds along the walkway.

"All right," William said at last.

They scattered.

Bill headed first toward the lilac bushes. Dean crouched low near the stone edging. Gerry checked beneath the bench as though certain he would outthink his brothers. Ron moved more methodically, eyes scanning carefully.

Dale toddled toward the nearest visible egg and claimed it with solemn triumph.

Florence watched from the porch, her hands folded loosely at her waist.

The shells caught the morning light, small, bright interruptions against brown grass and bare soil.

For a moment, she thought of the week before. Of flat bread broken cleanly. Of a story told at a narrow table under the kitchen light. Of Isaac's voice steady, deliberate, remembering.

Here, too, a story was being told. Not in Hebrew. Not from a worn book. But in color and laughter and the careful hiding of hope in unlikely places.

William stepped beside her. "Seems unfair," he murmured, watching Ron hand Dale an egg he had nearly missed.

"What does?"

"That something so fragile can carry so much meaning."

Florence smiled.

"It has to be fragile. Otherwise we'd forget to handle it gently."

In the yard, the baskets slowly filled.

Inside, the ham would soon be carved. Church bells would ring across Haverford's quiet streets. The children would sit in stiff collars and polished shoes, trying not to fidget.

But for now, the morning belonged to the search.

Hidden things found.

Promises revisited. Life emerging where it had seemed still.

Two weeks. Two tables. Two ancient remembrances.

Spring holding them both without argument.

CHAPTER EIGHT — CHILDREN BECOMING THEMSELVES

The children carried their days out into the world in small, ordinary ways—lunch pails clasped shut, school satchels worn soft at the edges. Florence noticed how each of them held what they were given differently. One packed carefully, another hurried. One lingered at the door, another never looked back. She did not correct these habits. She understood that becoming was not something to be managed, only steadied.

William watched them too, measuring progress not in grades or milestones but in posture, in how a boy stood when spoken to, in whether a child returned home eager or quiet. Together, he and Florence learned to read what was not announced. Parenthood, they discovered, was less instruction than observation.

Mornings moved in layers now. Bill and Dean argued gently over whose turn it was to carry the lunch pail.

"I had it yesterday," Dean insisted.

"And I didn't drop it," Bill countered, already reaching.

Gerry hovered near the door, shoes on the wrong feet until Florence knelt and switched them without comment. Ron lingered longest, watching William twist his coat buttons as if there were something to be learned there.

Behind them all came Dale, two years old and determined, dragging a wooden truck across the floor, its wheels catching on every seam. "Wait," he announced firmly, to no one in particular.

Florence smiled. "They'll still be there when you're ready."

Sylvia remained where she always was, in Florence's arms or nearby, bundled and watchful, her dark eyes tracking movement, sound, the shape of voices. When the door finally closed and the older boys spilled down the steps, she startled at the sudden quiet, then settled again as Florence shifted her weight.

The baby had arrived in the thick heat of August, when the air pressed against the windows and even the evenings offered little relief. The boys had run in and out of the house that summer, flushed and restless, while Florence waited through long afternoons that felt suspended between breath and prayer.

And then, a daughter.

William had stood at the foot of the bed, hat turning slowly in his hands, wonder softening the lines of his face. Five sons had filled the rooms with motion and noise. This small girl filled them differently, like light settling into corners that had gone unnoticed.

"Hello there," he had said, almost shyly.

Florence had drawn the baby closer then, an instinct deeper than thought. She held her not only as a mother, but as someone who understood how small a girl once was in a world that could shift without warning. She found herself memorizing the weight of her, the warmth at her neck, the steady rise and fall of breath, quiet promises made without words.

Now Sylvia blinked up at the quiet hallway as though measuring it. Dale, unsteady and determined at two, circled near Florence's skirts, glancing up at the bundle as if confirming she still belonged there.

The house felt altered again, not louder, but balanced in a way Florence hadn't known she had been waiting for.

She adjusted Sylvia against her shoulder and listened as the boys' footsteps faded into the distance. Summer had brought heat, fullness, and this small steady presence. Autumn would bring its own lessons.

The house exhaled.

William and Florence treated one another much the same way they treated the children, offering what was needed, withholding what was not. When William showed Florence the piano, he did so carefully. Where to place her hands. How not to watch them once she had. He corrected her rarely, and when he did, it was with a lightness that made room rather than closed it.

After that, she practiced alone. Sometimes in the afternoons, when the house held its breath between meals and school hours. Dale played at her feet, stacking blocks only to knock them down again, clapping at the sound. Sylvia lay nearby, fingers curled, listening. Florence approached the piano the way she approached the garden, patient with the beginning, attentive to what took hold, willing to wait through silence. Sometimes only a few notes at a time, letting one sound settle before reaching for the next.

She was not interested in fluency. She wanted understanding, the steadiness of it, the way order emerged when it was tended. In time, she learned enough to be satisfied. Enough to sit down when the house was quiet and leave it quieter than she found it.

In her childhood, music had arrived without instruments. There were no keys, no strings, no flourish to draw the ear. It came instead through voices, unadorned, droned, held steady by breath and belief. Words carried the melody, not to entertain, but to bind. The sound moved slowly, intentionally, the wooden benches beneath her still as the voices rose and fell.

Sometimes Florence thought about that first music and how it had shaped her listening. It taught her to hear what lingered beneath sound—to notice cadence, restraint, the strength of many voices moving as one. Now, music entered her life differently. It came through keys and pages, through William's hands and the patient turning of sheet music. It unfolded quietly in the evenings, settling beside her children as naturally as lamplight or prayer.

She did not feel the two worlds in conflict. One had taught her reverence; the other taught her expression. Together, they made room for something she recognized as grace, music not performed, but lived, carried forward without losing its first intention.

Grace, Florence had learned, often arrived the same way,

without announcement.

William's mother, Lillian, had been part of the children's lives from the beginning, appearing and receding in the quiet way some people did. She favored short, unannounced visits where she was always welcomed.

She arrived once with a small tin of cookies and left it unopened on the counter, as if simply knowing they were there was enough.

"Growing again," she said, watching Dale circle the table.

"They all are," Florence replied. Lillian nodded, as if that settled something.

She followed Florence into the kitchen, pausing at the doorway as if not to interrupt what was already in motion. Florence set out the coffee and sliced the leftover bread, spooning peach preserves from a jar still faintly warm from its recent putting up. The scent filled the room, sweet and familiar.

"Well, now," Lillian said, removing her gloves, "you've been busy."

"Only keeping pace," Florence replied, smiling as she poured.

They sat for a moment at the small table, cups cradled between their hands. Lillian spoke easily of her travels—of trains taken early and missed late, of rooms that all began to look the same, of people met briefly and remembered longer than expected.

"I never stay anywhere long enough to wear out my welcome," she said. "That's the trick."

Florence laughed. "You manage it well."

Lillian smiled, but it softened at the edges. "Elmer says I bring the weather with me," she added, removing her gloves and folding them neatly beside her cup. "In and out like a front rolling through." She shook her head lightly. "Truth is, he rather enjoys the quiet when I'm gone."

Florence raised a brow. "Does he?"

"Oh yes. He catches up on his papers. Puts his workshop

to rights. Says the house settles differently when it's just him." She paused, not wistful—just reflective. "He has a way of filling his hours properly. I suppose that's why I never worry over him."

"That sounds like a good arrangement," Florence said gently.

"It is. He keeps the hearth steady. I stir the air a bit. We meet again somewhere in the middle."

She reached for her bread then, studying the preserves. "These," she said, "are reason enough to linger." She took a bite and closed her eyes briefly. "I should travel less and visit more kitchens."

Florence laughed again, the sound light, unguarded. From the next room came the thump of a chair and a child's whisper quickly hushed. The house held.

Lillian glanced toward the sound, then back at Florence. "You've made something good here," she said, not as praise, but as recognition.

Florence met her gaze. "We're doing our best."

Lillian nodded, satisfied, and reached for another slice.

When the cups were emptied and the last crumbs brushed away, Florence pushed back her chair. "Let's send some of that energy outdoors," she said.

The children needed no encouragement. Chairs scraped, feet thudded, and they were off through the door, racing one another toward the yard, the air still holding the day's warmth. Lillian lingered just long enough to lift Sylvia, settling her securely against her shoulder.

"Come along," Lillian said, smiling down at her. "We'll let them wear themselves out."

Outside, the boys scattered at once, circling the garden beds, daring one another to climb, inventing games that required speed more than rules. Florence and Lillian followed at an easier pace, their conversation picking up where it had left off, meandering through news and small observations, laughter slipping in without effort.

Sylvia rested contentedly in her grandmother's arms, one small hand nestled into the fabric of her blouse, her gaze drifting between the movement of her brothers and the sound of the women's voices. Lillian rocked her gently as she listened, occasionally interjecting with a wry comment that sent Florence laughing again.

The yard filled with motion and sound, the house watching from behind them. It was the kind of day that asked nothing more than presence—and received it fully.

By the next morning, Lillian was already gone, bound west again, leaving behind only the echo of her laughter and the sense that she would return just as quietly, when the road allowed.

On certain free days, William and Florence took the children into the city. Not to spend, not to acquire, but to look. The steps of the Philadelphia Museum of Art were familiar to them—broad, patient, asking nothing at the door on those days set aside for everyone.

Before climbing the steps, they lingered at the rear of the museum, standing along the rise that overlooked the Schuylkill River and the neat line of boathouses below. The boys were the first to notice the long shells cutting through the water, oars lifting and dropping in perfect time, the soft slap of blades echoing back up the hill.

"Together," one of them said, already leaning forward.

William nodded. "That's how they move."

Florence's eye drifted just beyond the river's bend to Lemon Hill Mansion, pale and elegant among the trees, its federal lines catching the light. She knew it as a private estate still, carefully restored and lived in, its grounds tended with intention. From where she stood, she could only imagine the gardens—formal or free, clipped or generous—paths curving out of sight, beds laid with care. It was enough, for now, to notice it from afar, to let the idea of it settle quietly.

Then the moment passed. The boys were already moving,

and the wide stone steps, warm beneath their hands, were waiting. Together, they turned and climbed toward the museum, rising steadily into what the day still held for them.

Inside, the family moved differently. Voices lowered. Steps slowed. Dale insisted on being carried halfway through, his head heavy on William's shoulder. Sylvia slept through entire rooms, as if trusting the quiet. William paused over structure and balance, the way weight could be carried without excess, how light settled where it was needed. Florence watched the children instead, how long they lingered, which rooms held them, how their questions softened into attention.

Their parents did not explain everything. Florence believed some understanding arrived best without instruction. The children learned that beauty could be studied without being owned, that care could be given simply by noticing.

As she watched them move from room to room, Florence thought briefly of the years when her own world had been smaller and no less whole for it. Beauty, then, had been practical, clean lines, honest work, the quiet music of hands and seasons. There had been hymns, but no piano; stories, but few books meant for lingering. She had not known there were rooms like these or sounds that carried without words. And yet, she had learned how to notice, how to tend what was given. Now, with her own children, she recognized the same skill unfolding in a different key. Music, art, books—none of it overwhelmed her. It arrived as discovery, and she found she flourished alongside them.

They left the museum each time with empty hands and fuller minds. Florence counted that as nourishment. In a world intent on measuring worth by output and progress, she was grateful for places that asked only for presence.

The radio was often on in the afternoons, low enough to be ignored until it wasn't. One day, as Florence worked with her hands, a woman's voice carried steadily through the room—measured, unhurried.

"Who's that?" Bill asked, pausing near the doorway.

"Frances Perkins," the announcer said. Secretary of Labor.

She spoke of work and wages, of safety and dignity, as if these were matters that required calm attention rather than persuasion. Florence did not stop what she was doing. Dale sat on the floor, pushing his truck in slow circles. Sylvia stirred, then stilled again.

Dean looked up briefly, then returned to his work more slowly, as if measuring the sound before letting it pass.

Nothing more was said. Still, something settled into the house. Florence noticed that the voice did not press or plead. It assumed its place.

Florence had grown accustomed to certain presences arriving without announcement.

Estella, her mother, had always moved that way, appearing not with urgency, but with inevitability. She carried herself as someone who had learned how to live beside disappointment without letting it harden her. Conversation with her moved easily between the practical and the reflective, as if she understood that life required both to remain intact.

Her husband, Stephen Masters, came with her, steady and unassuming. He was not Florence's father, nor did he attempt to fill that absence. He did not arrive with promises, explanations, or plans that required believing in. He simply showed up when he said he would, and stayed until it was time to go.

That difference did not escape Florence.

Stephen occupied the space beside Estella with a quiet competence that asked little and offered much. He fixed what needed fixing, listened more than he spoke, and treated the children as individuals rather than a group to be managed. Florence noticed that he never raised his voice to be heard, never withdrew when attention was required.

When they visited, the house adjusted itself.

Estella took Sylvia without asking, settling her against her shoulder as though the motion were long practiced.

"She's lighter than she looks," Estella said, adjusting the

child's weight with a small shift of her hip.

Sylvia sighed, already yielding to sleep.

"She does that," Florence said. "Gives in all at once."

Estella smiled, not at Florence, but at the child. "Some people know when to rest."

Stephen knelt to Dale's level, examining a wooden truck with the seriousness of a man assessing a fine machine. He turned one wheel, then another, watching how they caught the floor.

"It rolls true," he said, giving it a careful push.

Dale laughed and sent it back. "Dad made it."

"I can tell," Stephen said. "He didn't rush it."

William, passing through the room, paused. "That's about the best thing you can say about anything."

Stephen nodded once. "Most things suffer from hurry."

Later, in the kitchen, Estella ran her hand along the edge of the table, stopping where a nick had been smoothed thin by years of use. "You keep a good house," she said.

Florence knew better than to hear judgment in it. "The house keeps us," she answered.

Estella met her gaze then, something unspoken moving between them. "That's the right arrangement."

Stephen set his coffee cup down carefully, aligning it with the grain of the wood. "We won't stay long," he said, not apologetically, just plainly.

Florence nodded. She had already understood that. "Long enough is still long enough."

Stephen's mouth curved, just slightly. "That's what we thought."

They gathered at the long kitchen table without ceremony, chairs pulled back and returned again as if the room knew their habits already. Florence set out the cake, still warm, its sugar crust faintly crackled, along with mismatched plates and a pot of coffee that had been keeping itself ready.

"Amish cake," she said, passing the knife. "Still forgiving, even when rushed."

Estella smiled. "The good ones always are."

Stephen waited until everyone had a plate before taking his own. He listened while coffee was poured, the conversation moving easily, weather first, then the long drive north, then how quickly children learned their own minds.

"Dale's already decided he prefers mornings," Estella said, watching him crumble cake with great seriousness. "Sylvia will hold out longer."

Florence laughed softly. "She's biding her time."

Stephen reached for the sugar bowl, paused, and instead slid it a few inches closer to Estella's cup, without looking at her. He'd noticed that her coffee had gone untouched.

She glanced down, then at him. "Thank you."

He nodded, as if the matter were settled.

William cut another thin slice and set its plate near the edge of the table. Stephen rose without comment, moved the plate closer to Dale's reach, and returned to his seat before the child noticed it had ever been out of place.

"It's good," Stephen said finally, gesturing toward the cake. "Tastes like it knows what it's for."

Florence felt something settle at that remark.

Estella leaned back slightly, folding her hands. "Florida doesn't make things like this," she said. "Too much sun. Not enough patience."

"Patience," Florence repeated, lifting her cup. "That's one way to put it."

Stephen reached again, this time for the chipped saucer beneath his cup. He turned it slowly, aligning the crack so it faced inward, then set the cup down squarely over it, steadying something that might have tipped later.

Florence noticed. She always did.

The talk continued, nothing important, everything essential. And when the plates were cleared, no one remarked on how the table looked a little more ordered than before, or how the room seemed to exhale once they rose.

They did not linger when it was time to go.

Estella folded her napkin, smoothing it once before setting it beside her plate. "We should start back," she said, already standing. There was no regret in her voice, only accuracy.

Florence walked them to the door while William gathered coats and Stephen lifted the overnight bag without being asked.

Estella paused, one hand on the doorframe, as if taking the measure of the room. "You're doing well here," she said.

Florence nodded. "We are."

Stephen stepped past them to the porch, then stopped and turned back. He reached for the loose hook beneath the window, tightening it with two quiet turns until it caught cleanly.

"There," he said, almost to himself.

No one answered.

Outside, the air had cooled. Estella kissed Florence's cheek, brief and certain. "Write when you can," she said. "Not when you mean to."

"I will," Florence replied.

Stephen tipped his hat once, already moving toward the car. "Good roads," he said.

Florence watched them go, aware of a small, unexpected loosening inside her, nothing dramatic, nothing that required comment. Some absences, she knew, were never repaired. But others were answered, quietly, by constancy.

The distance did not trouble Florence. Some people remained close without remaining near, and that, too, was a kind of holding.

Life, she saw, did not pull families apart so much as arrange them.

The children continued on, unaware of the quiet recalibrations taking place around them. Shoes were outgrown. Lunch pails dented. Satchels mended. Dale learned to climb the back steps without help. Sylvia learned the sound of her mother's footsteps and turned her head before Florence entered the room.

The piano, like everything else worth tending, took its

time.

Evenings often ended with a book opened and passed from hand to hand. Florence favored stories that did not hurry themselves, ones that trusted children to listen without being told what to think. *The Wind in the Willows* lived on the table for a season, its pages marked by a ribbon that moved forward slowly. William read when he was home, his voice steady, stopping where the light failed rather than where the chapter ended.

The children listened in different ways, one leaning close, another tracing patterns in the rug, Dale climbing into Florence's lap mid-sentence, Sylvia blinking awake just long enough to hear her father's voice. Florence noticed how they stayed. That, more than the story itself, told her it belonged.

Poetry lived among them, too, folded into evenings without ceremony. From *A Child's Garden of Verses*, they memorized a few lines at a time, the children taking turns until the words settled. One evening, a line about a shadow growing taller drew laughter, then quiet, as each child tried it aloud.

"Mine's bigger," Dale announced, standing tall.

"Only in the evening," Bill replied.

Florence listened, pleased not by their accuracy, but by how naturally the words stayed with them.

In time, bedtime quieted in different ways. Bill left his old copies of *Tom Swift* within easy reach, and it pleased him to see how readily Dean took to them, drawn to machines that worked because someone understood how they were built. He read *The Hardy Boys* just as eagerly, favoring stories where attention and persistence mattered more than bravado. Gerry preferred tales that bent rules playfully, laughing aloud over *The Incredible Adventures of Professor Branestawm.*

Ron listened longest when Florence read from *Just So Stories*, content to hear how the world acquired its shape one question at a time. Dale rarely made it to the end of any story, surrendering early to sleep with a book still open beside him, while Sylvia was passed from arm to arm, the boys unusually careful with her, as if instinct had already taught them she was to be kept. Watching them, Florence sometimes wondered whether, after the long silence she sensed ahead, another small girl might one day be welcomed into their practiced circle, arriving not into ease, but into a household that already knew how to hold.

Florence did not steer these choices. She noticed them and let them stand.

She believed, even then, that the truest measure of a household was not how tightly it clung, but how well it allowed its people to become themselves.

The house settled fully only after the last door was closed and the lights were turned low.

Florence moved through the front room, straightening nothing, simply passing through it as one does a space that has done its work for the day. William was there, standing at the window, watching the dark gather along the street.

"They're all down," she said.

He turned. "Everyone?"

"For now," she answered, and he smiled.

She came to him and rested her head briefly against his chest. His hand found the familiar place at her back, steady and sure. They stood without speaking, listening to the quiet they had made.

"Your mother and Stephen," he said at last. "They leave things calmer than they found them."

"They do," she said. "Even when they're gone."

He nodded, considering that. "Seems like a useful way to move through the world."

She tipped her head up toward him. "You do."

He laughed softly. "I had a good example."

They sat together for a while, the day easing out of them, the children's voices, the scrape of chairs, the sweetness of cake still faint in the air. Florence thought of how quickly the boys were changing, how their interests were already beginning to separate and take shape, how naturally they moved toward what suited them.

"It's strange," she said. "Watching them grow without feeling the need to hurry it along."

William reached for her hand. "That's because we're not pushing."

She nodded. That felt right.

When they finally rose to go upstairs, Florence glanced once more toward the hallway where the children slept, each in their own small orbit of dreams. Everything seemed held. Not fixed or promised, just held.

She had learned by now that a home was never finished growing. Rooms made space. Seasons shifted. What felt complete one year quietly widened the next.

Florence lingered a moment longer in the doorway. She knew, though she could not have explained how, that what feels secure can change without warning. Not from neglect. Not from failure. Simply from the passage of time.

She touched the banister as she passed, steadying herself in a way she no longer needed, but once had.

Then she followed William upstairs, carrying both the ease of the present and the quiet understanding that it would not remain untouched forever.

CHAPTER NINE — LOSS OF A PATRIARCH (1938)

William's father, Elmer Adams, died on a Tuesday in the spring.

There was no warning that Florence could recall later, no long illness, no season of preparation. One day he had been present in the way men like Elmer were always present: fixed, reliable, assumed. The next, he was gone, and the shape of the household adjusted around the absence he left behind.

William received the news at work. He came home early, his coat still on, his hat left on the table where it did not belong. Florence saw it immediately and understood that something had shifted beyond the ordinary range of worry.

"My father is gone," he said simply.

Florence did not ask how or when. She moved instead—toward William, toward the kitchen, toward the work that would need doing next. Loss, she had learned, did not wait for questions.

By the time they gathered the children and packed what was necessary, the day had already begun to fold in on itself. Shoes were matched, coats buttoned. One child asked where they were going; another asked if they would be back by nightfall. Florence answered what could be answered and left the rest untouched.

They traveled to William's parents' home the following day.

The house looked unchanged from the street, its windows in their usual places, the porch swept clean. Inside, it was quieter than Florence expected. Not empty, just still, as if everything had been asked to hold its position.

Lillian Adams sat at the table with her hands folded.

She rose when they entered, embraced William, nodded to

Florence. Then, almost as an afterthought, her gaze returned to the children. Something softened. She drew them in, one by one, into a quiet, lingering embrace, her hand resting briefly at the back of each small head, as if to steady them. Her dress carried a faint trace of lavender and starch, the scent clean and familiar, her touch firm but careful.

There was no collapse, no outward display. Grief, Florence saw at once, had been gathered inward and set carefully aside.

Elmer's things were already contained.

His coat hung where it always had. His shoes were placed side by side beneath the bench. Papers had been stacked and tied. Nothing lay abandoned. Florence recognized the impulse. Order was not denial. It was survival expressed through discipline.

The children moved carefully through the rooms, subdued without being told. One sat on the bottom stair, another traced the pattern in the rug with a finger. Florence noticed how instinctively they adjusted themselves to the quiet, as if they, too, understood the difference between absence and emptiness.

People came and went. Neighbors brought food. Men spoke in lowered voices about Elmer's work, his reliability, his steady judgment. Florence listened and understood that Elmer had been the kind of man whose importance was only fully visible once removed.

Lillian spoke little. When she did, it was to answer what was asked and no more. Florence watched her closely, respectfully. There was something deliberate in the way Lillian moved through the day, a care taken not just with objects, but with words.

That evening, Florence found herself beside her in the kitchen and said, "I can help with the dishes."

Lillian nodded. "That would be fine."

They worked without speaking for several minutes. Plates were rinsed. Cups stacked. A child's forgotten spoon was set aside and returned later without comment. Movements synchronized without effort.

"He liked things kept," Lillian said at last, gesturing toward the cupboard. "Not hidden. Just ... where they belonged."

Florence met her eyes. "That doesn't surprise me."

Lillian's mouth curved, not quite a smile. "Then you understand."

In the days that followed, Florence noticed what others did not. Lillian kept certain papers close at hand, returning them to the same drawer each evening. Letters were sorted and placed, not opened in haste. When questions arose, about accounts, about arrangements, Lillian answered them calmly, as if each response had been prepared long before it was needed.

Grief, Florence realized, had not emptied Lillian. It had revealed her.

The sky hung low, undecided about rain or snow. The family cemetery at Chestnut Grove sat just beyond the rise of the hill, its stones set with a restraint that mirrored the people who rested there. No flowers beyond what the season allowed. No excess.

The service was brief. Appropriate.

The minister spoke of steadiness. Of work done without spectacle. Of a life that left clear lines behind it. William listened with his head bowed, one child's hand tucked into each of his and Florence's, feeling the subtle pull between past and future made physical there in the small weight of their fingers.

When the coffin was lowered, Lillian stepped forward first.

She did not cry. She placed her hand against the wood once, just once, then turned back toward William.

"Your father believed in finishing what you start," she said quietly. "He'd want you to remember that."

"I will," William answered.

Her eyes held his, searching not for comfort but for readiness. Whatever she found there seemed to satisfy her. She nodded and stepped aside.

As the earth was returned, Florence felt the shift beside her, the moment William ceased being only a son. Elmer's absence pressed forward, asking to be managed. Not just sorrow now, but responsibility: land, name, example. The kind that did not wait for grief to soften.

Florence tightened her grip on the children's hands, steadying them, steadying him.

Nothing more was said. There was nothing more to say.

They returned to Lillian's house in a loose procession, cars pulling in and out of the drive, coats laid wherever there was room to set them. The door opened and closed steadily, admitting cold air and familiar faces, each arrival bringing with it a brief exchange of words that meant more for their presence than their content.

Florence moved easily among the rooms. She set out the coffee cake she had baked the day before, still fragrant despite the long morning, and refreshed the coffee before anyone thought to ask. Someone remarked on the weather, someone else on how Elmer would have approved of the turnout.

William stood with his brothers near the window, their heads bent together, voices low. There was talk of the shop, of tools that would need tending, of things Elmer had done a certain way that no one felt inclined to change just yet. Laughter surfaced briefly, surprised them all, and settled back into quiet.

Florence kept one eye on the children as they drifted between rooms, accepted onto laps, redirected gently when they grew restless. She gathered stray cups, wiped the counter more than necessary, and listened for what was needed before it was spoken.

Lillian remained at the table.

She answered questions when they came, thanked people without flourish, and received condolences with a nod that acknowledged care without letting it overstay. When someone offered to stay the night, she shook her head.

"No," she said. "I'll sleep best once the house is mine again."

By late afternoon, the chairs were returned to their places. The last car eased down the road. Silence reclaimed the rooms in stages, the way it always did.

Florence finished rinsing the final cup and turned to find Lillian standing alone in the doorway, her hands resting on the back of Elmer's chair.

"Well," Lillian said, exhaling slowly. "That's done."

Florence joined her, careful not to rush the moment. "You managed it beautifully."

Lillian's mouth curved, just slightly. "It needed doing."

She lowered herself into the chair and, for the first time that day, let her shoulders fall. The house seemed to respond, settling with her.

William appeared then, placing a hand briefly on his mother's shoulder. "We'll come back soon," he said. "See what needs seeing."

"I know," Lillian replied. "Not today."

Florence gathered the children, coats already in hand. At the door, she looked back once more. Lillian sat quietly at the table, the afternoon light thinning around her, satisfied and relieved—not because the loss was smaller, but because the day had been met and carried through.

On the drive home, the children slept in uneven patterns, heads leaning where they fell. William was quiet. Florence did not fill the silence.

"She's stronger than people think," he said finally.

Florence watched the road stretch ahead of them. "Yes," she said. "And careful."

He nodded. He understood the distinction.

That night, after the house had settled and the children were accounted for, Florence lay awake longer than usual. She thought of Elmer—of the kind of steadiness that did not announce itself, but shaped everything it touched. She thought of Lillian, whose grief had been folded rather than displayed, whose hands had already begun the work of preservation.

Florence sensed then—without knowing how or why—that Lillian Adams kept more than sorrow. And that whatever it was, it had been waiting a long time to be held.

When Lillian returned some weeks later, Florence walked

her quietly toward the far edge of the yard.

"I wanted you to see something," she said, brushing a stray curl from her face.

The maple stood slight against the widening sky, its leaves already flushed a tender red. The children's footprints still pressed faintly in the soil around its base.

Lillian stopped.

"For Elmer," Florence added simply.

Lillian removed her gloves, as she always did before touching something living. She stepped forward and laid her palm against the thin trunk—not clutching, not clinging. Just resting there.

"He would have liked this," she said after a moment. "Something that grows without asking permission."

They stood side by side in the quiet. A breeze moved through the yard, and the small leaves trembled, catching light.

Lillian drew in a slow breath. "He was never one for monuments," she added. "But he understood roots."

Florence nodded.

At length, Lillian stepped back, composure intact, though something in her gaze had softened—not broken, but steadied in a new way.

"Red was always his favorite in autumn," she said. "Said it reminded him that change could be bold."

Florence had not known that. She was glad now she did.

The tree was small and would take years to show itself. That suited her. Some things were meant to outlast the moment that called them into being.

PART III — THE WORLD AT WAR (1939–1941)

CHAPTER TEN — VOICES FROM EUROPE

The war arrived quietly at first.

It came folded into the morning paper, its headlines creased where Florence had pressed them flat against the table. Names of cities she had never seen crowded the page—Warsaw, Rotterdam, London—each reduced to type and ink, each carrying a weight that felt heavier than it looked. She read carefully, then refolded the paper, containing what she could before the day required her attention elsewhere.

By noon, the family gathered at the long table. The conversation moved along familiar tracks, school lessons, a loose hinge on the back gate, whether the tomatoes would survive another week of heat.

"Dean, finish chewing before you answer," William said mildly.

"I am," Dean protested, swallowing too quickly.

Gerry leaned across the table. "Dad, how fast can a plane go?"

William glanced at Florence, then back at his son. "Fast enough to matter," he said. "Why?"

Gerry shrugged. "Just wondering."

Florence set the serving bowl down between them. "Wondering is fine," she said. "Just don't forget to eat."

Bill reached for the salt. "They were talking about ships on the radio this morning," he said. "Big ones."

His father nodded. "There are always ships."

The answer satisfied no one entirely, but it allowed the meal to continue. Chairs scraped softly. Sylvia fussed, caught in that small storm of wanting and not wanting all at once, her hands reaching even as she protested, grazing the cup of water and nearly tipping it over. Life held its shape.

The radio spoke next.

Its wooden cabinet stood against the front room wall, polished and dependable, its dial glowing softly as though aware of its importance. William adjusted it in small increments, coaxing distant voices through static and hum. Reports arrived measured and official, delivered in tones meant to reassure. There were updates, not alarms. Movements, not losses. The language was designed to fit neatly inside the room.

Bill sat straighter when the radio mentioned troop movements.

"They need men who notice things," he said quietly.

William met his gaze then, just briefly. "Yes," he said. "They do."

Florence listened while she worked, clearing plates, wiping the table, resetting it for whatever came next. She learned to recognize the pauses, the moments when words failed briefly before continuing. She noticed how William stopped what he was doing when certain broadcasts came through, his hand resting on the radio's edge as though steadying something more than sound.

No one asked anything outright. But the room listened.

At night, the voices grew closer. Broadcasts stretched longer. Accents sharpened. Music gave way to reports, then returned again, as if to insist on normalcy. William learned which stations spoke plainly and which softened their truths. He marked the difference without comment.

The children sensed it before they understood it.

Bill lingered near the doorway when the radio was on, arms crossed, listening with a seriousness that surprised Florence. He asked questions that were practical—*Where was it happening? How far away?*—and waited for the answers without pressing.

Dean brought the folded paper with him, tracing maps with his finger, studying borders as if they were puzzles meant to be solved. "Why do they keep moving the lines?" he asked once.

William glanced at Florence before answering. "Because lines are easier to move than people," he said.

Gerry listened from the floor, half-engaged, half-distracted, until something caught his attention. Then he looked up sharply. "Why don't they just fix it?" he asked, genuinely perplexed.

His mother did not answer right away. "Some things," she said finally, "don't belong to just one person to fix."

The younger children moved through the room more loosely, Dale pushing a truck beneath the cabinet, Sylvia busy playing with her little doll made from fabric scraps, but even they seemed to recognize that this sound was different. When the radio came on, the house rearranged itself.

One evening, a familiar cadence broke through the static; Isaac's caution echoed without being named. William sat straighter as the report detailed border crossings, alliances tightening, words like *mobilization* and *occupation* repeated until they no longer fit easily inside sentences.

Florence reached for the radio knob and lowered the volume slightly, not to silence it, but to contain it.

"That's enough for now," she said gently.

Bill looked at her. "Is it going to come here?"

Florence met his eyes. "Not yet."

Dean watched his father. "But it could."

William nodded once. "Yes."

Gerry frowned, unsatisfied. "When?"

William rested his hand on the cabinet. "When it runs out of room where it is."

Still, the containment began to fail.

Newspapers grew thicker. Headlines expanded. Maps appeared where photographs once sufficed. The radio no longer pretended distance. The voices did not shout, but they no longer whispered either. War, once folded and shelved, began to occupy space.

Florence stood at the sink one morning, listening as the

broadcast carried reports of cities emptied, borders redrawn, families displaced. She dried her hands slowly, aware that something had shifted. What had been held at arm's length was now pressing against the cabinet door.

As the voices continued, she found her thoughts moving elsewhere, toward fields she had once known by heart, toward people who would never hear these reports as they were spoken. Her Amish foster family received their news in newspapers passed from hand to hand, read aloud at tables where the radio had never been invited. What was said aloud remained measured. What was discussed more fully stayed with the men, their conversations held back until work was finished and younger ears had moved on.

She wondered how they were weighing the words *war* and *duty* now, how a people shaped by peace would respond when the wider world no longer recognized refusal as a position, but as a problem to be solved. The thought unsettled her. Conscientious objection was not new to them, but the scale of this war, and the machinery it required, threatened to press even their careful lives into unfamiliar shapes. The world was changing, she knew, even for those who had ordered their lives to remain apart from it.

William turned off the radio when the report ended. The silence that followed felt heavier than the sound had been.

Dean refolded the paper and set it back on the table, careful with the creases. Bill remained standing, as if waiting for something more to be said. Gerry returned to his game, though less convincingly than before.

Florence watched them all and felt the quiet, unmistakable pull of time tightening its grip. The war had arrived as news, as voice, as paper carefully folded and stored.

But it was learning how to travel—how to move from cabinets and columns into lives.

Soon, it would no longer ask permission to be contained.

William and Florence drove to the grocer just before dusk. Dottie, their kind neighbor, offered to keep close watch on the children while they stepped away.

The streets were quiet in that in-between way, shops still open, but moving toward closure, light thinning at the edges of things. William parked at the curb and cut the engine. Florence gathered her list and purse.

"I won't be long."

"I'll wait," he replied.

She stepped inside, the bell over the door ringing once before settling. William remained in the car, hands resting loosely on the steering wheel, watching the sidewalk more out of habit than attention.

That was when the woman appeared.

She moved slowly, as if each step required negotiation. Her coat hung too large and too thin at once, its hem dark with grime. One child was pressed against her chest, the other clutched at her skirt, both silent in a way that suggested they had learned when not to ask.

She stopped several feet from the car.

"Sir," she said, her voice low and careful. "I don't suppose you might have something to spare. Just enough for bread."

William did not ask where she'd come from or how long she'd been standing there. He reached into his pocket, fingers closing around the few coins he carried, change he'd set aside without thought, meant for nothing in particular. He placed it in her hand without counting it, without hesitation.

"Thank you," she said, already backing away, pulling the children closer as though gratitude itself required retreat.

He nodded once. "Take care."

She disappeared down the block, her steps unhurried, as if she had learned not to expect urgency from the world.

Florence returned moments later, arms full. She paused when she saw William standing now, watching the empty sidewalk.

"Everything all right?" she asked.

"Yes," he said, opening the door for her. "Just a woman passing through."

She did not press him. She set the parcels at her feet and looked once more toward the street before the car pulled away.

They drove in silence for several blocks, the rhythm of the road steady beneath them.

Florence spoke first. "She had children."

"Yes," William said.

"I overheard the store clerk speaking unkindly about them." Florence reached over and put her hand tenderly on William's leg.

"They didn't say a word."

"No," he agreed. "They looked like they'd learned not to."

The car slowed at the corner. William waited, then continued.

"I didn't have much on me," he said, not as apology, just fact.

She rested her hand briefly over his on the seat between them. "You had enough."

He nodded once, eyes forward. "It seemed that way."

The houses thinned as they turned toward home, the light fading evenly along the street.

"Things are changing," Florence said.

"They are," William replied. "But they don't all change at once."

She considered that. "No. Some of them just show up."

He glanced at her then, a look of quiet recognition passing between them.

"We'll manage," he said.

She watched the familiar turn appear ahead of them. "I know."

They drove on, the groceries shifting softly at her feet, the street behind them already settling back into itself.

The war had not spoken this time.

It had simply stood there, asking quietly, and been answered.

CHAPTER ELEVEN — DECEMBER 7

Sunday arrived wearing its usual stillness.

Florence had set the table early, plates warming slightly from the kitchen, the roast resting where it always did. The radio sat low on the sideboard, dial turned to music, something light, meant to hold the morning in place. William adjusted the volume once, then left it alone.

Isaac was expected later. He had said he would stop by after lunch, nothing urgent in his voice, only the habit of keeping plans even when the world refused to cooperate.

The broadcast broke mid-phrase.

Music cut cleanly, replaced by a voice that did not bother with easing anyone into what it carried. The radio dial crackled as William turned it, instinctively seeking clarity, as though this were a problem of tuning rather than truth.

Pearl Harbor.

The words did not fit the room. They landed too heavily, too abruptly, refusing to be folded or set aside. Florence stood still at the counter, her hands damp, her mind already reaching for containment that no longer existed.

William did not sit. He leaned toward the radio, one hand braced on the cabinet as details emerged, ships burning, planes overhead, loss counted before names could be attached to it. The voice continued, steady and unadorned, as though this were simply another report.

The plates cooled where they were.

Outside, the neighborhood held its breath. Doors opened. Radios grew louder. A dog barked once, then stopped. Sunday loosened its grip and did not return.

When Isaac arrived, he did not knock. He stepped inside quietly, as though the house had already agreed to his presence. His coat remained on. He did not sit.

"They've crossed a line," he said, though the radio had already done the work of telling them so.

Florence noticed how he stood, too alert, too contained. She saw the same posture she had begun to recognize in William when broadcasts from Europe turned serious.

"This makes it certain," Isaac continued. "There will be no more pretending distance is protection."

William turned from the radio. "For us," he said.

Isaac met his eyes. "For everyone."

He spoke then of Europe, though the broadcast did not. Of letters that had stopped arriving. Of names mentioned less often, than not at all. Of cities that were no longer places so much as conditions. He did not dramatize it. He did not need to.

The chairs scraped softly as the children came in from the other rooms, summoned by habit more than hunger. Bill arrived first, already serious in the way he carried himself, pulling out his chair and squaring it to the table before sitting, as though alignment mattered. Dean followed, then Gerry and Dale, who lingered near the doorway until Florence gave a look that said *sit*. Ron slipped in last, sliding into his seat beside Dale, eyes darting between the adults and the radio as if trying to decide which one required more attention.

Sylvia came behind them, dragging her chair across the floor with a sound too loud for the room, then climbing into it with determined effort.

Isaac stood when Florence entered with the coffee tray.

"No need," he said quietly, already knowing it was too late.

She set the cups down anyway. It was what she did when a room felt unsteady, she placed something warm within reach. No one reached for it.

The radio spoke on, its voice level, precise. Words like *attack* and *casualties* moved through the room without urgency, as though they had nowhere else to go.

William leaned forward slightly. "They're saying Hawaii," he said, more to the table than to anyone in particular.

"Is that very far?" Sylvia asked.

Ron frowned. "Is it near California?"

"No," Bill said before anyone else could answer. "It's an island." He paused, then added, quieter, as if correcting himself, "A lot of water around it."

William nodded. "Far out in the Pacific."

Isaac nodded once as well. His hands closed around the cup Florence had placed near him, not to drink, but to steady. She noticed how carefully he held it, how his fingers pressed as though anchoring something already slipping. In that moment she understood that the war had already taken hold of him, long before America found the words to admit its own involvement.

"Does this mean fighting?" Ron asked.

"Yes," William said gently.

Bill said nothing. He had leaned forward now, elbows close to his sides, listening with the stillness Florence recognized, the kind that did not wander, the kind that stayed.

Official language followed, statements, responses, inevitability given voice. William did not move to adjust the dial. The sound no longer needed tending.

Florence looked from face to face, Bill already quiet and set, Ron's feet swinging beneath the chair, Sylvia's hands folded in her lap the way she had been taught.

Normalcy did not end loudly. It simply failed to hold.

That evening, the plates were cleared nearly untouched. Florence wrapped the food carefully, her hands moving by instinct, and placed it away as she always had. Some things, she believed, could still be saved.

She did not yet know which ones could not.

Later, when the house had quieted, William returned the radio to its place. He did not turn it off. He only lowered the volume, aware that silence would no longer protect them from what had begun.

The war had arrived first as voice and paper, carefully contained.

Now it had entered the room.

And nothing, not distance, not habit, not hope, could put it back where it had been.

After supper, when the children had been ushered toward beds and the house began to loosen its hold on the day, William and Florence returned to the front room. The piano waited where it always had, its bench pulled out just enough to suggest use. William did not sit. Instead, they took the sofa together and remained there for a long moment without speaking, letting the weight of what they had heard find its place.

"It won't stop with today," Florence said finally.

William shook his head. "No."

Their hands rested close, not touching at first. Then his found hers.

"They'll call for men," she said. "And boys."

"Yes."

She did not ask *when*. They both understood how quickly inevitability learned to move.

"It was always going to come," William said, not as reassurance but as truth. "For the country. For families like ours."

Florence thought of the table, the chairs pulled close, the way Bill had leaned forward, already listening for more than had been said. She said nothing, only tightened her fingers around William's.

And nothing, not distance, not habit, not hope, could put it back where it had been.

Monday arrived without ceremony.

School dismissed at its usual hour. The children came home hungry, coats loosened, books dropped by the door where they always landed. Florence had soup on again, simple, filling. Bread, butter, plates placed with care. The radio had been on since midmorning.

This time, she did not turn it down.

They were halfway through lunch when the tone shifted.

Florence paused with the ladle in her hand. The announcer's voice sharpened— unmistakably formal, as though the words themselves had been pressed flat.

"... the President of the United States will address Congress ..."

William and Isaac entered through the back door together, coats dusted with metal filings, the smell of oil and cold following them inside.

"We thought we'd take lunch here," William said. Then he heard the radio. He stopped.

Isaac did not remove his coat.

Florence set the ladle down. "You should sit," she said. "They're about to say it."

Bill, sixteen and already reading newspapers when Florence thought he wasn't, lowered his spoon slowly. Dean followed suit, his earlier chatter gone. Gerry sat straighter in his chair, eyes fixed on the radio now, jaw set with the seriousness of someone already measuring distance. Ron's foot, which had been swinging beneath the table, went still. Dale leaned closer to Sylvia, instinctively protective, while Sylvia folded her napkin carefully in her lap, watching Florence for cues.

The radio crackled once.

Then Roosevelt's voice filled the kitchen, measured, resolute, unmistakably final.

"The state of war has existed between the United States and the Japanese Empire..."

No one spoke.

Florence felt the moment land not like a blow, but like weight—settling, inescapable.

William exhaled slowly. "There it is," he said.

Isaac nodded. "Congress won't argue. Not after yesterday."

"So that's it," Dean said. Not a question.

"Yes," William said. "That's it."

Bill looked directly at his father. "What happens now?"

William did not answer immediately. "Now," he said carefully, "people do what they're asked. Some will be asked to leave. Others to build, repair, supply. Some will be asked to stay close to home and keep things moving."

Dean absorbed that, his gaze drifting briefly toward the window, toward familiar streets and distances he already knew by heart.

"And you?" Gerry asked.

"I'm needed where I am," William said. "Machines don't stop just because the world's gone mad."

Gerry nodded once, as if filing that away, work mattered, even far from home. His eyes returned to the radio, already tracking places beyond the room.

"And some of us," Isaac said quietly, "have already lost people without uniforms."

Florence met his eyes. She did not ask him to explain.

"Why does he sound so calm?" Sylvia asked.

Florence reached across the table and covered her hand. "Because calm helps people be brave."

Ron nodded, solemnly, as though he had been handed something he would carry for a long time. Dale did not speak, but his shoulders squared, his small frame settling into endurance rather than fear.

The address continued, words like duty and sacrifice moving through the room with careful precision. Florence noticed how William stood closer to the radio now, how Isaac's hands had found the edge of the table, fingers gripped, bracing. She noticed, too, how Bill's attention did not waver.

When the broadcast ended, no one rushed to fill the space it left behind.

William glanced at the clock. "Finish up," he said. "You'll be late getting back."

That instruction—ordinary, familiar—released something.

The children ate the last of their soup.

After lunch, coats were pulled on and buttons fumbled. The children gathered at the door in a loose knot, reluctant but ready. Florence smoothed collars, straightened caps.

At the door, Bill paused, then straightened. "So ... school," he said, not quite a question.

"Yes," Florence said. "School."

They walked back together, lunch settling heavy but steady inside them. The street felt the same, and not. Ron kicked a stone ahead of him, watching it skitter along the curb.

"My teacher won't believe it," he said.

"She will," Dean answered. "They heard it too."

Gerry broke into a short run, racing Dale to the corner post, the game instinctive, necessary. Dale laughed when he lost, breathless and bright, and for a moment the sound startled them all.

Sylvia skipped to keep up, her hand slipping into Bill's coat pocket the way she always did. "Do you think we'll still have spelling?" she asked.

"Yes," Bill said after a pause. "I think we will."

The bell rang. Lessons resumed. Arithmetic. Spelling. Desks aligned.

The world, astonishingly, continued to ask children to learn.

Inside the house, Florence rinsed the bowls and wiped the table clean. The radio remained on, low now, as though the house itself had learned to listen.

December 7 had brought the news. December 8 brought consent.

The war was no longer something announced.

It was something lived with.

And from this table forward, it would be carried—quietly, deliberately—into every ordinary day that followed.

Not everyone carried it the same way.

Isaac sat alone in his Philadelphia office long after the building emptied.

The radio was off. The silence felt earned.

He removed a folded letter from his desk drawer, its creases worn soft by repetition. He did not open it. He knew its contents by heart.

Names had stopped arriving months ago. First one. Then another. Cities he had once spoken aloud were now reduced to pauses in conversation, syllables swallowed before they reached the tongue.

He returned the letter to the drawer and locked it.

On his desk lay a small stack of papers, contracts deferred, filings delayed, inventions held in place by choice rather than fear. He had argued for restraint before. Now restraint felt like grief practiced in advance.

Isaac buttoned his coat, though he had nowhere to go.

At the window, he looked out at a city still lit, still moving, still believing itself intact.

"They won't see it until it's too late," he said to no one.

He took his hat from the hook, squared his shoulders, and stepped back into a world that had finally begun to resemble the one he had never fully left.

December did not wait for adjustment. The war moved faster than explanation.

The weeks that followed carried a different texture—less elastic, more exacting. Florence felt it first in the shops. Shelves thinned quietly. Familiar items disappeared without announcement. She knew ration books would appear, clean and official, like during the worst years of the Great Depression. She recognized the posture required—head down, hands busy, waste unacceptable.

Making little into much was not new to her. It had simply been renamed.

She returned to habits that had never truly left. Bones simmered longer. Leftovers learned new purposes. Flour was sifted twice. Butter was stretched with patience and faith. The chicory tin came down from its shelf, its bitter familiarity welcome. Coffee, thinned but present, still warmed the morning. Still marked time.

The children noticed the changes without being told.

Christmas approached without abundance, and no one

pretended otherwise. Florence laid paper scraps on the table one afternoon, brown, cream, the backs of envelopes saved for just such moments.

"We'll make what we can," she said. "And we'll mean it."

They did.

Cards were folded and unfolded until the creases held. Words were chosen slowly. Sylvia traced holly leaves again and again until they resembled something real. Dale carved wooden cars from scraps William brought home, wheels sanded smooth with more attention than skill. Ron fashioned small boxes, careful with corners. Gerry mended a tear in one of Bill's gloves under Florence's watchful eye, learning that repair carried its own dignity.

Nature filled in what stores could not. Pinecones gathered. Evergreen clipped sparingly. Twine saved, reused, knotted again. Gifts were wrapped in newspaper and tied with care. Nothing was hidden; everything was offered honestly.

Evenings changed shape.

Blackout curtains were hung and tested. Lamps lowered. Windows checked twice. Drills practiced, not with panic, but with discipline. Lights out. Silence held. Then release.

Florence noted how quickly the children adapted. How normal adjusted itself again.

Mending baskets stayed out longer. Socks were darned, sweaters turned. Buttons were never discarded. Hands learned new rhythms. Conversation softened but did not disappear.

The Great Depression had taught them how to endure without assurance. The war was teaching them how to endure with purpose. Both required the same hands.

On Christmas morning, the table was full enough. Not with excess, but with intention.

Florence carried in the warm tea bread, the loaf wrapped in a clean cloth, its heat pressing gently into her palms. She set it at the center of the table and uncovered it, releasing a scent that softened the room at once. A small dish of peach preserves followed, the color of late summer, saved for just such a morning.

"Careful," she said, smiling as Bill reached too quickly. "It's hot yet."

She sliced the bread thin and even, passing plates one by one. Chicory coffee steamed, dark and familiar.

Sylvia watched closely, chin in her hands. "Does this mean it's still Christmas," she asked, "even if everything else feels different?"

Florence paused, then smiled. "Yes," she said. "It does."

Sylvia nodded, satisfied, and took her bread with both hands.

Ron grinned. "Best day."

Wooden cars rolled across the floor between bites, their paths weaving beneath chairs and around slippers. Gerry nudged one toward Dale with his foot. Dean poured coffee the way he'd been taught, careful not to spill.

"This is the good bread," Bill said, spreading the peaches with deliberate care.

Florence met William's eye across the table. He nodded once.

Cards were exchanged—drawn, folded, written slowly. Laughter came, quiet but real, settling easily among the plates and cups left waiting in the kitchen.

Florence watched her children open what had been made by hands they knew. She watched gratitude take root without instruction.

After the last parcel was opened and the paper gathered, Florence noticed the radio still resting where William had left it the night before. This time, no one reached for it. The day held its own boundary, and they honored it.

William moved instead to the piano in the front room. The children followed, drawn by habit and hope, settling on the floor, the arm of the sofa, the edge of the rug. He did not announce the first song. His hands simply found it.

Florence joined softly—"Joy to the World"—her voice steady, familiar. The children came in where they could, some confidently, others a beat behind. One song led to the next. The music filled the space the radio usually claimed, and held it differently.

For this morning, at least, they chose what entered the room.

Outside, the world rearranged itself at a speed no one could manage.

Inside, they practiced holding.

December had not brought relief from hardship. It had brought direction.

And Florence, who had already learned how to keep a household standing when certainty failed, understood that this careful stretching, this steady making, was not merely survival.

It was contribution and it would be enough.

On New Year's morning, William turned the dial carefully, searching for the familiar station. Instead of carols or commentary, a burst of brass spilled into the room, uneven, exuberant, almost unruly.

"What's that?" Sylvia asked, sitting up straighter.

"The Mummers," William said after a moment. "Parade down Broad Street in Philadelphia."

The music carried laughter in it — horns blaring, drums tapping out a rhythm that felt out of step with the quiet of their home.

Ron frowned slightly, trying to make sense of the discordant cheer.

"They sound happy," Dale said.

The drums beat steadily—as though rehearsing something the nation did not yet fully understand.

Florence stood still beside the table, dish towel in her hands. "They always do," she replied softly.

Outside, the winter light lay flat against the windows. Inside, the radio crackled with feathers and satire, and a city determined to keep tradition alive.

The children listened for a few minutes longer, curious

but unmoved. One by one, they drifted back to their corners, books, marbles, quiet conversation.

William reached forward and lowered the volume.

The room settled again.

The new year did not arrive with celebration. It arrived with headlines.

January carried its own chill. The maps in the newspaper grew crowded with arrows and shaded regions. Names once distant became spoken daily. The boys leaned closer to the print now, tracing coastlines with fingers not yet steady enough for rifles but already learning the language of distance.

Sugar grew scarce. Rubber was counted. Tin was saved and stacked in a careful corner near the pantry door. Florence kept a small notebook beside her recipe box, adjusting measures, rewriting what abundance once allowed without thought.

"Will it come here?" Sylvia asked one afternoon, her brow furrowed as William folded the paper.

"It is already here," he answered gently. "Just not the way you imagine."

The factory whistles in town took on a different sound that spring, longer, more insistent. Trains passed through at odd hours. Young men stood straighter when they walked, as though something invisible had brushed against their shoulders.

Florence felt it too—not fear exactly, but pressure. A tightening of the weave.

And yet, beneath the steady accounting of ration cards and the careful saving of twine, something else was quietly unfolding.

She found herself pausing more often at the washbasin. Resting a hand at her apron longer than needed. Measuring her days not only by what was required, but by what she sensed gathering.

William noticed before she spoke of it.

"You're tired earlier," he said one evening, not accusing—observing.

"Perhaps," she answered. But there was a softness in her tone that had nothing to do with fatigue.

Outside, the red leaf maple stood bare against the gray sky, its small branches held upward as if in quiet insistence. Snow gathered lightly at its base, then melted. Gathered again. Melted again.

By March, Florence no longer doubted.

The war was asking for sons. Autumn, she suspected, would ask something else of her.

She did not announce it widely at first. The knowledge lived close, like a flame cupped from wind. Another child. Another voice to carry through uncertain years.

Not defiance.

Not distraction.

Continuation.

The world was breaking and binding at once. Ships were crossing dark water. Factories hummed through the night. Boys practiced marching in fields not far from home.

And in the quiet interior of her own body, life insisted.

Florence did not mistake the timing. She understood that children were never born into ease, only into seasons.

This one would arrive in autumn, when leaves turned bold before letting go.

She thought of Lillian's words.

Change could be bold.

PART IV — LETTING GO (1942–1945)

CHAPTER TWELVE — THE FIRST GOODBYE

Donna arrived during noise.

Not the noise of celebration, but of interruption, radios speaking too often, trucks passing more frequently, carts rattling down hospital corridors instead of quiet streets. The war had taught even buildings to announce themselves.

Florence labored at Bryn Mawr Hospital, the windows shaded, the lights kept low. The ward moved with practiced efficiency, nurses stepping in and out, voices clipped, purposeful. Outside the room, gurneys rolled past more often than they once had.

Dr. Harrison arrived without hurry.

"You've done this before," he said, reviewing her chart, his tone neither comforting nor cold, simply accurate. "We'll do it the same way."

Florence nodded. She did not need reassurance. She needed steadiness.

The pain came in waves, familiar and insistent. She breathed through them, counting, releasing, holding only what was necessary. Somewhere down the corridor, a radio murmured updates she did not strain to hear. This room had its own work.

"She's coming," the nurse said.

Donna arrived small but determined, her cry sharp and immediate, cutting cleanly through the layered noise of the hospital.

Dr. Harrison lifted her briefly, efficient even in wonder. "Strong lungs," he said. "She's ready."

Florence held her a moment later, the weight both astonishing and grounding. Life had insisted again—quietly, firmly—despite the world's refusal to slow.

William stood near the foot of the bed, hat in his hands, eyes fixed. "Welcome," he said softly. "You picked a loud year."

Dr. Harrison smiled once, already turning back to his instruments. "They all do," he said. "Lately."

Responsibility arrived with her.

It simply settled, into schedules, expectations, and quiet agreements that no one argued with.

Florence was still in the hospital when the first meal came together at home without her. A casserole arrived from the church, warm and carefully wrapped, carried in by a woman who kissed William's cheek and spoke Florence's name as if it were a blessing. Another neighbor followed the next day with bread and soup, then another with a pie whose crust had been pinched just so.

Bill watched closely. Dean asked questions. Gerry stood at the counter, sleeves rolled, uncertain but willing.

They took turns stirring, setting the table, washing what could not be saved for later. The work was not hard, exactly, but it was constant. Meals came every day. Plates needed filling. Someone always asked for more.

"This is what she does," Dean said once, standing over the sink, hands wet, voice changed by the thought.

Bill nodded. He had measured the hours now. Counted the tasks. He understood how little of it had ever been visible.

The children took on what they could.

Bill rose earlier, helping William before school when possible, learning which mornings required more and which allowed quiet. Dean found work close to home, errands, deliveries, small repairs for neighbors who no longer had sons or husbands nearby. Gerry and Ron took turns raking yards, hauling wood, running messages. Dale collected bottles, stacked them carefully, counted deposits twice. Sylvia folded, sorted, watched, learned.

When Florence came home with Donna bundled close against the autumn air, the house did not stop, but it shifted.

The children gathered at the bedroom door, ordered by

height without instruction.

"She's little," Sylvia said.

"She won't stay that way." Florence smiled warmly.

The boys moved differently around the table now. Plates were filled with more care. Bread was sliced evenly. Gratitude no longer needed reminding.

They had learned what it took to feed a family. And who had been doing it all along.

Nothing was wasted.

Bread ends were dried. Paper reused. String saved. Even time was measured now.

One afternoon, Florence paused at the door as the children prepared to leave again.

"Be home before dark," she said. "And stay where you're known."

"We will," Dale said quickly.

Sylvia nodded. Her school friend, Judy, stood beside her, solemn and eager, her braid already loosening from the day.

They cut across the familiar pasture behind Judy's house—a shortcut they'd taken dozens of times without thought. The grass was tall, sun-warmed, humming with insects. Dale ran ahead, then stopped abruptly.

"Don't—" he started.

Too late.

The bull lifted its head.

Massive. Still. Watching.

Sylvia froze. Judy gasped.

"Back," Dale whispered. "Slow."

The bull stamped once.

"Run," Dale said. "Now."

They ran.

The ground seemed to tilt beneath them, breath tearing loose, shoes slipping in the grass. The bull surged forward, faster than any of them had imagined possible.

"Fence!" Judy cried.

Dale reached it first, hauling himself up, then turning back without thinking. Sylvia scrambled, hands slipping, Judy's foot caught—Dale grabbed her sleeve and pulled.

Judy screamed as the wire scraped her arm. Sylvia tumbled over last, landing hard, breath knocked clean out of her.

They lay still on the other side, hearts hammering, the bull snorting and pacing before turning away at last.

No one spoke for a long moment.

Then Sylvia sat up. "We didn't know," she said.

Dale shook his head. "Doesn't matter."

They walked home without the shortcut.

Florence noticed the scraped arm immediately. "What happened?" she asked.

"Nothing," Judy said too quickly.

Dale met his mother's eyes. "We learned something," he said.

Florence nodded. "That's enough for today."

That night, as Donna slept and the house settled, Florence mended a tear in Sylvia's sleeve.

"Tell me the story," she said gently to Sylvia. "Tomorrow."

Later, when the lamps were lowered and blackout curtains secured, Florence sat with Donna against her shoulder, the radio murmuring quietly in the other room.

The war had rearranged everything.

But the children were learning, how to carry weight, how to move carefully, how to run when necessary, and when to hold still.

Life was still arriving.

Responsibility, too.

And Florence, watching them become capable in ways she had never wished for but had prepared them for all the same, understood that this was how a household endured war, not through grand gestures, but through borrowed hands, quick decisions, and the quiet refusal to waste what had been given.

By late October, the air had shifted.

Posters appeared in shop windows, bold lettering urging purchase of war bonds, urging silence, urging vigilance. Faces of soldiers stared outward from paper tacked to brick. The boys read every word.

Bill lingered longest before the posters.

He did not speak of it. He only stood a little apart, hands in his coat pockets, studying the uniforms, the dates, the small print at the bottom that mentioned age and enlistment. Once, Florence noticed him tracing the edge of a printed flag with his thumb, as though measuring it against something private.

At supper, he asked practical questions.

"How old do you have to be?"

"What's the difference between Army and Navy?"

"Do they choose you, or do you choose?"

William answered evenly, never rushing, never dismissing. "There's time yet," he said more than once.

Bill nodded each time.

But he had begun waking earlier. Florence heard him in the yard before school some mornings, splitting wood without being asked. He worked until his breath showed white in the air and his palms reddened against the handle.

"Save some for tomorrow," she called once.

"There might not be," he replied, not defiant, just certain.

Later, when Donna stirred and the house moved toward evening, Florence caught sight of him at the window, watching the road the way William sometimes did when trains passed in the night.

He was still her son.

But something in him had begun listening for a different summons.

Metal drives were announced from the church steps. Dean and Gerry dragged a bent washtub down the road one Saturday, proud of its dented usefulness. Even Sylvia surrendered a broken hair comb without complaint.

"We don't need it," she said simply.

At school, the children practiced drills, lining up quickly, heads lowered, hands over necks. They spoke of it matter-of-factly at supper, passing potatoes as though rehearsing for anything was the same as preparing.

William worked longer hours at the theater, grateful for his position as projectionist. It seemed more people came to the theater as an active diversion from the news, their faces turned toward the screen while the war pressed just beyond the doors, waiting for them when the lights came back on. Factories in town hummed past dark. Train whistles cut across midnight more often now, carrying freight instead of passengers. Sometimes Florence stood at the window with Donna tucked against her and counted the cars until the sound thinned into distance.

The red maple had begun to show itself. Its leaves, still young, had turned early, small flashes of determined crimson against a sky that felt too wide.

Donna slept through most of it.

Her breathing was steady. Her hands opened and closed as if grasping something unseen. When she cried, it was brief and certain, no apology in it.

"She doesn't know," Sylvia whispered once, watching her.

Florence smoothed the blanket. "She knows enough," she said.

Outside, men practiced marching on fields that had once held harvest festivals. Gasoline was rationed; Sunday drives faded. Letters arrived folded thin, their ink crowded into margins to save paper. Florence kept them stacked in a wooden box, tied loosely with string, each one a measure of distance and devotion.

The nearby field where children had outrun danger stood empty; the bull in the pasture had been sold.

Feed was too dear to keep an animal that served no purpose. The children noticed his absence but did not ask questions. They were learning that even strength could be repurposed.

That autumn, things took shape without asking permission.

Children grew taller. Shoulders squared. Donna grew and

stretched with the days. The maple deepened in color before releasing its leaves one by one, bold even in letting go.

Florence moved through the house with practiced economy, saving string, saving drippings, saving time. But she did not save tenderness.

At night, when blackout curtains were pinned and lamps lowered, she sat with Donna and listened to the low murmur of the radio, news from oceans she could not picture, names she whispered in prayer whether she knew the families or not.

The war had rearranged everything.

But in the small rooms of her house, shape was still being made.

Not loudly. Not for display. But steadily.

And that, she believed, would matter when the reckoning came.

CHAPTER THIRTEEN — THREE DEPARTURES

The leaving did not happen all at once.

It arrived in stages, measured not by dates, but by containers set carefully near the door. A duffel bag. A footlocker. A trunk that took longer to close than Florence expected. Each held what could be carried.

Bill went first.

His duffel rested at the foot of the stairs, soft-sided, already bearing the weight of movement. Florence packed it with the same precision she used for everything else—shirts folded flat, socks rolled tight, small necessities placed where hands would find them without searching. She did not linger. Lingering made room for doubt.

Bill came down early, already dressed, posture subtly altered, as though instruction had begun before orders were spoken. Germany. Medic. Florence repeated the words silently, the way she did with Scripture, not to soften them but to hold them steady.

"I don't need all this," he said gently, lifting a folded sweater.

"You'll be cold," she replied, tucking it back in. "And you won't think to ask for one."

He smiled, not amusement, but gratitude.

At the station, the platform filled quickly. Boots scuffed. Steam rose. Voices overlapped without listening. Florence stood close without clinging, aware that this goodbye would travel farther than the others. She straightened Bill's collar, then placed her hands on his shoulders—firm, unmistakable.

"Remember who you are," she said.

"I know," he answered. "Because you taught me."

That was promise enough.

The duffel disappeared into the train car, swallowed by metal and motion. Florence watched until the train bent out of sight, carrying her son into a place she could not follow, not even in imagination.

William did not speak. He reached for her hand and turned them away from the platform that had taken Bill. They walked the long way home, the streets unfamiliar in their familiarity, each step measured, each block accepted. Only when the house came into view, its windows patient, its door unchanged, did Florence tighten her grip, her fingers finding William's as if to confirm they were still tethered to one another.

The days that followed asked for tending. The garden needed attention, rows kept straight, soil turned where it had compacted. In the kitchen, meals were planned and prepared with care, portions adjusted, routines preserved. There were lunches to pack, clothes to inspect, chores assigned and reassigned, reminders offered without sharpness. The house held to its expectations. Florence met them steadily, keeping those still at home moving forward, school, work, the small necessary odds and ends that insisted on order.

Letters began arriving before the quiet fully settled.

Bill's handwriting was careful, slightly slanted, as though he were aware someone else might be reading over Sylvia's shoulder. The envelope bore foreign markings Florence did not linger on. She set it on the table and called Sylvia, now seven years old, in from the yard.

"From Bill," she said.

Sylvia came quickly, hands still dusty, breath short with anticipation. She slid into the chair and turned the envelope once before opening it, as though orienting herself to its distance.

Inside was a folded letter—and something smaller wrapped carefully in cloth.

A pocketknife. Silver. Plain. Its surface caught the light without asking for it.

"He wants you to keep it," Florence said, reading over Sylvia's shoulder as the words revealed themselves. "Says it's safer with you."

Sylvia lifted the knife carefully, testing its weight in her palm.

"He says it's German," she said. "That he traded for it."

Florence nodded. Men traded what they could.

Sylvia read aloud slowly, reverently.

I don't know how long I'll be here, or what I'll be asked to do. Some days feel longer than others. Keep this for me, will you? You were always better at holding on to things without losing them. When I come home, you can give it back.

Sylvia folded the letter once, then again, precise, intentional.

"I'll keep it safe," she said. "I won't even use it."

"That's not what he means," Florence replied gently. "He just means don't lose it."

Sylvia nodded, though she treated the knife like something already entrusted to memory.

That evening, she sat at the desk and wrote back.

Her handwriting was rounder than William's, less practiced, but determined. She told him about the garden, about the dog sleeping under the porch, about how Mother still folded laundry the same way even when there was less of it to fold. She did not ask questions she could not bear answers to.

She wrapped the knife again and placed it in the drawer beneath her sweater.

Safe meant still. Safe meant waiting.

The letter went out the next morning.

Dean's leaving came later. It was quieter. Almost ordinary.

His footlocker sat open in the hallway for days, its contents assembled slowly, revised often. Folded shirts were lifted and refolded. Socks counted twice. A photograph tucked into the corner, removed, then returned. He was bound for a supply center in New Jersey, close enough that Florence told herself it was not really leaving. Close enough that people spoke of it casually.

"You'll be home on leave," someone said.

"Maybe," Dean answered, noncommittal.

He moved through those final days with the steadiness she had come to recognize as his way. Not dramatic. Not restless. Simply deliberate. He tightened a loose hinge on the kitchen cabinet without being asked. Carried in wood. Checked the latch on the back gate. Small acts, as though securing the house before stepping beyond it.

Florence watched him more than she let on.

When the footlocker finally closed, the sound surprised her with its finality. A hollow clap that echoed down the hallway and seemed to settle in her chest.

Dean shrugged into his jacket as though he was headed to work, not war. He hugged her quickly—awkwardly—then smiled, as if to soften the moment.

"I'll be close," he said.

Florence nodded. She did not correct him. Distance was not always measured in miles.

After he left, the house did not feel emptier at once. It revealed its absence slowly. One less chair drawn back from the table. One less pair of shoes by the door. His laughter missing from the front room in the evenings.

She folded the blanket he had used on the sofa and placed it neatly along the armrest. She did not move it again for several days.

The letter came sooner than Florence expected.

It arrived in the midmorning post, thin and official-looking, his name written in a careful, almost formal hand. She recognized the steadiness of it at once. Dean had always written as he lived, measured, thoughtful, leaving little to chance.

She held the envelope a moment before opening it, pressing her thumb along the edge as though feeling for reassurance beneath the paper.

Only then did she break the seal.

Florence read it at the kitchen table, the light steady enough to keep her breathing even.

Dear Mom,

I wanted you to know I arrived safely. They've got me at the supply center just outside Trenton. It's busy, more paperwork than I imagined, crates coming in and going out faster than you can track. Nothing glamorous. Just making sure what's needed gets where it's supposed to go.

I think about home more than I thought I would. The way you set the table before anyone's hungry. Dad checking doors at night. The garden—tell Sylvia not to let the tomatoes overtake everything again.

I'm doing fine. Truly. Don't worry more than you have to. I'll be home when I can.

Florence read the letter twice, then once more slowly, listening for what had been set down between the lines.

Nothing glamorous. Just making sure what's needed gets where it's supposed to go.

She folded the pages carefully, aligning the edges, and placed the letter in the drawer beside the others. Another container. Another way of holding what could not be seen.

That evening, she set an extra place at the table without realizing it, then left it there. Some absences, she had learned, deserved acknowledgment.

She took out her paper that evening.

She set it square on the table, smoothed its edge with her palm, and sharpened the pencil even though the point was already fine. The house had settled into its evening sounds, pipes clicking, the low tick of the clock, William moving quietly in the other room.

She began.

Dear Dean,

The words waited.

She thought of the supply center with rows of crates, lists checked and rechecked, hands passing what others would never see. She imagined him standing among them, steady, useful, unseen. A good place for a son like Dean, she told herself. A safer place.

She wrote again.

I'm glad you arrived safely.

That was true. It was also small.

She wanted to tell him the garden was holding. That the tomatoes had been trimmed back, just enough. That Sylvia still read by the window in the evenings. That his father walked the house each night the way he always had, as though routine might anchor what had begun to drift.

She wanted to tell him she set his place at the table without thinking. That she noticed which chair he would have chosen.

Her pencil hovered. She crossed out a line before it was fully formed.

There were things a mother did not send into the world, fears that might travel faster than the mail, questions that had no safe destination. Worry was not meant to be passed along. It was meant to be carried.

Florence folded the paper once, then unfolded it again. The greeting stared back at her, unfinished. She placed the page in the drawer beside Dean's letter and closed it carefully.

Some words, she understood, were not meant to be delivered. They were meant to be held until the one who needed them most could return to receive them.

She wrote again the following morning.

She left the folded page in the drawer and, instead, reached for fresh paper, clean, uncreased, unburdened.

She sat at the table while the house was still, the light careful at the window. This time, she did not wait.

Dear Dean,

Your letter reached us safely. I was glad to hear you arrived without trouble and that your work keeps you busy. Busy is good. It leaves less room for wondering.

The house is holding steady. Your father is well. Sylvia sends her love and promises she's keeping to her chores, setting a careful example the others seem to follow. The garden is coming along, slow, but dependable. I think you'd approve.

I want you to know I'm proud of the way you've taken hold

of what's been asked of you. Not all service is visible, but all of it matters.

Take care of yourself. Eat when you can. Write when it suits you. We're right here.

With love, Mom

She read it once. Not for correction, for tone.

The letter said what needed saying. Nothing more.

Folding the page carefully, she slid it into the envelope and sealed it with deliberate pressure. At the door, she paused, letter in hand, before placing it with the outgoing mail.

Letting it go felt different than holding it.

Some words, she knew now, were meant to travel to steady the one who received them.

The newspaper arrived folded twice, its edges softened by other hands.

Florence unfolded it at the table, smoothing the crease the way she always did, though the headline resisted order.

"FIGHTING CONTINUES ON GERMAN SOIL"

She read slowly, carefully, measuring each word as though it might be rationed.

Advancing forces. Heavy resistance. Medical units under strain.

No names. No places she could picture with certainty. Only regions—*the Rhineland, along the western front*—and phrases that offered movement without meaning.

William stood behind her, reading over her shoulder.

"They don't say where," she said.

"They never do," he replied.

She traced the column with her finger, stopping where the article mentioned field stations—temporary, mobile, overwhelmed. She thought of Bill's hands. Steady. Capable. Hands meant to close wounds, not cause them.

"He won't be carrying a rifle," she said.

"No."

"But he'll be carrying others."

William nodded once.

That night, Florence folded the paper and placed it beneath Bill's letter, aligning the edges carefully. Another layer. Another way of keeping watch.

She did not speak of the article again, not to Sylvia or the others, not to Dean in her next letter. Worry, like so many things now, belonged at home.

But later, alone in the kitchen, she paused with her hands resting on the table, imagining Germany as something not marked on a map, but measured in sounds, boots on frozen ground, shouted instructions, the low urgency of voices calling for help.

She prayed without words.

For steadiness. For endurance. For hands that would keep doing what they had been taught to do.

Above all else she prayed for protection over her family, near and far.

Before Gerry's orders came, the house did not rest.

Ron and Gerry filled the days the way boys learned to, by staying in motion, though not in the same way. Gerry took naturally to the heavier work, ladders and paint cans balanced with an ease that came from liking noise and exertion. Ron followed more deliberately, quieter, carrying the smaller tools, the folded rags, the notebook where he kept track of which neighbor needed what.

They took on small jobs around the neighborhood. Lawns that had grown uneven without sons to tend them. Fences that needed repainting. Porches weathered thin by seasons that had not paused for war.

Ron preferred the work that required attention rather than strength. Measuring. Cleaning. Keeping lists. When the mower stalled, he knelt beside it, studying the problem as though it were a passage he had not yet understood.

"You could've stayed home," Gerry said once, wiping sweat from his neck. "Nobody would've blamed you."

Ron shrugged. "Someone has to remember what goes where."

Florence noticed how he carried a book with him, even now, set carefully on a porch rail while he worked, retrieved again before they left. He read in the evenings when his hands were too tired for anything else, pages turned slowly, thoughtfully.

"It's good to be useful," Ron said quietly one night, as though testing the words.

William glanced at him then—not with concern, but with recognition.

Some men would charge ahead. Others would wait, watch, and learn how things failed, and how they might be held together longer.

Florence folded the money they earned into an envelope and placed it in the drawer with the letters. Another small contribution. Another quiet holding.

When Gerry's notice finally came, it did not interrupt a stillness.

It arrived into motion, into a house already practicing what it meant to send its sons forward, each in his own way.

Gerry left last.

By then, the war had shifted, its urgency altered, but not erased. Headlines grew smaller, then disappeared. People spoke of *after* as though it were a place already reached.

Gerry's trunk stood in the front room, its hard sides scuffed before it ever moved. He was headed to Guam, after the fighting, to help with cleanup. Support work. Restoration. Words meant to sound lighter than they were.

Florence helped him pack deliberately. The trunk demanded choices, what would endure travel, what could not.

"I won't need this," he said, holding up a book.

"You'll want it," she replied. "For the waiting."

When the trunk was finally closed, she rested her hand on the lid a moment longer than necessary.

"This isn't over," Gerry said, uncertain whether he meant

the war—or his and his brothers leaving.

"No," Florence replied. "It isn't."

His father carried what needed carrying. He moved without hurry. Lifted the trunk. Checked the footlocker once more. Finished each task fully, as though completing it properly might anchor what followed. Florence noticed how he did not watch the containers leave. He watched her instead—the set of her shoulders, the way she released her breath only after the door closed.

That evening, he moved through the house restoring what he could. A chair returned to its place. A lamp switched off in a room no longer needed. He did not speak of the silence, but he shaped it, keeping it from becoming something that pressed too hard.

When Florence finally sat at the table, her hands folded in her lap, William placed his own over them once. Briefly. Not consolation. Acknowledgment.

"He went steady," William said, his voice low. "Just as he should."

She nodded, though her gaze remained on their hands where they had met. "He didn't look back."

"No," William answered. "He didn't need to."

That seemed to settle between them, not as comfort, but as something true.

After a moment, Florence drew a slow breath. "I kept thinking I would say more." A faint, almost rueful note touched her voice. "Something to carry with him."

William's hand shifted slightly, not to hold, only to remain near. "You already have."

She lifted her eyes to him then. "Have I?"

He met her look evenly. "He knows who he comes from."

The room stayed quiet around them, the kind that did not press for more.

Florence let that rest where it was. "Guam feels … far."

"It is," William said. Then, after a pause, "But not beyond reach."

Her fingers moved once beneath his, as if testing the steadiness of something unseen. "And Ron …" she began, but did not finish.

William understood. His voice, when it came, was firm without force. "One step at a time."

She studied him a moment longer, then gave a small nod.

"One step," she echoed.

His hand lifted then, not withdrawing so much as completing the gesture. The contact had done what it needed to do.

Outside, the house held its usual shape. Inside, they sat a moment longer, together in it, not speaking further, because there was nothing left that required saying. Later, as they prepared for bed, he paused in the hallway where three rooms now waited differently than before. He closed each door carefully, as though tucking the house in.

Some men left to serve.

William served by staying, holding the center so that everything else might one day return to it.

When the house finally emptied, it did not feel vacant. It felt rearranged.

The containers were gone, but their absence remained, spaces where they had rested, impressions left behind. Florence moved through the rooms, returning objects to their places, restoring order where she could.

A night later, she sat alone at the kitchen table, her hands folded in her lap. She thought of duffels, footlockers, trunks, of children carried inside them, sealed away from her reach.

She had followed them through childhood, through illness, through small dangers she could manage.

This was different.

These containers belonged to the world now.

Florence rose and turned out the light.

Letting go, she understood, did not mean releasing what was loved.

It meant trusting what had been given to carry it forward.

Ron was fourteen now, long-limbed, voice deepening

without permission. He carried wood without being asked and listened differently when the radio spoke of the Pacific. Florence sometimes caught him studying Gerry's photograph as though memorizing it for later.

Dale, twelve, still moved between boyhood and resolve. He asked questions at the table, practical ones, the way Bill once had. He lingered near his father more often, absorbing tone as much as instruction.

Sylvia, ten, kept close to little Donna in the afternoons, braiding and unbraiding her hair, inventing games that required no running toward roads or fields. She had begun to notice her mother's silences and filled them with small steadiness's of her own.

And Donna, four years old and certain of the world's goodness, moved through the rooms as if nothing irreversible had occurred. She sang while stacking blocks. She asked when Gerry would come back, not whether.

They remained, watchful and waiting.

Florence understood that war did not empty a house all at once. It thinned it in layers. One son forward. Then another. The younger ones measuring themselves quietly against the space left behind.

She did not mistake the arithmetic.

Fourteen was closer to eighteen than she preferred to admit.

Twelve was listening.

Ten was learning how to hold a room.

Four was still wholly hers.

War had taken Gerry into its keeping.

But it had left her with those still growing toward it.

And that, too, required preparation.

Florence had once stood at the edge of a doorway herself, small and silent, watching adults decide what would happen next.

She did not remember every word spoken that day long ago. Only the feeling of being carried forward by choices not her own.

Now she stood on the other side of that threshold.

Her children watched her the way she had once watched—measuring steadiness, measuring tone, searching faces for what was not said aloud.

She understood something she had not known at five: that departures echo longer in those who remain.

And so she kept her voice even. Her hands busy. Her posture unbroken, because she remembered what it was to stand small and uncertain in a room that decided your future.

Yet even as she counted the years forward—fourteen, twelve, ten, four—Florence felt something she could not yet name.

The house had grown quieter in its upper corners. Beds stood neatly made, trunks no longer tucked beneath them. The air carried absence differently now.

But beneath the thinning, there was also a deepening.

She noticed it in herself first, not in fatigue, but in attention. A widening patience. A tenderness that did not feel like concession, but like gathering.

Life did not move in a single direction. It pressed outward, yes. But sometimes, quietly, it returned.

One evening, as she folded laundry beside the stove, Donna wandered in and leaned against her skirts.

"Will there always be someone little?" she asked, without context.

Florence smoothed Donna's hair.

"I expect so," she said.

She did not yet know how true that would be.

Outside, the maple stood bare against the winter sky, its branches lifted in spare outline, waiting for a season not yet visible.

CHAPTER FOURTEEN — INK, PAPER, AND PRAYER

The letters became Florence's way of remaining close to her sons in the long stretches of absence and silence, each line of ink carrying what her arms no longer could.

She kept her paper in a drawer beside the stove, close enough to reach without thinking. Envelopes were stacked neatly, their edges aligned. Stamps were counted, replaced as needed. She wrote in the mornings, when the house was still and when words came without needing to be coaxed.

Ink became a way through.

She learned quickly what not to include. Fear did not travel well. Neither did questions without answers. Instead, she wrote about weather, about small repairs, about what had bloomed unexpectedly in the garden.

The lilacs surprised us this year.

The back step finally stopped creaking.

Sunday's roast turned out better than expected.

She wrote about church bells and familiar hymns. About neighbors who asked after them. About meals that held together even when the days did not.

Between the lines, she folded prayer.

And at the bottom of the page, she always left a careful space—not large, not demanding—just enough.

Enough for William.

He would add a sentence or two in his steadier hand. A practical note. A bit of news from town. Sometimes only his name, written firm and unmistakable, as if to say: *We are both here. We are both standing.*

The letters traveled that way—theirs.

Held together.

On evenings when the house felt thinned by distance, she

reached for the gentler books, the ones that asked little and gave comfort freely. She read from *Winnie-the-Pooh* without comment, grateful for a world where friendship was enough and no one was expected to be brave all the time.

"Just one more," Sylvia said once, already leaning closer.

Florence smiled but closed the book carefully, as she did the letters, trusting that what had been held would last through the night.

She did not press for reassurance in what she wrote. She left space for reply. She trusted the rhythm of exchange—the sending, the waiting, the receiving—as its own form of faith.

On Sundays, Florence sat in the same pew she always had, her hands resting on the smooth wood in front of her. The Bryn Mawr Presbyterian Church sanctuary remained dignified, unchanged in structure, though not untouched by the war's reach. Names were added to prayer lists. Candles burned longer than before. The congregation learned how to hold absence together.

Florence bowed her head and listened.

She did not ask for protection alone. She asked for steadiness, for her sons, for William, for the others and herself. For words when words were needed, and silence when they were not. When the service ended, she remained seated a moment longer.

"Take your time," William murmured beside her.

She nodded. Stillness, she had learned, worked best when not rushed.

Back home, replies arrived unevenly.

Some envelopes were thin, others heavier with pages folded small. Florence opened each carefully, smoothing the paper before reading, as though preparing it to be held. She read once for information, once for what was not said. She learned her sons' handwriting anew, how it shifted, tightened, steadied.

William read beside her, offering no commentary unless asked. When one letter arrived late, he set it aside.

"Later," he said.

"Yes," she agreed, knowing some words were better met with a steadier heart than the hour allowed.

At night, she returned the letters to their place—stacked, ordered, contained. Proof of life. Of continuity. Of connection stretched across distance and danger. Often, before turning out the light, she paused with one envelope still in hand, resting it against her palm as though prayer might travel back through the paper.

Words, she learned, could be lifelines. They crossed oceans and borders. They held what could not be spoken aloud. And when folded carefully, they carried faith, quiet, enduring, and strong enough to wait.

Sylvia wrote too.

Not long letters. Careful ones.

She told Bill small things. The way the piano sounded different with the windows open, how Donna's laugh arrived without warning, how the house settled at night. She did not ask for reassurance. She offered steadiness.

"You don't have to write much," Florence told her once.

"I know," Sylvia replied. "I just want it to be right."

Bill carried Sylvia's letters folded into his medic's kit, paper softened by travel. In places far from home, her words reminded him that life was continuing somewhere intact.

One arrived in early spring.

Dear Bill,

I hope this reaches you where there is still light through a window.

Spring is finding its way here, slowly. Mother says the lilacs are early this year and trims them as if they might notice. The house moves quietly, listening before it speaks.

Donna grows quickly and laughs at things all of the time. It feels like a good sign.

I open the piano most afternoons when the sun reaches the keys. Some days it sounds like waiting. Other days it sounds like remembering. I play softly, mindful of what is still being held together.

Please do not worry about us. We are steady. Supper comes when it should. There is comfort in that.

I think often of the work of hands and how they know what to do even when the heart is tired. I imagine yours sure and careful, and I am grateful for the lives they touch.

Write when you can. Until then, know you are carried here—in prayer, in thought, and in the quiet spaces between notes.

With love, Sylvia

Bill read it once. Then again, more slowly. He folded it along its original creases and held it there a moment.

Around him, the tent stirred, boots, voices, the unspoken language of survival—but the letter gave him something firm to return to.

When he tucked it back into his kit, his hands were steadier.

That night, after the lamps were lowered, he took out his own paper. He wrote to his mother first. He did not describe what he saw. He told her he was well enough. That his hands were still steady. That he carried her prayers with him and had found use for them.

When he finished, he folded the page carefully, the way he folded everything that mattered.

Dean's letters arrived next, postmarked Trenton. They were practical, nearly instructional—lists more than stories. He wrote of supplies tallied and retallied, of warehouses that never truly slept, of learning how much could be moved quietly if everyone did their part. He asked after home in small ways, whether the bread still rose properly in winter, if the garden fence had held through the last storm. Florence answered him with details she knew he'd appreciate, grounding him in the order he'd always trusted.

Gerry's letters came less regularly, the stamps unfamiliar, the return address stamped simply: Guam. His writing carried the heat with it, humidity pressing through the page, days broken by sudden rain, nights alive with unfamiliar sounds.

He did not complain. He described skies that never seemed to dim fully, work that demanded attention without ceremony, and a sense of distance unlike any he'd known before. Florence read his letters slowly, sometimes twice, tracing the words with her finger as if the motion might shorten the space between them.

She kept their letters together, stacked, folded, returned to envelopes when she could, proof that though they were scattered across maps and oceans, they were still speaking to one another. The house remained steady. The days moved forward. And each letter, arriving or sent, stitched another thread through the quiet that had not yet learned how to settle.

At night, when the house had settled and even the ticking clocks seemed to soften, Florence took the letters out once more. She did not read them again. Sometimes she only laid her hand across the small stack, feeling their weight, their edges worn from being folded and unfolded too many times.

She prayed over them with few words. Praying for steadiness. For protection in places she could not picture. For the grace to hold what was given without trying to outrun it. Each name passed through her quietly, one by one, as if spoken aloud might disturb the fragile order of the night.

When she finished, she returned the letters to their place and smoothed the drawer closed. Morning would come. Work would wait. And until the next envelope arrived, this was how she kept them close, held, entrusted, released.

CHAPTER FIFTEEN — THE HOME FRONT

The war rearranged the days without announcing itself.

Ration books now had become well-used staples in kitchen drawers, their coupons counted and recounted until Florence knew them by feel.

"You're short a sugar stamp," Sylvia said once, leaning over the table.

"I know," Florence replied. "We'll make it stretch."

Sugar measured smaller. Butter stretched thinner. Shoes were repaired rather than replaced, soles resoled, heels rebuilt, leather softened with care. Nothing about it felt dramatic. It was simply how the neighborhood adjusted, quietly, collectively, without complaint.

Gardens expanded in response.

Florence's baskets filled with what the season allowed, beans, tomatoes, and greens gathered early before the heat set in.

"These came in faster than I expected," she said, setting a basket on Mrs. Kelley's step.

"Take some bread in return," Mrs. Kelley answered, already turning back inside. "I baked too much."

Once a week, a different sound moved through the street.

The rag man came with his horse and wagon, the wooden wheels announcing him before he did. The horse stepped patiently, familiar with the route, its harness creaking softly as the wagon slowed.

"Rags! Old rags!" the man called, voice practiced but never loud.

Florence brought out a bundle tied with string—shirts worn thin at the elbows, towels softened past repair. Neighbors emerged as well, each offering what had finished one life and might begin another.

"Every bit counts," the rag man said, tipping his hat as he took the bundle.

Florence nodded. "It always does."

Nothing was wasted now. Tin was flattened. Paper saved. Rubber gathered.

"Feels strange, saving scraps," Sylvia said, watching the wagon move on.

"Feels stranger not to," Florence replied.

On Sundays, the rhythm gathered itself inside the family's church.

The old stone walls held their cool even in summer, and the great pipe organ rose above the sanctuary like something rooted rather than built.

Florence settled into her usual pew with William beside her. The children were in their Sunday school classrooms in the other building.

"Cooler today," he murmured.

She nodded. "It helps me listen."

When the organ spoke, she felt the echo of another room, long ago. The theater where his music had once filled the silence between scenes when she only knew him as "the music man."

"You hear it too, don't you?" she whispered once, as the notes rose.

William smiled faintly. "Always."

The pews filled differently now, more women, more children, more empty spaces where men once sat, but the order of the service remained intact.

When the minister spoke of endurance, his voice steady, no one needed instruction. "We hold one another," he said simply.

"Amen," came softly from the pew behind them.

After the service, the congregation moved slowly into the light.

"Any word from Bill?" someone asked, careful with the

question.

"Not yet," Florence replied. "But we're waiting."

"That counts," the woman said, squeezing her arm.

Down the narrow stairs beneath the sanctuary, the fellowship room was already awake with quiet conversation. Coffee steamed in mismatched cups. Plates held slices of cake and small cookies set out without ceremony. William and Florence stood among familiar faces, accepting what was offered, sipping slowly, listening more than speaking. There was comfort in the ordinariness of it, in the shared understanding that being present was enough.

After a while, they made their way back up and out into the open air. The children were waiting just beyond the doors, gathered in small clusters, folded papers in hand, voices low but eager. Florence felt the familiar pull of them then, the living weight of those still within reach, and William rested his hand at her back as they stepped forward together, the morning carrying them home.

After church, the neighborhood resumed its careful motion.

Walks home turned into quiet check-ins.

"Radio said fighting's heavier again," Mr. Ellis mentioned.

"Yes," William replied. "We heard."

A few houses down lived Dr. Stuart Mudd, close enough to feel less like a neighbor and more like part of the street's daily rhythm.

He and William spoke often, over the fence, on the sidewalk, sometimes standing longer than intended, as though neither quite knew how to conclude a conversation that had begun in curiosity rather than greeting.

"How's the laboratory?" William asked when Stuart stopped by their house later in the afternoon.

Stuart exhaled, thoughtful. "Busy. Careful work. A lot of waiting."

Florence knew he worked with blood—something about

preserving it, transporting it, making it usable beyond the moment it was drawn. She had heard fragments over time, never pressed for detail. What mattered most to her was how he spoke of it, not with pride, but with focus.

"We're trying to make it last," he said once, gesturing vaguely, as though the idea were too large to hold in one place. "To take what's fragile and give it time."

William nodded. "So it can be where it's needed."

"Exactly," Stuart replied. "A soldier doesn't need blood where it's drawn. He needs it where he falls."

Florence stood nearby, folding laundry, listening without appearing to. The words settled with a weight she did not comment on.

Later, when Stuart mentioned working with a colleague, "a biochemist who sees things differently than I do," Florence caught only the tone of it: collaboration without competition.

"We've learned how to dry plasma," he said simply. "Freeze it. Preserve it. Ship it without losing what matters."

"And it works?" William asked.

Stuart smiled faintly. "It does. Which means now we have to make enough."

Florence thought of Bill then. Of field stations. Of hands working quickly, carefully, never knowing what would arrive in time and what would not. She imagined blood not as something lost, but as something *carried*, held between moments, crossing distances the way letters did.

"It must feel strange," she said quietly, surprising herself. "Working so far from where it's used."

He considered this. "At first. But you get used to trusting the chain. You do your part. Someone else does theirs. Lives move along that line."

When he left, William stood watching him go.

"He talks about it the way you talk about engines," Florence said.

William nodded. "Same problem, really. How to keep something working long enough to matter."

Later that week, Florence paused over the newspaper.

She had meant only to fold it for kindling, but a headline caught and held her:

DRIED PLASMA SPEEDS AID TO WOUNDED OVERSEAS

She read the article once, then again more slowly. It spoke of laboratories, of preservation and transport, of blood made portable, usable far from where it was drawn. The language was careful, almost modest, as though aware that what it described was too important for flourish.

Florence thought of Dr. Mudd's quiet voice.

Of Bill's steady hands.

Of letters crossing water while other things crossed farther.

She folded the paper and placed it beneath the stack of letters waiting to be answered.

Some work, she understood, traveled unseen, but arrived all the same.

Later, Florence wrote one more line in her letter, nothing specific, nothing that could alarm.

There are people here doing careful work. Quiet work. It helps to know that.

She folded the page and sealed it, trusting that what traveled between them did not need explanation to be felt.

That evening, she returned the ration books to their place.

"Tomorrow we'll start earlier," she said to Sylvia, setting the garden baskets by the door.

"I'll help," Sylvia replied. "Before it gets too sunny."

Florence washed her hands and stood at the window, watching lights appear one by one along the block.

Fear was present. It always was.

But it was held—contained within routine, conversation, shared work, and the quiet conviction that ordinary days, faithfully tended, were not small at all.

Later, when the children were settled and the house had taken on its nighttime hush, Florence moved toward the front room. William was already there, seated at the piano, his back to the door. A soft tune drifted into the hallway, unhurried, familiar, played more for steadiness than performance.

She paused, then stepped fully into the room. "Don't stop," she said quietly.

He didn't. She took her seat, the gentle rhythm settling her as it always did, smoothing the edges of what the day had carried.

When the final notes faded, he closed the fallboard and came to sit beside her. They spoke softly then, of the children still under their roof, of the boys gone far and near, of how quickly time seemed to move even when the days felt long. There was no need to name what lay ahead. Some things announced themselves gently, arriving first as a sense, a widening, a future not yet shaped but already making room.

They sat together a while longer, the piano silent, the house breathing around them, steady, expectant, holding what was still to come.

CHAPTER SIXTEEN — WHAT STAYED

The house learned new rhythms after each coming and going. The older boys departing for faraway places, the arrival of Donna, and the daily happenings all seemed to adjust. Life did not pause for explanation. It rearranged itself and continued.

Ron read more than before.

He claimed the chair nearest the window when he could, light falling cleanly across the page. When the house grew too loud, he took his book outside, perching on the back step, the fence rail, sometimes the low stone wall where the street curved away from view.

Not all the neighborhood boys understood this.

They wanted motion. Noise. The quick proof of belonging that came from running hard and coming home scraped and breathless. Ron did not refuse them outright. He simply did not follow.

"Come on," one of them said once, tugging at his sleeve. "We're playing down the block."

"In a minute," Ron replied, eyes still on the page.

The minute passed.

The next time, they did not ask.

A shove. A sharp knock to the shoulder. Fingers striking the book hard enough to send it skidding across the pavement.

"Stop reading," one of them said. "Run."

Ron retrieved the book without speaking. His knuckles were scraped. His lip split once—thin enough not to bleed much, but enough to sting.

He came home quieter on those days.

Florence noticed the marks without comment. She cleaned them carefully, the way she cleaned everything else, methodical, calm.

"They don't like it," Ron said once, when she pressed a cloth to his hand.

"That you read?"

"That I don't run."

She considered him, then nodded. "You don't owe anyone noise."

He absorbed this silently.

After that, he learned when to move and when to stay. He read where he could finish a chapter. He ran just enough to be left alone. He learned how to take a hit without dropping what mattered.

William noticed too, not the bruises, but the steadiness.

"He watches first," William said quietly one evening.

Florence nodded. "And remembers."

Late in the afternoon, when the light slanted low and the street quieted between errands, Ron sat on the front steps with his book open across his knees, one finger holding his place. Sylvia was inside at the piano, the window raised just enough to let the sound spill out, soft, careful, unfinished.

She heard the voices before she saw them.

"Still reading?"

The music faltered. Sylvia stood, listening.

A book slapped shut. A laugh—too sharp to belong to play.

"Come on," one of the boys said. "You don't need that."

Sylvia crossed the room and stepped onto the porch.

Ron stood now, his shoulders squared, the book held tight against his chest. One boy reached for it again.

"Leave him," Sylvia said.

They turned, surprised more than threatened.

"What?" one asked.

"He's busy," she said, and moved down the steps until she was beside Ron. She did not raise her voice. She did not explain. She simply stood there, close enough that Ron could feel her steadiness without looking at her.

"He's always busy," another boy said. "That's the problem."

Sylvia considered this.

"No," she said. "That's not a problem. That's his way."

One of them scoffed. "He thinks he's better than us."

Ron opened his mouth, but Sylvia spoke first.

"He doesn't," she said. "He just likes different things."

They waited for more, for an apology, a dare, a challenge. Sylvia offered none.

"You can play if you want," she added, evenly. "But you don't get to take what isn't yours."

The silence stretched. The boys shifted, uncertain where the line had moved.

"Come on," one muttered finally, backing away. "Let's go."

They left without ceremony, the street absorbing them the way it always did.

Ron let out a breath he hadn't known he was holding.

"You didn't have to," he said.

Sylvia shrugged. "I wanted to."

He looked at her then. "They won't stop."

"I know," she replied. "But they'll think first next time."

She waited until he sat again before turning back toward the house.

At the piano, her hands rested on the keys longer than usual before she played. When she did, the notes were steadier, not louder, not faster, just sure of themselves.

Outside, Ron reopened his book and placed his finger back on the page, exactly where he'd left off. He read because it ordered the world, because it explained what noise could not.

And somewhere in that quiet persistence, that refusal to be hurried into someone else's rhythm, something durable was taking shape.

Dale liked to be moving all the time. He went from the floor to the yard and back again. One minute he was building a city out of blocks. The next, the rug was a huge field and he was marching across it.

He built things up and then knocked them down on purpose, not because he was mad, but because he wanted to start over and make them better.

Sometimes he let Donna help. He would spread her blanket out and tell her it was the border. She wasn't allowed to cross it unless he said so.

"She's watching," he said seriously.

"She always is," Florence replied.

Aunt Mae visited weekly, as reliably as the P&W that carried her in and out of the neighborhood from the city. She arrived at Haverford Station with her handbag squared firmly on her arm and expectations just as neatly arranged. Music, she insisted, was not an ornament. It was a language. One learned early, or spent a lifetime translating poorly.

The boys often found ways to disappear when she came. Errands suddenly required running. A ball needed retrieving from a yard too far away to hear instruction. One by one, they slipped beyond her reach, leaving Sylvia, willing, patient, attentive, to bear the weight of her focus at the piano.

Mae did not mind. Sylvia listened.

She would stay for a meal when Florence insisted, sharing conversation that wandered easily between music and memory—stories of William as a young man, earnest and determined, working hours at Luther's small grocery before hurrying off to lessons. It was under Mae's roof, after all, that William had first been allowed to live in Philadelphia, her quiet confidence making room for his studies at the conservatory. She spoke of those years without pride, only certainty, as if she had simply recognized what needed tending.

By early evening she rose, gloves smoothed, schedule resumed. The P&W carried her home again, its rhythm already familiar to the household she left behind.

Sylvia practiced every afternoon. Now and then, Sylvia corrected herself, nothing dramatic, just a slight shift of hand or pace, as if someone had once stood nearby long enough to be remembered.

The piano had become less a lesson and more a companion. She opened it without prompting, pulling the bench back just enough. Some days were devoted to discipline—scales, repetition, correction. Other days wandered. Melody gave way to memory, though Sylvia was too young to name it as such.

The house listened.

Not in a way anyone announced it, but in the way the house seemed to grow quieter when the music began. Florence would stand nearby with Donna on her hip, the child warm and solid against her.

Donna rarely stayed still at first. She twisted a curl around her finger. She tapped Florence's shoulder in time with the louder notes. Sometimes she whispered questions that didn't quite match the moment.

But after a while, the rhythm would find her. Her head would rest against Florence's collarbone. Her fingers would grow quiet. The music, more than instruction, would hold her there.

"Softly," Sylvia whispered once, glancing back.

"I am," Florence answered. And she was.

Evenings gathered them in quieter ways. Dale sprawled on the rug, sorting marbles by color. Ron read aloud when asked, his voice even, unhurried. Donna settled between them, leaning here, then there, the center of a circle she would not remember forming.

"Tell her a story," Dale said.

"She doesn't understand," Ron replied.

"She will," Sylvia said. "Later."

Florence watched them then, their closeness imperfect but sincere, and felt something settle into place. Not relief. Not certainty. Something firmer.

Occasionally, the house felt as though it were holding its breath. Letters still arrived. Radios still spoke too loudly. Names hovered unspoken at the edges of conversation. But inside these rooms, ordinary things insisted on being done. Pages turned. Keys struck. Toys gathered and scattered again.

William moved between hours. He kept his work at the

theater, lights cued, reels threaded, evenings accounted for, but more and more of his time spent elsewhere.

In the shop, with Isaac, days unfolded in pieces: measurements revised, parts tested, failures set aside without comment. What they were building did not yet have a name. It required patience more than optimism. William came home carrying the quiet of that work with him, hands marked, thoughts still turning.

One afternoon, as Sylvia played and Ron read and Dale argued quietly with himself, Florence glanced down at Donna and thought—without urgency, without fear—that this child would not be the last.

The thought surprised her with its calm.

Not now, of course. Not while the world remained unsettled. But later. When the house had learned yet another rhythm. When the silence made room again.

That night, after Donna had been laid down and the others drifted toward sleep, Sylvia returned once more to the piano. She played softly, careful not to wake anyone. The melody was unfinished, resolving itself only where it could.

Florence listened from the doorway.

She glanced toward William, and without speaking they moved together into the front room. They took their seats side by side, close enough that their shoulders touched, and settled into stillness. Neither spoke. There was nothing to add. The music filled what needed filling.

William listened the way he always had, counting without counting, noticing how Sylvia returned to a phrase, how she tested its weight before letting it move on. Even unfinished, the music held. It knew where it could bear pressure and where it needed release.

The war had not ended. Fear had not left. But life—persistent, unannounced, unmistakable—continued to take its place among them.

And the house, for all it had lost, remained open.

Later, when the piano lid was lowered and the children

drifted toward their rooms, William crossed to the radio. He turned the dial slowly, careful not to rush the static.

The announcer's voice carried a different tone that evening. Less urgency. More restraint. Words like *advance* and *collapse* and *near surrender* threaded through the broadcast. Cities named. Lines redrawn. Speculation offered, then carefully tempered.

Florence stood at the doorway, drying her hands on her apron though there was nothing left to dry.

They did not look at one another. They had learned the discipline of waiting.

But something in the cadence had shifted.

Not victory. Not yet.

They were listening now for the bell, the clear, unmistakable strike that would end what force had begun.

And until it sounded, they would remain in their corners. Steady. Guarded. Ready to step forward when called.

PART V — HOMECOMINGS & HOLDINGS (1945–1947)

CHAPTER SEVENTEEN — VICTORY WITHOUT EASE (1945)

The war ended the way it had been carried, suddenly, yet not all at once.

On doorsteps and stoops across the city, newspapers landed with a heavier thud that morning, pages already creased by urgency. *The Philadelphia Inquirer* declared it plainly, the headline stretching wide across the front page:

NAZIS SURRENDER

V-E DAY TODAY

Below it, columns marched in tidy formation, chronologies tracing the rise and fall of Hitler's Germany, maps inked dark with arrows finally pointing backward, tributes to Allied generals whose names had become familiar through repetition rather than closeness. The war, it seemed, had been reduced to order at last. Labeled. Summarized. Finished.

People gathered where the papers lay open. Fingers traced dates. Voices read aloud what eyes could not yet absorb. Church bells rang without waiting for instruction. Car horns answered back, uneven and insistent.

The bells began before the words did.

Florence was at the sink when she heard them, one at first, then another, carrying from different directions across the Main Line. Not urgent. Not frantic. Just steady.

She dried her hands and stepped onto the porch.

Down the street, Mrs. Halpern had done the same, apron still tied at her waist. Across from her, old Mr. Kearney stood at the edge of his lawn, hat in hand, listening as if the sound required confirmation.

A screen door opened somewhere behind her. Another bell joined the first.

William came to stand beside her without asking why.

"Europe," he said quietly.

She nodded. It was not a question.

A boy on a bicycle rode past, waving a folded newspaper above his head. "Germany's surrendered!" he called, voice cracking between boyhood and something older.

Flags appeared almost shyly, drawn from drawers, shaken open, fastened to porch rails that had waited patiently through four years of rationing and restraint.

No one cheered at first.

They simply stood.

The wind moved lightly through the maples lining the street. Somewhere, a radio carried the president's voice through an open window, the words blurred by distance but unmistakable in tone.

Mrs. Halpern began to clap, once, then twice. The sound felt uncertain, as though she were testing whether hands still remembered how. Mr. Kearney joined her. Then another neighbor. The rhythm gathered, small and uncoordinated but sincere.

William did not clap.

Florence felt his shoulder steady against hers.

"Gerry's still in the Pacific," she said.

"Yes."

The bells continued.

Children, who understood only that something large had shifted, ran in widening circles on the sidewalk. A sparrow startled from the hedges. The train whistle down the line carried longer than usual, as if even it had something to declare.

Victory had arrived.

Relief stood at the edge of it, uncertain where to step.

Florence reached for William's hand. He let her take it.

Across the street, someone began to sing *The Star-Spangled Banner*, softly at first, then stronger as others found the tune. The notes rose into the same air that had held telegrams and rumors and ration counts.

Florence did not join the singing.

But she did not go inside either.

The house behind her remained open.

And for the first time in a long while, the waiting loosened, just slightly, its grip.

But the sound that carried farthest was not celebration. It was the exhale that followed years of holding still.

Some papers were already setting type for what had not yet come, another date, another headline waiting its turn. August sat farther down the calendar, unnamed but present. Victory, it seemed, would need to be declared more than once before it could be believed.

Train cars arrived in steady succession, metal shrieking as brakes caught, doors sliding open to release what they had held too long. Men stepped down with duffels worn soft by use, faces altered by time lived under instruction.

"There," someone said, pointing.

"No, over there."

"I thought he'd be taller."

Greetings varied. Embraces clung too tightly. Others faltered mid-reach, stopping just short of contact. Victory, Florence saw, had not returned everyone equally. Men came home carrying what had not been issued and could not be returned.

Florence stood near the edge of the platform with William, watching the rhythm repeat itself.

"They don't look finished," she said quietly.

William shook his head. "They're not."

The war released men from duty, but not from its weight. Relief arrived easily. Rest did not.

Florence thought then of other kinds of force she had known—measured, bounded, ended by agreement. This was not that. War, she learned, had no bell. It did not signal when enough had been done, only when something else was about to begin.

William watched posture. How some men still leaned forward, ready for command. How others stood uncertainly, as though waiting to be told where to place their hands.

"Home feels strange," a man near them muttered to no one in particular.

"Yes," Florence said softly, though she did not know him. "It does."

Farther away, and with less witness, the barracks emptied. Lockers stood open, names scratched out or peeled away. Cots were stripped and stacked. What had once been held in precise order was released without ceremony.

The war did not tidy after itself. It left spaces behind.

That evening, Florence set the table before the light fully faded. Soup simmered longer than necessary. Bread was sliced and resliced, as if precision might invite arrival.

"They should be through by now," Ron said, glancing toward the clock.

Florence nodded. "Trains don't keep promises anymore."

"They'll come," William said, taking his seat. "They always do. Just not when we expect it."

Dale dragged his chair closer. "Will Bill come first?"

"Dean might," Florence said. "They'll find their way."

"And Gerry?" Sylvia asked, her voice careful.

Florence met her daughter's eyes. "Later," she said. "But yes."

They ate without ceremony, listening for footsteps that did not come. Conversation circled ordinary things—school, a loose hinge, a neighbor's fence—never landing where it wanted to rest. When the bowls were cleared and the kettle set on, the waiting did not leave with the dishes.

At home, William had remained where routine could still be counted on.

As a projectionist, he threaded film through machines night after night, keeping stories moving while the world beyond the theater lurched and stalled. Newsreels slowly gave way to features again. Applause returned where silence had been.

"Feels like people forgot how to clap," a young usher said one evening.

"They'll remember," William replied. "They always do."

He understood something then: continuity, too, could be a form of service. Keeping the reel steady. Letting the story finish.

In the garage, his own unfinished story waited. Drawers held sketches untouched by the years they could not see. The locked desk remained closed, not out of fear, but out of decision.

During the thickest stretch of the war, a man from Washington had come calling.

"You could scale this," the man said, tapping the drawings. "Government contract. Good money. Steady work."

William listened without interrupting.

"There would be inspections," the man continued. "Paperwork. Names. Partners."

William gathered the pages, aligning their edges before sliding them back into the drawer.

"I won't be taking it," he said.

The man frowned. "You'd be turning down more than a paycheck."

"I know."

He did not explain that scrutiny traveled unevenly in wartime. That some names drew attention they could not afford. That protecting a partner sometimes meant refusing opportunity.

He did not say Isaac Rosenfeld aloud.

Some names were guarded the way others guarded gold.

Florence believed their financial strain had been wartime scarcity.

It was not.

It was the quiet cost of deciding who would be protected when protection was not evenly given.

When racing resumed in earnest, William attended once, standing near the fence as engines roared back to civilian life. The machines were faster now. Louder. Tuned for spectacle.

A young mechanic glanced at him. "You ever work on motors?"

William smiled faintly. "Once."

The checkered flag fell. Most of the cars crossed intact. The crowd cheered as though completion itself were triumph.

William remained where he was, listening as the engines ticked and cooled, the noise thinning into something quieter, truer.

Endurance, he had learned, was rarely loud. It revealed itself after the strain, in what still stood.

That evening, more celebration spilled into the streets, but William and Florence walked home slowly, letting the noise move around them without pulling them in.

"Everyone else seems relieved," Florence said.

"They are," William answered. "It's just not the same thing."

Victory had arrived. Ease had not.

Later, as Florence set the kettle on and William checked the clock above the stove, neither spoke of what they were measuring.

The war had released what it held.

Tomorrow, it would return something of their own. First in small increments. A letter marked "arriving soon." A date circled in pencil. A uniform folded carefully for the last time before civilian clothes were pressed and hung.

At home, the porch light glowed as it always had. Florence paused before unlocking the door, listening once more to the distant bells, now softer, less certain.

Inside, the house held its shape. The chairs remained where they belonged. The hallway runner lay straight. The kettle found its place on the stove.

Later, as Florence set the water to heat and William checked the clock above the cupboard, neither spoke of what they were measuring. She had learned not to count ahead. Not to prepare joy before it stood at the door.

Trains would begin running fuller in the coming weeks.

Schedules would shift. Names would appear in columns no longer bordered in black. Some sons would step down onto platforms thinner than when they had left, duffel bags slung low, eyes searching before they allowed themselves to see.

Others would wait their turn across warmer waters, their return measured in tides and timetables not yet announced.

Still, somewhere beneath her discipline, something shifted, an awareness that two sets of footsteps would soon sound again on their porch boards, familiar in cadence, altered in weight.

Not all at once.

But soon.

CHAPTER EIGHTEEN — SONS COME HOME

They waited at the platform longer than the schedule promised.

Florence stood with her hands folded inside her coat sleeves, the way she did when there was nothing left to prepare. William remained beside her, aware of the same quiet he had felt at the track months earlier, waiting not for spectacle, but for arrival.

"He should've been here by now," Florence said.

William glanced down the line. "Trains keep their own time."

Around them, families gathered in clusters, each holding anticipation differently, too tightly, or not enough.

The train arrived without announcement.

Metal groaned. Doors slid open. Men stepped down in uneven rhythm, some moving quickly toward familiar voices, others pausing as if uncertain which direction belonged to them now.

"There," Florence said suddenly.

William followed her gaze.

She saw her son before he saw them.

He moved carefully, his bag carried low, his attention still scanning. Even here, even now, his posture had not fully released him.

Florence stepped forward before hesitation could settle in.

"Bill," she said—not loudly, not as a call, but as a name returned.

He turned. For a moment, he only looked. Then recognition arrived, slow and sure.

She placed her hands on his shoulders, then his face, confirming what the war had returned.

"You're home," she said.

"Yes, ma'am," he replied automatically, then caught himself. "Yes. I am."

For a brief moment, neither moved. Then Florence stepped forward and gathered him in, her arms firm around him, as if to confirm what her eyes already knew. He held her back just as tightly, his chin resting against her shoulder, the years between them closing without a word.

William stood just behind her, allowing the space.

When Florence drew back, she kept her hands on Bill's arms, as though reluctant to let him go entirely.

"Good to see you, son," William said.

Bill nodded once. "Good to be seen."

His father stepped forward then, not with hesitation, but with a quiet certainty, and pulled him into a brief, solid embrace, one hand firm at his back. No words passed between them, but the gesture held what might have been said.

They walked home without hurry.

The late afternoon light had begun its slow descent, laying gold along the tops of the maples that lined the street. Bill noticed how wide the sky felt here. In Germany, even open fields had carried a different weight. Here, the air seemed to rest lightly on his shoulders.

A train whistle sounded down the line, familiar, unthreatening. Not a warning. Just arrival and departure as it had always been.

He drew in a long breath without meaning to. Cut grass. Damp earth. Someone baking bread nearby. The faint sweetness of clethra lingering past their peak.

The sidewalks were unchanged, cracked in the same narrow place near the post, the corner where he and Dean had once raced one another home from school. A boy sped past them now on a bicycle too large for him, wobbling but determined.

Bill watched him go.

Houses stood in tidy succession, stone and brick steady as

ever. Flags still hung from some porches, their fabric no longer snapping in celebration but settling into quieter motion.

He slowed near the bend in the road, taking in the rhythm of it, the porch swings, the open windows, the ordinary cadence of voices drifting from inside.

"It's beautiful," he said softly, almost to himself.

Florence glanced at him but did not answer. She understood that he was not speaking of architecture.

William walked beside him now, close enough that their sleeves brushed.

"You'll sleep tonight," William said.

Bill considered it. "I think I might."

They turned onto their street.

The front door was already open.

Ron reached him first, fourteen and all elbows, nearly colliding with him in his hurry. Dale was just behind, breathless, grinning wide enough for all of them. Sylvia came more carefully but no less quickly, her composure dissolving halfway across the lawn.

Donna followed last, her small legs pumping with fierce determination, curls coming loose from their ribbon.

"Bill!" she shouted, as if the name itself were a victory.

He barely had time to drop his bag before they were on him, arms around his waist, hands tugging at his sleeves, voices tumbling over one another.

"Did you see tanks?"

"Are the planes really that loud?"

"Did you bring anything back?"

"Are you staying for good?"

Donna wrapped herself around one of his legs and refused to let go.

Bill laughed then, a sound rusty at first, then fuller.

"I'm home," he said again, this time to all of them.

Ron stepped back only slightly, trying to look older than his relief. Dale punched his arm lightly, as if testing whether he was solid. Sylvia studied his face, as though memorizing the changes.

Florence remained near the walk, watching the circle close around him.

William stood beside her.

"Two more," he said quietly.

She nodded.

"Yes."

Not all at once.

But soon.

Bill lifted Donna into his arms. She held his face between her small hands as if confirming he was real.

The porch steps creaked in the same place.

And together—louder now, less measured—they went inside.

Inside, the uniforms were packed away first. Florence folded each piece carefully, smoothing the fabric as though it might still remember its shape if handled gently. Buttons were fastened. Insignia turned inward.

"Are you sure you don't want to keep it out?" William asked quietly.

Florence shook her head. "It's finished its work."

The uniform was placed in a box and the lid closed without ceremony.

The medals followed later, laid flat, separated by tissue.

"They don't have to go away," Bill said, watching her.

"I know," Florence replied. "They're not being hidden. Just … rested."

Later, at the kitchen table, Bill sat with his hands wrapped around a cup that had long since gone cold.

"They changed stations on us twice," he said. "Hard to keep track of where you were."

Florence nodded. "I always said letters arrived in pieces."

He smiled faintly.

"There were men who didn't make it back onto the trains," he added.

"I know," she said simply.

William leaned back slightly. "That's enough for tonight."

Bill exhaled. "Yes, sir."

As dusk settled, William found his son in the garage.

Bill stood at the workbench, hands resting at his sides, not touching anything.

"Your mother said I'd find you here," William said.

"I didn't want to disturb anyone," Bill replied.

William opened a drawer and removed a small metal piece, turning it slowly in his palm.

"This one never made it past testing," he said. "Held up fine. Just not the way I needed."

Bill watched his father's hands.

"In Germany," he said after a moment, "we didn't always have what we needed."

William waited.

"You learned to work with what stayed whole," Bill continued. "And to let go of what couldn't be held."

William set the piece down carefully.

"I think hands remember things the rest of us don't know how to say yet," Bill said.

"That's why I don't rush mine," William replied.

They stood together a moment longer.

Not finished. But sound.

Later, when the house had settled and the radio no longer demanded attention, Sylvia lifted the piano bench and set it back down again.

"Do you want me to ..." Bill began.

"No," Sylvia said gently. "I just need to play."

Her fingers found the keys carefully at first, then with assurance.

The music was different now.

It did not practice endurance. It practiced return.

Florence listened from the doorway.

"That sounds like home," Bill said quietly.

"It remembers you," Florence replied.

William stood nearby, not watching the piano, but listening all the same.

When the last note faded, Sylvia did not rush away. She closed the lid gently.

"I'll play again tomorrow," she said.

Later that night, the uniform box was placed on the shelf. The medals remained stored, their stories intact but unopened.

Some experiences arrived by train. Others were set down slowly, once the house remembered how to hold them.

Dean arrived on a different train.

There was no platform crowd this time, just Florence, William, Bill, and Ron standing a little apart, the afternoon already sloping toward evening.

"He said he'd be on the four-thirty," William noted.

Florence checked her watch. "Then he will be."

Dean stepped down with more certainty than Bill had. His bag was lighter. His uniform less worn. He scanned the platform, spotted them quickly, and smiled—broad, unguarded.

"Well," he said, setting the bag down, "this looks familiar."

Florence reached for him and he met her halfway, arms firm, quick.

"You look well," she said.

"I slept in a bed every night," Dean replied. "That helps."

Bill stood slightly back, watching.

Dean clapped him once on the shoulder. "You beat me home."

"By a little," Bill said.

"Enough to settle in," Dean added. "Figures."

They walked home together, Dean talking easily, about the supply depot, about paperwork, about the relief of predictability.

"You wouldn't believe the inventory lists," he said. "Miles of them."

Bill nodded, listening.

Ron walked a few steps behind, hands in his pockets, saying nothing. He watched the difference, the way Dean's stride stayed loose, the way Bill's shoulders still angled forward, as though the world might call him back at any moment.

At the house, Dean set his bag down and looked around. "Smells the same," he said.

Florence smiled. "I took that as a compliment."

Dinner came together easily that night. Dean ate heartily, asked for seconds, laughed when Sylvia teased him.

"You missed Donna learning how to laugh properly," she said.

"I'll catch up," he replied. "I'm good at that."

Bill ate more slowly.

Florence noticed.

Later, while Dean recounted a story about a mislabeled crate and Ron listened from the corner chair, Florence watched Bill's hands, how they paused between bites, how he set his fork down carefully each time, as though sound mattered more than hunger.

He did not speak of what he had seen.

He did not say *Germany* again. He did not say *wounded*. He did not say *too late*.

Florence did not ask.

After dinner, Dean helped William carry the uniform box to the shelf.

"Feels strange putting it away," Dean said.

William nodded. "It always does."

Ron stood in the doorway, unnoticed, watching Bill as the box was lifted, placed, aligned.

Bill did not look relieved.

He looked responsible.

That night, Florence found Ron sitting on the stairs with a book open but unread.

"You all right?" she asked.

"Yes, ma'am," he said quickly, then corrected himself. "I mean … yes."

She sat beside him.

"Bill doesn't talk much," Ron said, not looking at her.

"No," she agreed.

"But Dean does."

"Yes."

Ron considered this. "I think Bill's still listening."

Florence rested her hand briefly on Ron's shoulder. "So do I."

Later, when the house had quieted, she stood alone in the kitchen, rinsing cups that did not need rinsing.

She thought of what Bill had not said.

Of the way his eyes tracked doorways. Of how he waited for others to finish speaking before he moved. Of how carefully he folded his napkin.

Some truths, she knew, arrived before words could carry them.

They would come later. Or not at all.

For now, it was enough to know that one son had returned with stories, another with silence, and both would need to be held differently.

Florence turned out the light.

The house had learned this before.

It would learn it again.

The house had settled enough for truth to surface.

It happened in the kitchen, late.

Florence was mending something that did not need mending. Bill sat at the table, turning his cup once, twice, as if checking whether it still held heat.

"You don't have to stay up," he said.

Florence did not look up. "I know."

The clock moved forward without comment.

"I keep thinking I hear the train," he said then. "Even when I know it's gone."

She set the needle down.

"Yes," she said, simple recognition.

Bill stared at the table. "There were nights I didn't think I'd be able to sleep anywhere quiet again."

"And now?" she asked.

"Now it's quiet," he said. "That's the trouble."

Florence waited.

"There was a boy," Bill said finally. "Younger than Dean. He kept asking me if he was going home. I told him yes because I didn't know what else to say." He swallowed. "He didn't."

Florence reached across the table and rested her hand over his—not to stop him or to pull him forward, just to let him know he was not alone in the telling.

"I did what I could," he said. "But sometimes what you can do isn't enough."

"No," she said gently. "It isn't."

Bill breathed out, the sound small but unguarded.

"I don't need you to fix it," he added quickly. "I just ... needed to say it out loud. Once."

She nodded. "Then you've said it."

They sat together a moment longer.

Florence found herself remembering something he had told Sylvia not long after returning home, how the soldiers were given chocolate bars with their meals. Bill had slipped several into his pockets instead of eating them, saving them to hand out to the small children who gathered near the camp fences.

He had said it almost casually then, as if it were nothing.

But sitting beside him now, Florence understood.

Even in a place where he could not save everyone, he had still found a way to give something sweet to the ones who remained.

Later, Florence would realize that this was all he ever intended to give her—not the story in full, not the weight in detail. Just the truth, released enough to be shared.

Dean's reckoning came later.

He was back at work—civilian now, useful again—when a crate arrived mislabeled, its contents shifted just enough to cause a delay. Nothing serious. Nothing dangerous.

But Dean felt his chest tighten all the same.

He stood there longer than necessary, hands resting on the

edge of the table, waiting for the feeling to pass.

It didn't.

That evening, he sat on the back step with Ron, who was reading nearby.

"You ever feel like things are about to go wrong," Dean said, "even when they're not?"

Ron turned a page. "Sometimes."

"I didn't see what Bill saw," Dean continued. "Not really. I stayed organized. I stayed clean."

Ron looked up then. "That doesn't mean it didn't count."

Dean shook his head. "No. But it means I thought I was finished when I wasn't."

Ron considered him quietly. "Bill listens first."

Dean smiled faintly. "Yeah. I noticed."

Later, Dean stood in the garage with Bill, watching him work.

"You ever miss the time to yourself?" Dean asked.

Bill did not stop what he was doing. "Sometimes."

Dean nodded. "I think I do too. And that surprises me."

Bill set the tool down. "It won't always."

That night, Dean lay awake longer than he expected to.

He thought of lists. Of trains that arrived on time. Of ease mistaken for completion.

It did not undo him.

But something shifted.

The war, he understood now, had ended for him earlier than it should have and would take longer than he'd admitted to finish.

Florence prayed after the house had settled.

She stood at the kitchen sink, hands resting on the porcelain edge, the room dim enough to soften the corners of things.

She did not name what Bill had said.

Names gave shape. Shape invited detail. This was not a prayer for explanation.

She asked instead for what she had always asked when words failed—

for steadiness to continue. For patience that did not demand relief. For wisdom to know when silence was shelter rather than avoidance.

She thought of Bill's hands and how they trembled only after the work was done. She thought of the boy he had mentioned without description, trusting her not to ask for more.

"Help me hold what he cannot," she whispered.

The prayer did not move. It settled.

Florence turned out the light and went to bed, carrying the knowledge the way she carried everything else, without display, without complaint, and without letting it become heavier than it already was.

Ron heard more than people realized.

Not because he listened at doors, but because silence spoke to him differently. He noticed how Bill paused before entering a room. How Dean filled space with words. How their mother asked questions only when the answers could be borne.

That night, Ron sat on the edge of his bed with a book open but unread.

He thought of the way Bill had said *once,* sitting in the kitchen a few nights ago. Of how his mother had not asked *again.* Of how some truths, once spoken, did not need repeating to remain alive.

Ron closed the book and placed it back on the shelf.

He did not know yet what shape his own life would take. Only that noise was not required to prove strength. That watching could be a form of preparation. That remembering mattered.

Someday, he thought, he might need to stand where Bill had stood, to hold what others could not, to speak when necessary, and to stay quiet the rest of the time.

He lay back and stared at the ceiling until the house's sounds returned to their ordinary places.

Ron did not write this down.

He stored it.

The way he stored everything that mattered—carefully, intact, and waiting for the moment it would be needed.

By the time summer's end settled in, Bill and Dean were home. Fully.

Not all at once. Not without pauses. But present, occupying chairs again, sleeping in familiar rooms, learning the shape of the house as it now was. Their laughter returned in fragments. Their silences, too. Florence learned to recognize both as signs of arrival.

The days lengthened. Windows stayed open later. Supper stretched into evening. The world, for a time, appeared willing to loosen its grip.

Then, in August, the headlines came again.

They landed with less ceremony this time—smaller print, fewer exclamations, as though even the papers understood restraint.

JAPAN SURRENDERS

WAR ENDS AT LAST

People still gathered. Bells rang again. Flags were pulled back out, corners creased from waiting. But the sound that followed was different, briefer, quieter, already edged with fatigue.

Florence read the words at the table while Bill leaned against the counter and Dean stood at the window, watching the street react without joining it.

"So that's it," Dean said finally.

"That's what they're calling it," Bill replied.

William folded the paper carefully. "It means no more letters that begin with regret," he said. "That matters."

It did. But it was not the same as peace.

That came later, if it came at all, in small adjustments. In learning who sat where now. In which doors stayed open. In what was spoken, and what was left alone.

The war had been declared finished twice. The living still had work to do.

Florence stood at the sink that evening, warm water running over her hands, the window above it open to the thick ease of summer. The house was full again—voices in rooms that had held too much quiet, footsteps where she could place them without guessing.

The paper lay folded on the table behind her. Another surrender. Another declaration, this one reaching across an ocean she had learned to measure in weeks and worry.

Guam was closer now.

The knowledge settled into her body with unexpected gentleness. Her shoulders eased. Her breath slowed. For the first time in months, the waiting loosened its hold.

She did not mistake it for certainty. She knew better than that. But relief, she had learned, did not need to be permanent to be real.

This surrender mattered.

It placed Gerry on the near side of the map, within reach of return, within the portion of the world that had begun, however cautiously, to release what it held.

Florence dried her hands and rested them on the counter, listening to the sounds behind her: Bill's voice, Dean's quiet laughter, William moving through the room with familiar weight.

The war had ended.

And for the first time, she allowed herself to believe that what remained might be carried together.

CHAPTER NINETEEN — WHAT REMAINS UNSAID (1945)

The house was full again, but it had learned new rules.

Voices returned first, tentative at the edges, then steadier. Chairs were pulled back into place. Plates were set for the right number of people. Florence restored habits carefully, as if too much normalcy too quickly might crack what had only just begun to hold.

"Did you mean to set out the extra plate?" Sylvia asked once.

Florence glanced at the table. "No," she said. Then, after a pause, "Leave it."

Some things, she had come to understand, were not mistakes. They were accommodations. Space made quietly for what had been and for what might never be spoken.

Outside the house, the world seemed to understand this too. After Bill and Dean had returned from the war, the neighborhood received them the way it knew how, through small talk offered like a steadying hand. Just something to hold and acknowledge the moment.

Late afternoon light settled across the porch, warm against the steps where neighbors lingered, hands resting on railings or folded loosely at their waists. A screen door creaked open, then closed. Somewhere, a radio played low, its tune drifting in and out with the breeze.

They spoke easily enough about trains and weather. About meals missed and meals remembered. Names of places were mentioned without detail.

"How was the ride?" a neighbor asked.

"Long," Bill said. "But steady."

There were nods at that, a whisper of understanding that asked for nothing more.

Certain questions hovered, then dissolved, caught in the space between what was offered and what could not yet be spoken.

Florence did not ask what could not yet be carried. She had learned that silence, when chosen, was not absence. It was containment.

At night, the house shifted and creaked as if adjusting its memory. Florence lay awake longer than she admitted, listening to footsteps moving down hallways that had once echoed with absence.

Once, passing the front room on her way to bed, she noticed the piano bench had been moved slightly from the wall.

No one mentioned it, and the lid remained closed.

Someone pacing. Someone stopping. Someone standing still longer than necessary.

She marked the sounds without turning them into meaning.

William moved beside her, solid and present. "You all right?" he asked quietly.

"Yes," she said. Then, more honestly, "I'm listening."

He nodded. That was enough.

In daylight, neighbors appeared with casseroles and cautious smiles, their presence a kind of welcome offered without ceremony.

"Such a relief," someone said.

"You must be grateful," said another.

"We're all so fortunate," said a third.

"Yes," she said. "We are."

She did not correct them.

The words gathered gently, meant for the boys, for the house, for all of them at once. No one lingered long enough to disturb what had only just settled.

Florence thanked them, stacked dishes neatly in the kitchen, returned empty plates clean and orderly.

The children carried their silences differently.

One rose early and left before breakfast. "I'll eat later," he said, already reaching for his coat.

Another lingered too long over small tasks, repairing what did not need fixing.

"This hinge was fine," Florence said gently.

"I know," he replied. "Just making sure."

She let him. Not everything needed to be opened.

She found herself tidying drawers that did not require it, straightening stacks of paper already aligned. It was a habit she recognized.

Order, she knew, was not control. It was care expressed through placement.

Later in the day, a letter from her mother arrived, a sweet distraction, Florida warmth pressed flat inside the envelope.

The paper carried the faint scent of orange blossom and starch, as if it had rested briefly on a sunny windowsill before being folded. Estella's handwriting slanted slightly forward, neat and deliberate, each loop formed without flourish.

My dear Florence,

The days here have turned warm already. The light lingers longer than it ought to, and the orange trees are heavy with bloom. I thought of you this morning while hanging linens in the breeze. I imagined you tending something growing, as you always have.

Thinking of you all. No need to write.

There was no excess in it. No apology. No reach for what could not be undone.

Estella had always known when to write. She understood distance, how it could bruise if pressed too firmly. Her letters never asked for reassurance. Never demanded reply. They arrived like small offerings set quietly at the door.

I trust you are well, she had added in smaller script at the bottom. *Give the children a kiss from me.*

Florence smiled at that.

Once, at five years old, she had watched a road stretch longer than she understood, her small hand empty where her mother's had been. Words had not followed her then. Silence had.

But now they did.

Not many. Not heavy. Just enough.

Florence folded the letter once more along its original crease and placed it inside the kitchen drawer where she kept such things, contained. She did not need more words. The space between them no longer required filling.

Some mothers hovered. Some instructed. Estella wrote.

And in her writing, she remained.

The war was over. That much everyone agreed on.

But endings, Florence knew, did not erase what had been held inside them. They simply made room for something else to arrive.

She washed her hands and stood at the window. The house settled around her—full but not yet finished.

Some things had come home. Some things remained unsaid. And some, she sensed, were still waiting to be entrusted.

Not all truths arrived with the war's end. Some had been living quietly in the house long before it.

Florence learned one of them by accident.

Not from William, not directly, but from a conversation that lingered longer than it meant to.

She was clearing cups when William stepped out to walk a visitor to the door. Their voices carried back through the hallway, softened by distance, shaped by familiarity.

"You didn't have to do that," the man said quietly.

William paused. "Yes," he replied. "I did."

Florence stopped where she was.

"Most men wouldn't have turned that contract down," the visitor continued. "Especially then."

William's voice came steady, unembellished. "Most men didn't need to consider who else it would cost."

There was a silence, not awkward, but weighted.

"I won't forget who stepped aside," the man said. "Not everyone did."

"You don't need to," William answered. "Just keep building."

The door closed.

Florence finished stacking the cups.

Later, when William returned to the kitchen, she poured coffee, watching the way he took it, black, as always, and how he wrapped his hands around the mug as though heat were something to be held, not hurried.

"Everything all right?" he asked.

"Yes," she said. And it was.

That night, when the house had settled and the clock marked time without opinion, Florence followed the thread backward.

The years she had named scarcity. The work left deliberately untouched. The opportunities that had passed without explanation.

She thought of inspections. Of lists. Of names spoken too loudly or written too clearly. Of how certain families learned to lower their voices without being told.

She thought of Isaac Rosenfeld, the way he arrived carefully, left quietly, never staying long enough to invite attention.

And suddenly, the shape of it appeared.

Not sacrifice or heroism, but rather protection.

William had not chosen the safer path for himself. He had chosen it for someone else.

In the dark, she reached across the bed and rested her hand against William's back, to acknowledge something that had always been there and she had only just learned how to name.

In the morning, she said nothing.

She did not thank him. She did not ask questions that would require answers already lived. Instead, she understood her marriage differently.

Not as a union built on protection promised, but as one built on protection practiced—quietly, consistently, and without the need to be seen.

Some men came home from war carrying medals. Others carried the weight of choices no one else ever noticed.

Florence rose and began the day.

Holding, as she always had, what mattered most.

She did not speak of what she had learned.

She folded it into her days the way she folded everything else, carefully, deliberately, without drawing attention to the seam.

Understanding changed little on the surface. The work remained the same. The house kept its rhythm.

But Florence now knew what the rhythm had been protecting.

William sat at the table with papers spread before him, figures worked thin by use. Florence poured coffee, set it beside him, and gathered the papers into a neater stack.

"You'll misplace something," he said mildly.

"I won't," she replied. "I'm not changing the order."

She read nothing aloud. She offered no instruction.

But when she reached the final page, she paused.

"This one," she said, tapping the corner lightly. "You should keep."

William looked up. "I wasn't sure we could afford to."

Florence met his eyes. "We can."

He waited.

"You made the choice you made," she said. "The rest of us live inside it."

William leaned back slightly, seeing her, perhaps for the first time, as she was now standing.

"It would mean holding a little longer," he said.

"Yes."

"And fewer guarantees."

"Yes."

He nodded once. "All right."

Isaac arrived earlier than usual a few days later, as if testing whether the door he had once approached carefully might now open without caution.

Not early enough to draw notice, just early enough to

stand fully in the day. He did not linger at the threshold or glance down the street before knocking.

Florence opened the door and stepped aside without thinking.

"Good morning," he said.

"Good morning," she replied.

He removed his hat and set it on the hall table. As one did in a place that required no accounting.

William looked up from the kitchen. "You're ahead of schedule."

Isaac nodded. "I had the time."

Florence poured a third cup of coffee without asking.

Isaac accepted it, letting the warmth settle before he drank. He spoke of nothing that required caution. He stood where the light reached him.

Outside, a neighbor passed and waved.

Isaac lifted his hand in return.

Nothing about it was bold. Nothing about it was hidden.

When the conversation ended, Isaac did not rise immediately. He remained seated, not measuring risk, not calculating departure.

He remained longer than he usually did; no one moved to end the conversation.

When Florence set a pot back on the stove and reached for another plate, she did not pause to consider it. She simply set it out.

William noticed. He said nothing.

"Will you stay?" Florence asked, already turning back toward the counter.

Isaac hesitated, not out of fear, but habit. Then he nodded once. "If it's no trouble."

"It isn't," she said.

The table filled gradually, as it always did, chairs drawn back, places found without instruction.

The meal was ordinary: roast chicken, potatoes, green beans cooked long enough to soften. Bread passed hand to hand.

Isaac sat where the light reached him, not at the edge, not at the head. He folded his napkin carefully and waited until Florence sat before touching his fork.

Dean spoke first, as if continuing something already underway.

"They've reopened the route near the station," he said. "Fewer delays now."

"That'll help," William replied. "People are tired of waiting."

Isaac nodded. "They are."

No one asked how he knew.

Ron listened more than he spoke. Bill ate steadily, eyes lifting now and then, measuring nothing in particular. Sylvia refilled water without being asked.

The conversation stayed where it could bear weight—work, weather, the price of food. Laughter arrived once, unexpectedly, and stayed just long enough to be acknowledged.

Isaac did not rush his meal. He did not glance at the clock. When a neighbor's voice drifted in through the open window, he did not stiffen.

When the plates were cleared, Florence rose with them. Isaac stood at once.

"You needn't—" she began.

"I know," he said gently. He picked up his cup and carried it to the sink anyway.

They stood there a moment, side by side, the quiet of work settling naturally between them.

At the table, William watched without comment.

Later, when Isaac reached for his hat, he did not hover at the threshold. He paused long enough to nod once to Florence, not in thanks, but in acknowledgment.

She returned it.

After the door closed, the house did not tense.

William exhaled slowly. "That went well," he said.

Florence rinsed the last cup and set it on the rack. "Yes," she said. And meant more than the meal.

In the quiet that followed, nothing needed to be said.

Isaac had answered, in the only way that mattered. Florence had seen it in the way he stood, and in the way he left.

The moment passed without ceremony.

Yet something in the house adjusted.

Meals were still served at the same time. Doors were still checked at night. The radio still spoke when it had something to say and was turned off when it did not.

The change revealed itself one morning at breakfast.

Florence set the coffeepot on the table and turned back toward the stove when she felt the room pause, not silent, but waiting.

Bill looked up first.

"Do you think the rain will hold?" he asked.

It was an ordinary question. The sort that might once have passed between brothers or landed casually with William.

But now it had come to her.

Florence glanced toward the window where the sky sat low and gray above the yard.

"For a few hours," she said. "Long enough."

Bill nodded and reached for his coat.

The others resumed what they were doing, chairs shifting, cups lifted, the small sounds of morning returning.

Florence poured another cup of coffee.

She understood then that it was not advice they were seeking.

It was steadiness.

Questions began to arrive at Florence before they went elsewhere.

"Do you think this can wait?" Dean asked one afternoon, holding a form he was meant to sign.

Florence read it once. "Yes," she said. "For now."

He nodded and set it aside.

Ron lingered near her more often, standing where her attention could find him if it needed to. When he finally spoke, it was measured.

"Would you rather I stay tonight?" he asked.

"I would," she replied.

Bill deferred in smaller ways. He paused before leaving rooms. Waited for her to finish speaking. When the house grew loud, he looked to her—not for permission, but for bearing.

Even William noticed.

"You don't rush them," he said one evening, almost to himself.

Florence continued folding towels. "They've had enough of that."

Nothing was announced. No roles were reassigned.

But the family began to move with her, as water does around a fixed stone because it knows where it can settle.

It happened one evening without planning, the way healing sometimes begins, quietly, before anyone thinks to name it.

Someone left the radio off.

The chairs in the front room were pulled closer together, not arranged, simply drawn into use. Florence finished in the kitchen and found the space already holding itself.

William sat at the piano.

He had not announced it. He had not opened the bench with ceremony. His fingers rested on the keys as though they had been waiting there all day.

The first notes came lightly, testing the room.

Then faster.

A ripple of sound followed, bright and nimble, the kind that tripped over itself without falling. Dizzy fingers, running ahead of thought. Zez Confrey—"Kitten on the Keys," then something even quicker, laughter hiding inside the rhythm.

"Is he trying to outplay himself?" Ron murmured.

William grinned without looking up and let the notes scatter, then gathered them again. The room filled with motion.

Sound skipping like stones across water.

Someone laughed outright. Not carefully. Not quietly.

Bill leaned back against the doorframe, arms crossed, the tension in his shoulders easing as the tempo climbed. Dean tapped a foot before realizing he was doing it. Sylvia clapped once, then caught herself and didn't stop. Donna gave way to fits of laughter while Dale soaked up the moment.

The music asked nothing of them.

It did not explain the years or soften what had been carried home. It did not insist on gratitude or remembrance.

It simply moved.

When William let the final chord land, it wasn't held for effect. It ended the way it began, naturally, as if the room had decided it was finished.

For a moment, no one spoke.

For the first time in a long while, the silence that followed felt easy.

Then someone said, "Again."

William obliged.

Florence stood at the threshold, drying her hands on a towel she had forgotten she was holding. She watched the way the family gathered—not around the piano, but around the *ease* of it. How laughter found its way back without being invited. How stillness returned without tightening.

She did not step forward. There was no need.

Florence understood then that authority did not require declaration.

It came from having held what others could not. From knowing when to speak and when not to. From making the truth livable without insisting it be admired.

She rose in the morning and set the day in order, as she always had.

And the house, having learned where its steadiness lived, followed.

CHAPTER TWENTY — THE ONE WHO STAYS (1946)

The house had begun to lean forward.

Not all at once, and not noisily, but in small, unmistakable ways. Drawers were opened and closed again. Shoes were lined more carefully by the door. Florence found the same basket folded and refolded in the hallway, its contents checked without being changed.

William did not speak often of the coming birth.

But Florence noticed the ways he moved around it.

He checked the car more frequently—oil, tires, the sound the engine made when it first turned over. Once, she watched him sit behind the wheel without starting it, hands resting lightly where they would go when the time came.

He did not rush.

In the evenings, he lingered near the crib they had brought down from storage. He ran his hand once along the rail, then stepped back, as if measuring something that could not be adjusted by inches.

One night, Florence woke to the sound of the piano.

Not music—not yet. Just a single chord tested softly, then released. William sat in the front room with the lamp low, his shoulders rounded forward, the way they had been when the children were small and sleep came in fragments.

She did not join him.

She listened.

Later, he returned to bed and lay awake beside her longer than usual. When she reached for his hand, his fingers closed around hers.

"I was thinking," he said finally, his voice quiet enough not to wake the house.

"Yes?" she replied.

"I don't remember what it was like," he said. "To be new."

Florence turned slightly toward him. "None of us do."

He nodded. "I was hoping ... this one wouldn't need to learn so much so early."

The words stayed between them, not as fear, not as prayer, but as acknowledgment.

In the days that followed, William said little more. But when Florence rested, he stayed close. When the children drifted near her, he let them. When questions arose, he answered what could be answered and left the rest untouched.

He was not waiting for arrival.

He was preparing for holding.

Donna climbed into Florence's lap more often, her small hands resting on Florence's stomach as if listening for something beneath the skin.

"Is he awake?" she whispered once.

"Sometimes," Florence said.

Donna nodded, satisfied, as if that explained everything.

Sylvia hovered closer than usual, attentive without instruction. She counted towels when Florence folded laundry and corrected herself aloud if she miscounted.

"That one goes on top," she said once, adjusting a stack that did not require it.

Florence let her.

Dale asked practical questions.

"How will we get to the hospital?"

"Who stays here?"

"Do we need to bring the small lamp or the big one?"

Florence answered each as if the answers mattered—because they did. Dale wrote nothing down, but he remembered.

Ron did not ask questions at all. He lingered near the doorway when Florence rested, offering presence instead of speech. When she rose, he rose too, already reaching for her coat before she asked.

"Not yet," she said one afternoon.

"I know," he replied. "Just ready."

The room that had once held absence began to hold expectation instead. Not the careless kind, no one spoke of miracles or guarantees, but the steady kind that made room without insisting on outcome.

Even William noticed the shift.

"They're watching the calendar," he said quietly one night.

Florence smiled faintly. "They're watching me."

On the morning it began, the house was unusually still. Breakfast was eaten without hurry. Donna lined her dolls along the windowsill and informed them she would be back later.

Sylvia packed a small bag for herself, just in case. Dale checked the latch on the back door twice. Ron stood at the end of the drive longer than necessary, as if memorizing the way the house looked before it changed again.

The war had ended, but Florence no longer trusted endings that arrived all at once.

Victory came the way everything did now—in stages. Men stepped off trains thinner than they had left, uniforms folded into boxes that were slid beneath beds or pushed to the backs of closets. Laughter returned to the house, but it came more carefully, as if it needed permission. Even joy, Florence noticed, had learned restraint.

It was into this altered quiet that Robert was born.

Florence was forty-one. She felt the years not as weariness, but as knowing. She no longer reached for reassurance in first cries or strong grips. When the nurse placed Robert in her arms, Florence did not search his face for resemblance or promise. She listened first, then watched his breathing.

He was small. Not alarmingly so, but enough that voices softened around him. Enough that the doctor paused, listened, then listened again.

Florence found herself counting without intending to. She had learned how easily life could slip when no one stayed attentive.

William stood at the foot of the bed, hands folded as if

still waiting for instruction. He did not speak. He counted too—quietly, almost imperceptibly—then stopped himself, as though remembering something he had once hoped would not be necessary.

"We'll keep an eye," the doctor said at last, his voice steady but narrowed, as if choosing which truths required time.

Florence nodded once. *An eye,* she thought. *I can do that.*

"Not concern," he added, almost to himself. "Just attention."

Medicine bottles appeared, brown glass with careful labels. Florence read each one twice before setting it down. A thin medical file followed, then another page added weeks later. Robert's body became a container that required vigilance, not panic. Florence understood the difference. Panic scattered. Vigilance remained.

The nurse set the bottles down gently, aligning them without comment.

"He tells you what he needs," she said, tightening the cap. "You just have to listen longer than most."

At home, she made space.

A shelf was cleared for droppers and folded cloths, always washed, always ready. A drawer reassigned without explanation. She did not announce these changes. She had learned that calm, like waiting, was something you demonstrated, not declared.

William noticed. He always did. He said nothing, only brought home what was needed and trusted Florence to know where it belonged. During the war, silence had taught him that some work was done best without words.

"I can take the late feeding," William said one night, already reaching for the lamp.

Florence watched him measure without rushing. "You don't have to," she said.

"I know," he replied. And stayed anyway.

The older children hovered at a distance at first, then closer. They had seen enough to recognize fragility even if they lacked the language for it. Florence let them look. Let them touch Robert's small hand, warm and certain despite its size. She did not shoo them away.

"Why does he get the little spoon?" Sylvia asked, watching Florence stir carefully.

"Because it fits him," she said.

She considered this, then nodded. "He's not in a hurry," she decided.

Florence turned away so no one would see her face.

This child would not be protected by distance. He would be protected by presence.

At church, a woman leaned too close to the carriage and lingered. "He's delicate," she said, not unkindly.

Florence met her gaze. "He's exact," she replied.

The woman stepped back, unsure what had just passed between them.

At night, when the house finally settled, Florence sat with Robert and listened again. His breathing filled the room, soft, steady, insisting on its own continuation. She thought of the sons who had once slept the same way, unaware of the distances they would travel, the dangers their bodies would learn to endure. She remembered how she had once believed that if you held tightly enough, nothing could be taken.

She knew better now.

The door eased open behind her. William stepped in without turning on the light, as if he already understood the room.

"He's settled?" he asked softly.

"For now," Florence said.

William came to stand beside her, resting his hand lightly against the edge of the cradle. For a moment, he did nothing more than watch, his gaze moving between Robert and Florence, as though measuring something he did not name.

"They all breathed like that," he said quietly. "In the beginning."

She nodded. "I used to think it meant they would always be safe."

William glanced at her then, a small, knowing shift in his expression. "And now?"

She looked down at Robert, her hand resting gently over the blanket. "Now I think it means they are here."

William let out a slow breath, something easing in it. He reached for her hand, not to interrupt her touch, but to join it, his fingers settling lightly over hers where it rested near the baby.

"Here is enough," he said.

Florence leaned into him, just slightly, her shoulder finding its place against his arm.

Robert stirred, then settled again, his breathing returning to its quiet rhythm. The house did not wait for certainty.

Morning gave way to noon the way it always had, through motion rather than announcement. Doors opened and closed. Shoes were shed by the back steps. A pot was set on the stove and stirred without hurry.

Robert slept.

Florence kept him in the front room where the light fell evenly across his face. She watched the small, steady rise of his chest while her hands worked, folding, stirring, setting things within reach. She did not hover. She did not turn away.

When the children returned for the midday meal, they entered quietly, as if the house had instructed them.

Donna leaned close to the bassinet but did not touch. "He's dreaming," she whispered.

"Yes," Florence said. "Let him."

Sylvia laid the table and counted the places twice. "We're all here," she said softly, almost to herself.

Dale washed his hands and waited. "Do we start?" he asked, glancing toward his mother.

"In a moment," she said.

Ron stood at the doorway briefly, listening, not to the room, but to the rhythm of breathing he had learned to recognize. "He's steady," he said quietly.

Florence looked at him, a flicker of understanding passing

between them. "Yes," she said.

William came in last. He looked once at the bassinet, then at Florence.

"He's resting," she said.

William nodded. "Good." That was enough.

They took their places.

"Pass the bread?" Dale said.

Sylvia handed it across. "Careful," she added lightly. "I just cut it."

Ron reached for the salt. "Smells better than ever," he said, almost offhand.

Florence set a dish at the center. "Eat while it's warm," she said.

They ate together, unremarkable food served at a familiar hour. Conversation stayed low, then rose naturally, then settled again. Someone laughed. Someone asked for more bread.

Robert slept through it all.

Florence ate with one eye on her plate and the other on the bassinet, the way she had learned to do so many things at once. She did not name the watching. She simply practiced it.

The house resumed its shape around her, not pressing, not waiting, trusting that what needed attention was being attended to.

She knew better now.

Holding, she had learned, was not about force. It was about constancy. About staying when leaving might be easier. About watching without looking away.

Bill's letter arrived folded thin from handling, the envelope creased as if it had already traveled farther than its paper intended.

Kansas, he wrote. The word sat alone in the margin, set apart from the rest. There was work—good work, he assured her. Surveying land, assisting with designs that stretched across rivers and ravines, places where distance had to be measured and trusted.

"Bridges," William said quietly when Florence handed it to

him.

Florence nodded. Of course it was bridges. Bill had always been drawn to what connected one side to another without belonging fully to either.

She folded the letter back into itself and placed it where she kept things that were both certain and unfinished.

Robert slept, unaware of the vigilance he inspired. Florence did not imagine the future for him. She had learned to keep such questions contained. The war had taught her that speculation was a luxury best postponed.

For now, it was enough that he was here.

She carried the basket of seedlings out to the narrow strip of garden behind the house, Robert's bassinet placed just inside the open kitchen door where she could see him through the screen. The morning air held the faint sweetness of damp earth warming beneath a thin spring sun. Sparrows worked the hedgerow. Somewhere beyond, a neighbor shook a rug against the line.

Florence knelt carefully.

The seedlings had come up crowded, eager, fragile, indistinguishable at first glance. She ran her fingers lightly across the soil, feeling for the strongest stems. Some leaned toward the light with quiet insistence. Others bowed already under their own thin weight.

She began to thin them.

Two fingers at the base, a gentle pull, roots lifting with a soft surrender. The scent of turned soil rose richer as she made space between what would remain. She did not discard what she removed carelessly. Each small sprout rested in her palm a moment before being set aside.

There was no cruelty in it. Only intention.

The garden, she had learned long ago, could not sustain everything that tried to grow at once. Crowding weakened what might otherwise flourish. Space was not abandonment. It was provision.

From inside, Robert made a small sound.

Florence stilled, listening, not with alarm, but with attunement. The sound faded. She exhaled and returned to her careful work.

The war had released two of her three sons back to her, but not without cost. It had taught her that survival did not end when danger passed, it simply changed shape. Waiting, she knew now, did not always announce itself. Sometimes it arrived quietly and asked to be honored.

She pressed the soil gently around the remaining stems, firming their footing. The stronger seedlings would root deeper now. They would not need to compete for light. They would stretch on their own.

Children were not so different. Some pushed upward early, restless for horizon.

Some required steadier shelter. And some—rarely—asked not to be propelled at all, but anchored.

Robert shifted again. Florence rose, brushed the soil from her knees, and lifted him from the bassinet. His weight settled against her with a completeness that stilled the air around them. His breathing found its rhythm beneath her palm.

She looked back at the garden.

The rows appeared sparse now, almost bare to an untrained eye. But she knew what was coming. In weeks, there would be fullness. Leaves widening. Stems thickening. Roots unseen but certain.

She did not rush to put him down.

Some children were born into motion. Some were born into uncertainty.

And some were born into vigilance.

Florence understood that this one would need something different from her.

Not preparation for leaving, but the quiet teaching of how to remain. How to root deeply. How to grow without being pushed.

And so she did what she had always done.

She took what was given.

She placed it where it would be safe.
She tended it carefully.
She made room for it to grow.

And she stayed.

CHAPTER TWENTY-ONE — THE LONG WAIT (1947)

Waiting had not ended with the war. It had simply learned a different posture.

The house no longer waited for sirens or telegrams, but Florence recognized the familiar shape of it all the same. Waiting lived now in ordinary places, in the space between footsteps on the stairs, in the pause before the mail was gathered from the front hall, in the way William lingered an extra moment before opening envelopes addressed in unfamiliar hands.

"Is it from Gerry?" Sylvia asked from the stair landing, already knowing enough to ask quietly.

Florence did not look up. "Not today."

Sylvia nodded once and went back upstairs without another word, the way a child does when she understands she is not meant to linger.

Some days, the mail brought nothing that mattered. Catalogs. Circulars. Notices meant for someone else. Florence sorted and stacked, placing each thing where it belonged. Other days, there were letters that changed the weight of the afternoon.

Gerry's letter with news of orders arrived without ceremony.

Not homecoming orders. Extensions.

Dean stood in the doorway while Florence folded the letter.

"How long?" he asked.

"They didn't say."

He absorbed that. "They never do," he said, not accusing, just older now, aware of how institutions spoke.

Florence did not read Gerry's letter right away. She set it on the table and finished what she was doing, the way she always did with things that mattered.

"Is it from Gerry?" Ron asked, already halfway into the room.

Florence nodded.

Donna climbed onto a chair, swinging her legs. "Read it," she said, as if that settled the question.

Florence looked at William. He gave a small nod, not permission, exactly, but agreement.

She opened the letter and unfolded it fully before she began.

"Dear Mom," she read, her voice even, *"I'm well enough and staying busy. The weather's the same every day, and the work keeps us from thinking too much. Don't worry about me. I've learned what matters. I carry home with me more than I ever expected."*

She paused, just long enough to breathe.

"The men are good. Some younger than they should be, some older than they feel. We look out for one another. That's how it goes."

Dale shifted on the floor. Dean leaned against the wall, arms crossed, listening harder than he meant to.

"I don't know when I'll be back," Florence continued, choosing not to soften the line. *"But I know where I belong. Tell Dad I keep his advice close. Tell the kids to mind you. I'll write again soon."*

She reached the end without ceremony.

Donna frowned. "That's it?"

"That's it," Florence said.

"He didn't say if he's scared," Sylvia said quietly.

Florence folded the letter. "No," she said. "He wouldn't."

Ron looked down at his hands. "He sounds different."

"He is," William said. "So are you."

Florence placed the letter beside her plate, then stood and cleared the table. The sound of dishes was ordinary, grounding.

"He's doing what he needs to do," she said, not as comfort, but as fact.

No one argued.

The letter had said enough.

Florence folded the paper once, then again, until it fit neatly inside the ledger she kept for such things. Guam was a long way off, but the war had taught her that distance did not always mean danger. Sometimes it simply meant time—time that asked to be endured rather than resisted. She placed the page beside the others and closed the cover, satisfied that it had been acknowledged and contained.

Donna climbed into Florence's lap without asking.

"Is tomorrow closer?" she asked.

Florence smoothed her hair. "To what?"

Donna thought. "To when everybody's back."

"A little," Florence said.

Donna accepted this and rested her head, satisfied with increments.

Waiting, Florence knew, did not require explanation. It required steadiness.

Robert slept nearby when the letter came, his small chest rising and falling with effort that Florence still measured without thinking. She listened as she always did now, not for reassurance, but for rhythm. His breathing set the pace of the room, quiet and insistent, reminding her that vigilance was not something to be put away once danger passed.

The older boys adjusted in their own ways. One took long walks without destination. Another busied himself with tasks that did not need doing. Florence let them be. She understood that some waiting was done outwardly, and some was carried alone.

Ron was tightening a hinge that had already been tightened twice.

"You're going to strip the screws," Dale said, leaning in the doorway.

Ron shrugged. "Then it won't squeak."

"It never squeaked."

Ron turned the screwdriver once more anyway.

William said little, but Florence could feel the way the extension order sat with him. Not fear, something heavier. Acceptance mixed with restraint. They spoke of practical things instead: repairs that needed finishing, plans that could wait. There was no need to rehearse what they already knew.

"We'll finish the back steps in the spring," William said, though neither of them had mentioned it yet.

"If the boards hold," Florence replied.

"They will," he said.

She believed him, not because he promised, but because he stayed.

Even peace, Florence understood, arrived unevenly.

Neighbors spoke of moving forward, of how good it felt to be finished with all of it. Florence nodded, smiled when expected. She did not disagree. She had learned that peace was not something you claimed. It was something you practiced.

At night, when the house finally settled, Florence sat with the ledger open on her lap. Names. Dates. Places. Each entry written in the same careful hand. She did not count ahead. She did not imagine what would come next. The book did not require it.

Sylvia appeared in the doorway, barefoot. "Are you counting?" she asked.

Florence shook her head. "I'm keeping."

Sylvia nodded, the distinction settling somewhere she would use later in life.

Some waiting, Florence had learned, was not meant to be shortened. It was meant to be honored.

She closed the ledger and set it aside. In the quiet that followed, Robert stirred and then stilled again, finding his rhythm. Florence listened until she was satisfied.

The second letter arrived thinner than the first.

Florence recognized that before she opened it, the way paper could carry less and still weigh more.

She read it alone at the table, the house quiet around her.

Dear Mom,

I got your note and the picture. Tell Donna I keep it folded in my pocket, even when it doesn't make sense. Some things don't have to.

The days run together here. Not in a bad way. Just steady. We're doing what we're meant to do, and most of us are still standing at the end of it.

I won't pretend I'm the same as when I left. I don't think that's the point anymore. But I'm all right. I need you to trust that.

Don't worry about writing back right away. Knowing you will is enough.

Love you all.

—Gerry

Florence did not read this one aloud.

She folded it once, then again, and placed it in the ledger, not beside the others, but between pages already written, as if to anchor it among what was known.

Later, Sylvia noticed the envelope on the counter.

"Is it from Gerry?" she asked.

"Yes," Florence said.

Sylvia waited. "Is he coming home?"

Florence met her eyes. "Not yet."

That was all.

When William came in, she handed him the letter without comment. He read it standing, then set it down carefully.

"He's learned how to carry," he said.

Florence nodded. That, she understood, was both the cost and the proof.

That night, as Robert slept nearby, Florence added one line to the ledger, nothing more than a date and a place. She did not summarize. She did not interpret.

Some words, she had learned, were not meant to be shared widely.

They were meant to be held.

"That's it," she murmured, not to Robert, but to the room itself.

The door opened softly behind her. William stepped in,

closing it with care, as if the night itself might be disturbed.

"You're still up," he said.

Florence did not turn at once. "I needed to set it down," she replied, her hand resting lightly on the page.

William came nearer, his gaze dropping briefly to the ledger. "Gerry?"

She nodded. "Just the place."

He stood beside her a moment, then rested his hand gently at the back of her chair, familiar and steady. "You're thinking ahead again," he said quietly.

Florence let out a small breath. "I don't know that it's ahead," she said. "It feels ... already in motion."

William's hand shifted from the chair to her shoulder, his thumb brushing once in a slow, circle, as if easing something he could not name.

She closed the ledger. "He won't be home for some time. Not in the way we had hoped."

"No," William answered.

Florence looked up at him then. "It isn't only him," she said. "There's a shifting again. You can feel it, can't you?"

William did not answer right away. Instead, he moved closer, his hand sliding down to take hers where it rested on the table. His grip was firm, warm, and anchoring.

"We've only just come through one war," he said.

"Yes," she replied. "And yet it doesn't feel finished."

Robert stirred softly. Both of them turned, instinctively. William reached down and adjusted the edge of the blanket, careful not to wake him, his hand lingering there a moment longer than needed.

Florence watched him. "Ron will be next," she said, her voice low. Not certain, but not unsure.

William straightened slowly. He did not contradict her. Instead, he drew her gently to her feet, his hand steady at her back, bringing her into him.

"We don't know that." His voice held more comfort than argument.

Florence rested her head briefly against his shoulder. "No," she said. "But I've learned not to wait for knowing."

His hand moved once along her back, a quiet, reassuring pass. "We'll meet it," he said.

Florence nodded against him, her hand still lightly holding his. "Yes," she said. "We will."

They stood that way for a moment longer, the room settled around them, Robert's breathing soft and sure.

The house held its quiet.

And something in it, once again, had already begun to prepare.

PART VI — BUILDING FORWARD (1949–EARLY 1950S)

CHAPTER TWENTY-TWO — PEACE ALONGSIDE WHAT WAS COMING

By late winter 1949, the radio had begun to speak differently again.

Not urgently. Not yet. But with a tone Florence recognized, the careful distance of men describing places most people could not find without a map. Borders were mentioned. Alliances. A peninsula she had never needed to picture before.

William turned the volume lower than usual. "They're restless," he said, not specifying who.

Florence folded laundry and listened anyway.

After a moment, she said quietly, "You mean overseas."

William nodded, his eyes still on the radio, though the sound had nearly faded. "There's talk of Korea again. Lines drawn after the war ... they never quite held."

Florence smoothed a sleeve, pressing the fabric flat with more care than necessary. "Another place we're not finished with."

"No," he said. "Another place no one's finished with."

The room settled around that.

Ron had grown taller without seeming to notice. His shoulders had broadened; his voice no longer lifted when he spoke. He lingered near the radio now, pretending not to.

"They won't call it anything yet," William added after a moment. "Just tension. Posturing. That's how it begins."

Florence glanced toward Ron, then back to her hands. "It always has a name later."

William's gaze followed hers. "Yes."

"It's nothing," Dale said once, passing through the room.

Ron did not answer.

Dean watched his younger brother from the doorway, said nothing. He understood what age could do on its own, without orders.

Later, when the room had thinned and the radio sat silent, Florence spoke again, softer still. "He's eighteen."

"I know."

She folded the last shirt and set it aside. "Gerry's still in Guam. And now..." She did not finish.

William crossed the room then, not quickly, but with purpose. His hand came to rest lightly at her back, steady, familiar.

"We don't know anything," he said.

Florence did not turn. "No," she agreed. "But I know the sound of something beginning."

He let that stand.

Florence marked Ron's birthday in the ledger when the time came. Eighteen. The number settled heavily on the page.

She did not imagine what would follow. She had learned better than to rush forward in thought. But she noticed the way the house adjusted around him already, how meals shifted, how questions paused, how the future leaned, almost imperceptibly, in his direction.

Peace, she understood, was not the absence of conflict.

It was the interval between demands.

The long months of winter finally relented, and the glorious sun melted the last stubborn seams of snow and ice. Florence grew restless for the outdoors, eager to turn the earth with her hands, to press seeds into soil, to coax sleeping plants awake, to stand within the landscape where her thoughts most often found their footing.

Robert, now nearly four, played nearby, content and bright, his laughter skipping along the path as he ran ahead and doubled back again, pockets already heavy with stones and bits of nothing he deemed important. Florence worked and watched in equal measure, comforted by the familiar exchange, his motion, her tending, his noise, her quiet industry.

It was only when the sound thinned, when the garden slipped into a sudden, expectant stillness, that her hands paused mid-motion.

She lifted her head, listening. Spring carried many silences, she knew. Not all of them meant absence. Some were simply the earth holding its breath before moving again.

She shaded her eyes and scanned the path, the budding hedgerow, the places a boy might disappear for no reason at all.

She had learned by then: quiet was never just quiet. It was a space.

And life, she knew, had a way of stepping forward from such pauses changed.

Spring moved in the way it always did, quietly at first, then all at once. The soil softened. Buds loosened their grip. Days stretched longer, as if daring the world to believe in them again. Florence welcomed the work that came with it, the bending and lifting, the reassurance of things that answered care with growth.

She had lived long enough to know that seasons did not arrive as guarantees. They arrived as invitations. What followed depended on forces no one tending a garden could fully command.

Still, she planted. She marked rows. She trusted the warmth enough to act, even as she listened, always, for the subtle shifts beneath the shade of trees. History, she sensed, rarely announced itself at the door. It gathered the way weather did, beyond the horizon, altering the air long before the sky darkened.

Spring promised life.

And Florence, hands in the earth, understood that promise was never the same thing as protection.

Peace came in pieces, some fitting easily, others requiring adjustment. Florence learned to recognize the difference. She did not expect quiet to mean ease, only that the house would eventually learn how to hold itself again.

William's ledgers began to thicken that year. Pages once spare now filled with careful handwriting, numbers balanced and rebalanced until they behaved. Florence watched him work in the evenings, sleeves rolled, pencil tucked behind his ear. Order returned not through celebration, but repetition.

The sons drifted back into the household in stages. Some stayed. Some came and went. Each arrival brought relief; each departure required recalibration. Florence resisted the urge to mark endings too boldly. She had learned that many things were provisional.

Sylvia worried in ways she did not announce. At fourteen, she had learned that fear could be managed by attention, by helping more, by listening harder, by keeping herself useful. Florence noticed the way she lingered near the radio, how she watched William's face for shifts in tone.

Donna, eight and untroubled by the mechanics of war, was spoiled openly now by her older siblings when they were home, extra desserts, small indulgences passed across the table without comment. Florence let it happen. Innocence, she had learned, did not replenish itself.

Robert, four and still small for his age, lived closer to the floor than the others. Florence measured his days differently, by meals taken on time, by rest, by steadiness rather than speed, by the careful watching of color and appetite. She did not speak of his condition aloud. It was enough that routines held and that vigilance remained quiet.

Gerry came home briefly in 1950, thinner than Florence remembered but steady in a way that mattered more. Guam still clung to him, in his posture, in the way he scanned rooms before settling. He stayed long enough to sleep in his old bed, to eat at the table without hurry, to let Donna trail him from room to room as if he might vanish again if she looked away.

He spoke little of the island. More of what came next.

"College," he said one evening, almost casually, as if testing the word aloud. "Out west. A fellow I served with said it counts. The state covers the expense when you live there."

William looked up from his plate. Florence did not.

"Free," Gerry added, not smiling. "Seems a waste not to use

it."

Florence nodded once. She understood bargains that came wrapped in years rather than money.

He left again soon after, this time toward California, carrying fewer things than before. The house barely had time to recalibrate before it was required to do so again.

Life resumed its habits. Meals returned to familiar hours. Shoes lined up by the door again. Florence stored what she could and released what she could not. She did not confuse the two.

On Sundays, after church, they sometimes drove west instead of home.

Florence packed simply, sandwiches wrapped in wax paper, fruit tucked into tins, a thermos carried more out of habit than necessity. William drove with the windows cracked, the air shifting as they left town behind. The children grew quieter the closer they came, as if something in the landscape asked for it.

Longwood Gardens was not announced when they arrived. It revealed itself gradually, paths unfolding, water moving where it was meant to, gardens arranged with intention rather than insistence. Pierre du Pont had understood something Florence recognized immediately: that beauty required structure, and patience, and long thinking.

"It doesn't ask you to look," Florence said softly, more to herself than to anyone. "It lets you come to it."

William glanced at her, a quiet recognition passing between them. "That takes confidence," he said.

"And time," she added.

They spread a blanket beneath a stand of trees and ate without hurry. Donna wandered just far enough to feel independent, then returned to show what she'd found.

"Look," she said, holding up a small leaf cupped in her palm. "It's shaped like a heart."

Florence smiled. "Then you chose well."

Sylvia lingered near the flowers, reading labels carefully, as if learning names mattered.

"This one's been here since before the war," she said, tracing the sign lightly. "It says so."

"Then it knows something about staying," Florence replied.

Dale studied the fountains, tracing the way water rose and fell, already attentive to systems that worked because they were designed to endure.

"It's not random," he said, half to William. "There's pressure behind it. Timing."

William stepped beside him. "Everything you see working ... has something behind it you don't."

Dale nodded, eyes still fixed on the arc of water. "I figured."

Ron walked beside William for a time, hands in his pockets, saying little. When he stopped, he stopped fully, watching water spill into stone basins and find its level without instruction.

"It always settles," Ron said after a moment.

William followed his gaze. "It does."

Robert stayed close to Florence, his steps measured. She let him set the pace.

"Am I too slow?" he asked, looking up.

"No," she said gently. "You're exactly right."

There was no need to hurry here. Growth did not reward speed.

They walked the paths until the afternoon shifted, until light filtered differently through glass and leaves.

"It feels ... different here," Sylvia said at last. "Quieter."

"It was made that way," Florence answered. "So people could remember how to be still."

No one spoke of war. No one spoke of what might come next. It was enough to notice what had been built to last, what had been tended season after season so that others might arrive and feel peace.

William stood beside her as the light shifted again, softer

now, settling into the paths.

"They built this to hold," he said quietly.

Florence watched the water move, steady in its course. "So people could come when things don't."

He nodded.

After a moment, she added quietly, "It won't always stay this way."

William's hand found hers, not to answer, but to remain.

On the drive home, Donna slept. The older children stared out the windows, full in a way that had nothing to do with food. William rested one hand on the wheel, the other on the quiet between them.

They returned again a few weeks later. Then again.

It became a practice. A place where time behaved itself. Where patience could be seen and understood without explanation. The family learned, simply by returning, that tending something together, trusting it to grow in its own season, could become a kind of inheritance.

By the time Ron stepped fully into adulthood, that lesson had already taken root.

The notice arrived not long after.

There was no gathering to mark it, no ceremony beyond supper taken at the usual hour and William's brief acknowledgment that sounded more like routine than recognition. Adulthood, Florence knew, often arrived this way, quietly, and already asking something in return.

The paper itself was official. Impersonal. Inevitable.

Florence read it once before passing it to William, the thin sheet moving between them with a familiarity that surprised her. Korea had begun to surface more often on the radio by then, threaded between weather reports and music, no longer spoken of as distant unrest but as obligation.

Ron said little in the days that followed. He moved through the house with the same economy he always had, finishing chores, answering when spoken to, packing carefully as though order itself might steady what lay ahead. He folded each shirt flat, checked and rechecked what he was allowed to bring, and left the rest behind without comment.

"Tail gunner," he told Dale one afternoon, almost offhand, as if naming the position might fix it in place, give it boundaries.

Dale nodded, absorbing the word without fully understanding it. He stood in the doorway when Ron left, committing details to memory he did not yet know he would need, the angle of Ron's shoulders beneath the strap of his bag, the sound of his boots on the walk, the way the screen door closed more softly than usual. At sixteen, he was learning that departures marked a person long before decisions did.

William and Florence did not say goodbye loudly. They had learned better than to compete with trains.

After he embraced them both, Ron turned quickly and strode forward.

They remained where they were, her hands folded, William's arm resting gently at her waist, watching until distance took him, trusting that restraint, too, could endure.

They returned home together in silence and deep thought. He retreated to his workshop. Instinct carried her toward the kitchen, the familiar order of counters and tasks waiting to receive her. But she paused at the threshold and turned instead toward the garden.

The summer months had brought it into its own fullness. Roses stood open and unguarded, their scent rising in the heat. Trees had leafed out completely now, their branches casting dappled light that protected the tender growth beneath while still allowing enough sun to reach the waiting blooms. Shade and warmth existed together, each making room for the other.

Florence moved slowly along the path, brushing past familiar edges, letting color and texture steady her. The garden had learned its own rhythms, when to hold, when to release. Nothing hurried. Nothing clung. What had gone to ground in colder seasons had returned, altered but intact.

She had come to understand life this way. Delicate, yes—but not without design. Fragile, but never without purpose. Seasons arrived, departed, and arrived again, each bearing what was needed for that time alone.

She stood for a moment with her hands resting against the bark of the old tree, feeling the quiet exchange of shade and light above her. Loss did not mean absence forever. Nor did departure mean erasure.

All things, she believed, were restored in their proper hour.

Several days later a letter arrived from California giving Florence a shift in thought. She recognized the writing and carefully unfolded the letter and began to read.

Dear Mom,

Classes have started, and I'm finding my way well enough. The campus is larger than I expected, but it's laid out so you can learn it by walking—paths that return you to where you began if you stay with them long enough.

There's a garden not far from my room. I go there between lectures when the noise catches up with me. It isn't showy. Everything seems placed with a reason, water moving where it's meant to, trees given room to become what they already are.

I thought of you there. Of Sundays after church, when we walked without needing to arrive anywhere in particular. This place feels built by people who understood that patience could be designed, not just hoped for.

I sit sometimes and watch others pass through—students mostly, some in a hurry, some not. It steadies me to see that things can be tended across generations, even when the world keeps changing its mind.

I'm doing the work. I'm learning what I came for. That feels like enough for now.

Give my love to everyone. Tell Donna I found a tree she would climb if she were here. Tell Dale to keep looking up. And give Robert a big hug from me.

Love,

Gerry

Florence folded Gerry's letter with care. It carried the kind of reassurance that did not insist on being believed, only understood. He had found his footing, she thought. Or at least the patience to stand where he was.

She placed the letter where she kept the others and let the afternoon settle back into its familiar order. Robert played until sleep finally claimed him, his small body yielding to rest without argument.

In the weeks that followed, the house resumed its measured pace. Days arranged themselves around small tasks and necessary routines, each one completed without comment. Gerry's letter held its place among the others, steady in tone, easy to return to. Ron's absence did not settle in the same way. It moved at the edges of things—less defined, less willing to be named. Letters were waited for, not expected. Time moved forward in its quiet, unremarked way—until one afternoon, something new arrived among the ordinary.

She held it a moment longer than necessary, absorbing its weight before breaking the seal and drawing out the page.

I got here all right. The trip was long, but orderly. They keep us busy, which helps. The weather isn't what I expected, colder than it looks on the map, and it changes its mind often.

My position is in the tail. It suits me fine. You can see a long way from there, which feels useful. The crew is solid. We're learning how to trust one another quickly.

Don't worry about supplies. Everything is accounted for. We eat when we're told and sleep when we can. That's enough.

I've tucked a few small things in the parcel coming your way. There's an extra insignia patch for Dale — thought he might like something official to pin up over his desk. For Sylvia, I found a dainty hand-carved bracelet at a market stall near base. It looked like something she'd turn over in her hands and study. For Donna, a small square of bright silk, colorful as she is. And for Robert, a badge I came across, bold and painted. He can decide what rank it gives him.

Tell Dale to keep at his studies. Tell Sylvia I got her note and read it twice. Donna should listen to you, even when she thinks she doesn't have to. Give Robert a pat for me.

I'll write again when I can.

Love,

Ron

Florence read the letter once, then again—more slowly.

You can see a long way from there.

She folded the page carefully and set it aside, not where reassurance was kept, but where truth belonged. Some words were meant to inform. Others were meant to steady.

This one did both.

She took out a clean sheet of paper and began to write.

Dear Ron,

Your letter came and was read carefully. I'm glad to know you arrived as you said you did. Order matters more than people realize, and I'm relieved you've found some. I'll keep watch for the parcel. We'll all be excited to open it together.

I'm not worried about your work. I trust you to do what's been given to you with attention and steadiness. That has always been your way.

Things here keep their rhythm. The garden is coming along. The back stoop is finished at last. Your father has been at his desk more than usual, which I take as a good sign.

Dale studies hard and asks questions. Sylvia keeps me company and pretends she isn't watching the radio. Donna listens when she wants to, which is often enough. Robert is well and growing in his careful way.

Write when you can. You don't need to say more than you have. Knowing you're thinking of home is enough.

Remember to rest when it's offered and to notice what steadies you. Those things count, even when they don't feel important.

We are here. We remain.

Love,

Mom

At the bottom of the page, William added his own hand.

P.S.—

I read your letter too.
Do your job carefully and trust your crew.
Your place matters.
—Dad

On quiet afternoons after, Florence sorted through what had accumulated—documents, receipts, photographs—each item finding its proper place. She did not rush the process. Things handled too quickly had a way of returning.

By evening, the house felt balanced. Not finished, but stable. Florence closed the drawer where the family records were kept and rested her hand there briefly, feeling the weight of what had already been contained and what still would be.

Peace, she understood, was not an event. It was a practice.

William's mother, Lillian, came and went quietly, never announcing her visits in advance. She arrived with a small case, stayed a measured length of time, and left the house as she found it. More often than not, her stays coincided with the beginning of another journey—she was determined, in her lifetime, to see every state capital, one by one, without haste.

With the grandchildren, she was attentive rather than indulgent. She listened more than she spoke, asking questions that invited answers without pressing for them. Florence noticed how the children leaned toward her, not out of excitement, but recognition.

Lillian paid attention to what was kept. To where things were placed, and how often they were returned to the same spot. She did not interfere. She understood that households, like people, revealed themselves best when left undisturbed.

It was during one such visit, in the spring of 1952, that Florence noticed a different kind of mapping taking shape. Dale had begun watching the sky more carefully, pausing mid-conversation to follow the movement of clouds or the distant passage of an aircraft. He charted patterns others ignored.

Lillian noticed it too.

"They don't move the way people think they do," Dale said one afternoon, shading his eyes as a plane crossed high overhead. “The sky, I mean. It looks open, but it’s full of lines.”

Lillian smiled, not looking up. “Most places are,” she said. “You don’t see the routes until you start paying attention.”

Florence set a plate on the table and listened. Dale rarely spoke without purpose.

“They teach you those lines,” he added, quieter now. “How to read them. How to stay where you’re meant to be.”

“That matters,” Florence said. “Knowing where you belong.”

Lillian met her gaze briefly, something knowing passing between them. “And knowing when you’re ready to follow them.”

Dale said nothing more. He didn’t need to.

Florence heard his decision without surprise. She recorded 1952 in the same careful hand she used for births and marriages, then drew a clean line beneath it before closing the book. The Air Force suited him, she thought—structured, steady, built for the long haul. Like Lillian’s journeys, it was a life measured not by stops alone, but by the distance between them.

She placed the paper where it belonged and did not count ahead.

That, she had learned, was the discipline. You recorded what had happened, not what might.

Only later would Florence understand how much Lillian had been noticing all along, what she set aside, what she kept near, the quiet order she gave to things others might have overlooked. Nothing announced itself. Nothing asked to be explained. Yet it was all there, gathered with intention, as though meant to be found when the time was right.

Not everyone who passed through the house stayed for decades. Some left more carefully than they arrived.

The spare room upstairs took on a tenant that year—Shirley Tattersfield, twenty-two, newly out of art school and determined to make a place for herself in a city that had not yet decided what to do with her. She arrived with a single trunk and a confidence that came and went, her laughter carrying easily up the narrow stairs. Florence noticed the scarves first, bright, unapologetic, then the way Shirley worked, sketching at the small desk by the window until the light failed.

William and Florence asked for little. A modest rent. A willingness to share meals. An understanding that the house kept its own rhythms. Shirley fit herself into them easily, rising early, returning late, sometimes discouraged, sometimes alight with possibility. Florence did not ask about rejections. She had learned that ambition needed room as much as reassurance.

One afternoon, Florence poured the coffee and set the cake between them, steam lifting softly from the cups.

"I never know how much to say," Shirley admitted, turning her saucer a quarter turn. "You don't want to sound foolish. Or ... hungry."

Florence smiled, cutting the slice cleanly. "Hungry isn't foolish," she said. "It means you're paying attention."

Shirley laughed at that, surprised. "I want my work to matter," she said after a moment. "Not just hang somewhere. I want it to say something. Even if people don't like it."

Florence considered her, then nodded. "Some things are worth being misunderstood for."

They carried their cups into the garden when the air grew too warm for the kitchen. Shirley walked slowly there, stopping to study a rose that had climbed higher than expected, its stem trained but determined. "I'm afraid of getting stuck," she said, brushing her fingers against the trellis. "Of staying small because it's safer."

Florence followed her gaze. "Things that are meant to grow usually push against something first," she said. "Walls. Weather. Time."

Shirley looked around, really looked—at the beds laid out with care, at what had been pruned back and what had been allowed to reach. "You don't rush it," she said quietly.

"No," Florence agreed. "But you don't stop it either."

When Shirley eventually moved on, as people with purpose always did, Florence folded the extra linens back into the cupboard and closed the door gently, satisfied that the room had done what it was meant to do.

Only later did she notice what Shirley had left behind.

Two framed pieces leaned carefully against the spare room wall, wrapped in brown paper and tied with string. Florence carried them downstairs one at a time, setting them on the dining table where the light was kind.

The first made her smile outright. Slender, elongated figures moved along garden paths as if on parade, fabrics flowing, colors confident and alive. The women wore fashions Florence admired, not practical, not cautious, but expressive, each stride suggesting choice, intention, a delight in being seen. She recognized herself there, not as she was, but as she had always understood beauty: something cultivated, worn with assurance, allowed to take up space.

The second she studied longer. A man and a woman walked hand in hand through a garden softened by late light, their figures turned slightly toward one another, as if conversation mattered more than destination. The path curved ahead, unfixed, but there was no hesitation in their steps. Florence felt the familiar settling in her chest, the quiet recognition of a life walked alongside another, season after season.

She hung them both where she would pass them often. Proof, she thought, that tending—whether of rooms, gardens, or people—sometimes left behind more than memory. Sometimes it left beauty, shaped by having been welcomed at all.

The house adjusted again. Chairs were shifted. Schedules rewritten. The pantry filled more easily now, though Florence still arranged it with care. Old habits did not vanish simply because they were no longer necessary.

CHAPTER TWENTY-THREE — MARRIAGES AND MOVING OUT

The house began to empty, not all at once, but the way tides recede, quietly, deliberately, leaving marks behind.

Florence noticed it first in the corners. A cedar chest no longer pressed beneath a window. A wedding trunk lifted and carried down the steps, its weight redistributed into someone else's future. Rooms did not fall silent so much as they loosened their hold, releasing what had once been packed tight with childhood and expectation.

Hope chests had lined Florence's own life like punctuation marks, each one holding linens, letters, promises folded carefully for a season not yet arrived. Now she watched them open again, altered by time, filled not with anticipation but with departure.

On evenings when the quiet settled too firmly, Florence walked the garden paths alone. Her steps followed familiar turns, but her thoughts returned to an earlier walk, long before the house was full. She remembered William stopping near a low stone wall, reaching for her hand, not with urgency, but with certainty, as if the gesture itself were a question he was willing to wait on. She had not answered with words. She had simply stayed. That, she understood now, had been the beginning.

Later, passing through the front room, her eye caught on the painting Shirley had left behind—the romantic garden scene she had hung where the light fell softest. A couple walked hand in hand along a curved path, their figures angled slightly toward one another, as if the world ahead mattered less than the moment they were choosing together. Near the edge of the frame, barely noticeable unless you lingered, a low stone wall traced the boundary of the garden. Florence stopped. Shirley had not known the story. Or perhaps she had sensed it without being told.

William stopped beside her. He did not speak. He only leaned in slightly, studying the painting longer than he might have otherwise. Florence felt the recognition settle between them when his gaze paused where hers had—at the stone wall, at the space where a hand reached and waited. Their eyes met briefly. Nothing needed saying. Some beginnings were still theirs alone.

Florence saw it clearly then, how love had first arrived quietly, offering a hand and waiting. How that same patience had shaped the home her children were now leaving behind. Each of them carried something learned there: how to choose carefully, how to walk alongside another without rushing the path.

She rested her hand against the familiar grain of the doorframe, the house breathing differently now but still alive with what had been planted. Loving William had taught her how to begin without guarantees. Loving her children had taught her how to let go without fear. Both, she knew, were acts of faith—trusting that what was truly held would endure, even when carried beyond the garden gate.

Bill and Donita

Bill had been the first to send his life forward a season earlier.

He and Donita returned one summer afternoon from Kansas with dust on their shoes and quiet certainty in their voices. The house adjusted itself almost immediately, chairs drawn closer, an extra place set without discussion. Donita moved easily through the rooms, observant, rather than tentative, taking in the family with a careful warmth that Florence recognized as respect.

"We didn't want a fuss, Mom," Bill said gently, setting his hat on the sideboard. "Just something simple. Something sure."

Florence embraced them both. "Simplicity often lasts the longest," she replied, meaning more than she said.

That evening, family gathered as they always did when something mattered. Plates were passed, stories retold, laughter arriving in familiar waves. Donita listened closely, asking questions that showed she had already learned Bill's people the way one learns a new landscape, by paying attention. Florence watched her hands as she poured coffee, steady and unhurried, and felt the quiet relief of knowing her son had chosen well.

Later, in the kitchen, Florence rinsed the last cup while Donita dried it carefully, aligning it with the others as if it belonged there.

"He's always been steady," Donita said, not as praise but as fact.

"He has," Florence replied. "And he needs someone who won't hurry him."

Donita met her gaze. "I won't."

Florence nodded. It was enough.

The next day, Bill suggested they take Donita into the city. They moved through gallery rooms at an unspoken pace, Bill lingering over structure and line, Donita drawn to color and movement. Florence noticed how they paused for one another, how one would wait while the other finished looking, how conversation resumed without being rushed. It reminded her of a long-ago walk beside William, when learning how to move together had mattered more than destination.

Later, as Bill packed his trunk, engineering manuals stacked neatly, rolled plans tied with twine, a few carved wood pieces tucked carefully between shirts, William lingered in the doorway.

"You're building more than machines," William told him. "You're building a life."

Bill smiled. "You taught me how."

When the trunk lid closed, Florence rested her palm on the worn leather. Pride settled alongside loss, an ache she recognized as love doing its work. This was how it began now, she understood. Not with rupture, but with welcome. Not with absence, but with a widening of the circle, making room for what would come next.

Bill returned again the following year, this time alone, arriving with the sound of an unfamiliar engine idling outside the house.

Sylvia rushed to the window. "What on earth is that?"

Bill stepped inside with a grin. "Come see."

Out front sat a modest used automobile—polished, practical, dependable. Nothing flashy. Exactly right.

"For me?" Sylvia whispered.

"For your sixteenth," Bill said. "Every young woman deserves a way forward."

Sylvia laughed, then startled herself by crying at the same time. "I don't even know how to drive!"

"You will," he assured her. "I'll teach you."

William circled the car slowly. "Reliable engine," he murmured. "Solid choice."

Florence kissed Sylvia's cheek. "Freedom can be a gift," she said softly. "Just remember to carry it wisely."

Donna climbed onto the running board. "Can I ride with you?"

"Eventually," Sylvia teased. "Once I'm confident I won't drive into a fence."

The family laughed together, the moment settling into memory like a pressed flower between pages.

Florence watched Sylvia run her fingers across the steering wheel and thought: *Another kind of departure has begun.*

Dean and Jeanne

Dean's leaving came more gently.

His marriage to Jeanne did not carry him far, only to Bryn Mawr, close enough that Florence could imagine Sunday dinners and familiar knock patterns, the easy rhythm of coming and going never fully broken.

"You're not going far," Florence said as she folded his

shirts, smoothing the creases with practiced care.

"Not far enough to forget home," Dean replied, leaning in the doorway, watching her hands the way children sometimes did when they knew something important was being done for them.

Their trunk was modest. Practical. Rooted. Shoes wrapped in paper. Everyday things stacked without ceremony. Nothing extravagant. Nothing uncertain.

Florence found comfort in that, distance measured not in miles, but in ease of return.

Not long after the wedding, the four of them—Florence and William, Dean and Jeanne—spent a Sunday afternoon at Bartram's Garden.

It was Jeanne's idea, offered casually, as if she already understood the quiet importance of the place.

"I'd like to see where it all began," she said.

Florence smiled at that.

They walked slowly along the paths, the river moving beside them with the same steady assurance it always had. Early blossoms stirred in the breeze. The ground held the memory of winter but had begun to soften. The river carried the smell of earth and early blossoms, the same as it had years before, and Florence felt time fold rather than pass.

William slowed as they approached the stone steps.

"Here," he said simply.

Jeanne stopped. "This is where you proposed?"

Florence nodded. "Not much has changed."

William glanced down at the worn stone. "I was afraid I'd forget what I meant to say."

"And you didn't," Florence replied.

"I said just enough."

Dean watched quietly, his hand resting at the small of Jeanne's back, absorbing the history without needing to claim it.

They spread a blanket nearby, unpacking the picnic Florence had prepared, simple fare, nothing that required plates to linger or crumbs to be gathered too carefully. Jeanne poured lemonade. Dean passed bread. William leaned back, content to let the afternoon unfold.

"This is what I hoped marriage would look like," Jeanne said after a while. "Not grand. Just...steady."

Florence regarded her thoughtfully. "Steady is something you build," she said. "But it's worth the effort."

Dean reached for Jeanne's hand. "We're trying to do it right."

Florence believed them.

As they packed up, William lingered again at the steps, his hand brushing the stone as if acknowledging an old promise still intact.

On the walk back, Florence felt the quiet reassurance she had been carrying settle more fully into place. Some children left boldly. Others left gently.

Dean's leaving did not empty the house so much as widen it—stretching its reach just enough to include a new table, a new door, a new place where love could arrive without knocking.

Gerry and Janet

Gerry's leaving had carried a different rhythm.

Not abrupt, not final, more like a tide that had already gone out once and returned briefly, altered by distance. California lay beyond Florence's sense of geography, a place of sun and study and the improbable gift of education without cost. He had left with books and promise, his life already angled west.

When he returned that summer to marry Janet—his high school sweetheart—it felt less like a homecoming than a pause, a breath taken before moving forward again. Janet arrived with him, easy in her presence, as though she already understood how this family worked, what was said, what was held, what was simply done.

One afternoon, Janet suggested the water.

"My uncle Miles has a boat," she said. "He's offered to take us out."

Florence watched as Gerry helped Sylvia into the boat, steadying her hand, laughing as she adjusted to the unfamiliar sway. Sylvia's laughter carried across the water—lighter than it had been, freer—her hair lifting in the breeze as Janet pointed out landmarks only she seemed to know.

From the shore, Florence observed them move together—Gerry at ease, Janet confident, Sylvia newly unanchored from childhood, already learning what it meant to trust momentum.

Florence caught the sound of water slapping the hull, steady and sure, the rhythm carried across the shallows of the Chesapeake Bay.

Donna tugged at her skirt. "When do we get a turn?"

"In a little while," Florence said, smoothing her hair, though she already knew the answer would change.

Robert crouched near the waterline, intent on a smooth gray stone he turned over in his palm. "Look," he said, holding it up. "This one's heavy."

Donna knelt beside him, momentarily forgetting the boat, and began arranging pebbles into a careful row—dark, light, striped—collecting bits of shell and driftwood as if they were prizes rather than distractions. She pocketed a small piece of sea glass, its edges softened by time.

Florence watched them settle into the work of discovery, their urgency easing into focus.

Out on the water, Gerry leaned easily at Janet's side. Sylvia laughed as the boat tilted, her voice carrying back to shore, lifted by wind and sun and something new she had not yet learned to name.

Florence remained where she was, one eye on the children at her feet, the other on the widening water. Some were already moving outward. Others were still gathering what the shore had to offer.

Both, she knew, were exactly where they needed to be.

Later, as the sun softened and the boat returned, Florence

handed Gerry a book she had set aside for him. "You don't have to carry everything at once," she told him, pressing it into his hands.

He kissed her cheek. "I'll carry what matters."

Their trunk held books more than belongings, pages instead of weight, ideas instead of keepsakes. Florence kissed him longer than usual, as if lengthening the moment might shorten the distance.

Love, she knew, sometimes asked to be unreasonable.

Ron and Lucy

Ron returned from Korea with a quiet steadiness.

He had always been the one with his head in a book, content to listen while others filled the room. The war did not change that so much as refine it—silence worn not as distance, but as discipline. He moved carefully through the house, aware of thresholds, attentive to small routines, as if order itself were something worth protecting.

That was why the family was caught slightly off guard when he brought Lucy home.

She entered with warmth and motion, her laughter arriving just ahead of her, her stories trailing easily behind. She spoke with her hands, noticed everything, asked questions that invited answers rather than demanded them. Lucy was originally from Colorado, and she carried something of its openness with her, airier, wider, unconcerned with walls.

Florence watched Ron beside her and understood immediately. This was not opposition. It was balance.

When he introduced Lucy, he did so simply, without flourish. "She keeps me balanced," he said.

Lucy smiled, reaching for his arm. "He keeps me grounded."

Donna studied Lucy from the doorway at first, unsure what to make of someone who filled a room so easily. When Lucy laughed, Donna laughed too, a half-second late, testing the sound as if it might belong to her.

Robert lingered near his mother's knee, watching. "She smiles when she talks," he said, matter-of-fact, as though this were useful information.

Before long, Lucy had knelt beside them both, asking Donna about school, admiring the ribbon in her hair, listening carefully as Robert explained the difference between smooth stones and rough ones in his pocket.

Later, Donna whispered to Sylvia, "She talks a lot."

Sylvia smiled. "Ron doesn't."

Robert looked up from his stones. "She talks for him."

Donna nodded. "I think that's why it works."

At the table that night, Lucy filled the spaces Ron left open, describing her family, the mountains she missed, the way snow sounded different out west. Ron listened, occasionally offering a sentence that anchored the conversation, his quiet confidence steadying the room.

Colorado called them westward soon after. His trunk reflected him, entirely organized, labeled, efficient. Shirts folded square. Papers aligned. Nothing unnecessary.

Before the lid was closed, Florence slipped a small envelope between the layers, nothing important on paper, only the shape of her handwriting, the reassurance of home folded thin enough to travel.

Ron caught her hand. "I'll write," he promised.

Florence nodded. "You always have."

She watched him lift the trunk without hesitation, Lucy beside him, already oriented toward the road ahead. Some children left loudly. Others left with purpose.

Ron had always known where he was going.

Dale and Liz

Dale's leaving began with orders, not vows.

Germany reshaped him before he knew it would, discipline sharpening into confidence, distance teaching him how to carry himself differently. When Liz entered his life, it felt less like a beginning than a recognition.

She arrived like an unexpected line in a letter, beautiful, composed, belonging both nowhere and everywhere.

"You bring the world with you," Florence told her.

Liz smiled warmly, her German accent soft but certain. "And your son brings home."

Dale's trunk told its own story. Corners softened by travel. Stickers half-peeled. Leather worn thin where hands had gripped and lifted it again and again. Distance had already lived there.

It was Liz who asked, one afternoon, almost shyly, "Would you show me Longwood Gardens? Dale has spoken of it so often."

So they went together—Florence and William, Dale and Liz, Sylvia, Donna, Robert, Dean and Jeanne—spreading out across the paths of Longwood Gardens.

Blankets were laid beneath tall trees. Baskets opened. Children wandered and returned, pockets slowly filling, leaves pressed flat, smooth stones, something green Donna insisted was important. Robert trailed close to Florence, his small hand warm in hers, while William and Dean spoke quietly nearby, their heads inclined together.

Liz moved easily among them, admiring the fountains, pausing to touch the edge of a leaf, asking questions that revealed how carefully she was watching. Sylvia stayed near her, curious, absorbing Liz's confidence and grace. Dale stood back at times, observing it all with a look Florence recognized, gratitude mixed with relief.

"This is beautiful," Liz said, taking in the long view of water and sky. "It feels ... rooted."

Florence nodded. "Some places are meant to remind us where we stand."

As the afternoon settled, the family gathered closer, the day folding itself gently around them. Laughter rose and fell. Plates emptied. The gardens held their voices without urgency.

Later, as they packed up, Florence understood the gift Liz had asked for. Not a visit. A meeting of worlds.

Some children left with certainty. Some returned changed. Some brought the world back with them, asking it—politely, hopefully—to sit at the family table for a while.

And sometimes, it did.

Florence stood in the doorway as each container left the house, hope chests once filled under her careful supervision, wedding trunks now closed by younger hands.

William watched her from across the room.

"We packed these lives well," he said quietly.

"Yes," she answered. "And taught them how to carry love without weighing it down."

Sylvia and Jack

Sylvia was smitten the moment she met Jack Swartz.

He was broad-shouldered and sun-weathered, a young man raised on a dairy farm in Port Royal, where mornings began before light and strength was earned rather than spoken of. He moved with an ease shaped by long days outdoors, his hands steady, his presence grounded. Sylvia noticed everything about him, the way he listened before answering, the way his laughter arrived unguarded, the way the earth itself seemed to recognize him.

Florence noticed too.

At first, she assumed it was a passing crush. Sylvia was still young. There were suitable local boys, familiar families, predictable paths. Florence expected her daughter would settle close to home, choose something sensible, something approved.

But it had not begun that way.

Sylvia had gone with a few of her cousins to visit a relative who had taken ill, a small house set just beyond the edge of Port Royal, where the road narrowed and the town seemed to gather in on itself. They had not planned to stay long, just long enough to sit, to bring what was needed, to be present in the quiet way illness required.

Jack had come by in the late afternoon, not as a visitor

exactly, but as someone expected. He knew Ronny, had grown up alongside him in the easy, unspoken way of boys who shared seasons and small-town rhythms. He stepped in without ceremony, nodded to the room, and took his place as if he had always belonged to it.

Sylvia noticed him not all at once, but in parts. The way he listened before speaking. The steadiness in how he carried himself. When he did speak, it was not to fill silence, but to meet it.

"You're Sylvia," he said at one point, not as a question.

She looked up, surprised. "I am."

"Ronny's mentioned you."

There was nothing remarkable in the words, and yet something in the way he said them, plain, without embellishment, held.

They spoke only briefly that first day. About where she had come from. About how long they would stay. Nothing that would have marked the moment as significant to anyone watching.

But when it was time to leave, Sylvia found herself turning once more than necessary.

Jack had already stepped outside, standing near the fence line, his attention turned outward, as if accustomed to watching what might be coming down the road.

He lifted a hand in acknowledgment. Not a wave. Just enough.

It was, Florence would later understand, not the beginning of something sudden.

It was the beginning of something that would return.

Sylvia spoke of the visit only in passing. The cousin's condition. The drive. The way the town seemed quieter than expected. Jack's name came once, lightly placed among the others, without emphasis.

But it returned.

In small ways at first, an extra moment at the window in the late afternoon, as if measuring the hour. A question asked without appearing to be one. The mention of Ronny's friend, then again, not repeated too closely, but not forgotten either.

Florence noticed what was not said as much as what was.

"You enjoyed yourself," she remarked one evening, not looking up from her mending.

Sylvia hesitated, just briefly. "It was... different."

"Different how?"

Sylvia considered, then shook her head. "I don't know."

Florence did.

She had seen that kind of uncertainty before, not confusion, but recognition arriving without permission.

After that, the name settled more easily into the house. Not often. Not enough to invite comment. But enough.

William noticed it too, though he said nothing at first.

"He's steady," Sylvia said once, as if offering explanation where none had been asked.

William glanced at her. "That matters."

Florence folded the cloth in her lap, aligning its edges carefully. "Distance does too," she said, her tone even.

Sylvia did not argue. But she did not agree.

Time passed. Letters began, not many, not long. Enough to continue what had already taken hold.

Florence watched it form the way one watches a structure rise at a distance, first a suggestion, then a shape, then something unmistakable.

It was not a passing thing.

It did not fade when left alone.

It held.

And in that holding, Florence understood, this was not something that would remain near, or simple, or easily guided.

It would require something else entirely.

Something she could not arrange for her. But Sylvia did not waver.

What began quietly did not loosen with time. It did not yield to distance or to expectation. If anything, it clarified, each absence shaping it more precisely, each return confirming what had already taken hold.

Florence spoke when she could. Gently at first, then with greater care. Of distance. Of timing. Of the life Sylvia had always been expected to build.

Sylvia listened.

But she did not turn.

And so it happened without announcement.

Against her parents' wishes, she and Jack eloped, marrying quietly in Elkton, a place chosen precisely because no signatures were required. There was no announcement beforehand, no careful negotiation. Only certainty. Only forward motion.

Jack proved himself not through persuasion, but through presence.

He was strong and tireless, and in time he built a successful tree service, tending the great estates along the Main Line. His name traveled by word of mouth, passed neighbor to neighbor, spoken with trust. He loved the land—soil, roots, growth—and it was this reverence that slowly drew Florence and William closer to him. In the gardens, Jack worked without instruction, understanding intuitively where care was needed and where patience mattered more than force.

That spring, Florence and William joined Sylvia and Jack for a picnic at Valley Forge. Donna and Robert came along, eager for escape from the long drive and the dull gravity of adult conversation. The day was bright and unseasonably warm, sunlight filtering generously through budding trees.

They arrived first at the covered bridge.

Florence gasped. She remembered bridges like these from her childhood, the rhythm of wheels over wood, open buggies, the feeling of passage suspended between places. Jack noticed immediately. He said nothing, but the warmth of her reaction did not go unseen.

They moved on, passing Washington's headquarters and the crude wooden cabins beyond, structures that barely deserved the name shelter, standing as quiet witnesses to the brutal winter of 1777. Florence slowed there, imagining the cold, the hunger, the endurance required to remain.

At the crest of the hill, they reached the National Memorial Arch. This was where they stopped.

Donna and Robert scattered at once, laughter spilling out as they shook off the confines of the car. Florence and William laid out the picnic beside the hilltop, overlooking a valley dotted with grazing deer.

Sylvia and Jack stepped beneath the arch together.

The inscription held them still:

Naked and starving as they are
We cannot enough admire
the incomparable patience and fidelity
of the soldiery.
—George Washington

They stood in silence, dwarfed by stone and history, the weight of endurance pressing gently between them. Sylvia felt it settle—this understanding of what it meant to choose someone not only for love, but for the long work of living.

The stone rose above them, unchanged, as though time itself had been asked to pause. Florence felt, without knowing why, that the hilltop would one day receive another moment —another meeting—separate from this one, yet quietly linked. Such was the nature of enduring places: they gathered meaning without announcing it.

From below, familiar voices carried upward. Donna's laughter rose first, bright and unrestrained, followed by Robert's, lower and insistent as he called for her to slow down. Florence waved them over, the picnic already laid out, cloth against the grass, baskets opened, the ordinary comforts of food and family reclaiming the moment.

William handed Jack a thermos without ceremony. Jack accepted it with a nod, their exchange easy now, unspoken. Sylvia joined them, settling onto the blanket as Florence passed around plates, the simple act grounding what had felt momentous only moments before.

A light breeze moved through the hilltop, carrying the

clean scent of new grass and warming bread as it stirred the edges of the blanket.

They ate beneath the open sky, the arch standing watch behind them, history giving way to the present. Deer grazed at the edge of the field, unbothered. The children ran and returned, ran again. Conversation drifted—light, then quieter—until the weight of the morning softened into something held in common.

In time, Florence and William came to see the wisdom in Sylvia's choosing.

Months later, without explanation, Jack brought Florence into the backyard garden. Spanning the narrow creek that wound through her beds, he had placed an exact scaled replica of the Knox Covered Bridge. The craftsmanship was precise, measured, faithful, but it was the intention that undid her. He had taken something she loved, something rooted in shared memory, and carried it home.

Florence rested her hand on the railing, overcome by the recognition of what he had given her, not just a bridge, but a continuation. A gesture that understood how she held the past, how she honored what endured. In building it, Jack had not only recreated a structure; he had crossed something invisible himself. He had learned the language of her world. He had placed himself within it.

From that day on, Florence no longer thought of Jack as someone Sylvia had married, but as someone who had joined them, carefully, deliberately, like a bridge built to last.

Jack proved himself not through grand gestures, but through constancy—by staying, by listening, by loving the land, and by loving their daughter well.

Donna and Robert scarcely gave it thought.

By the time they had arrived, leaving had become the house's rhythm.

Absence felt ordinary.

Florence saw the difference.

Longing arrived when it was ready.

Donna and Shenton

Donna met Shenton at a dance at Haverford College, one of those evenings meant for lightness—music drifting across the floor, laughter rising easily, the future still unclaimed. He was attending college there; she had only just finished high school and had come with friends for the dance, as she sometimes did. He asked her to dance once, then again. By the end of the night, neither pretended it was chance.

Their courtship unfolded simply and with purpose. Letters were exchanged. Dinners shared. Walks taken without hurry. A year later, they married—not with fanfare, but with confidence—two young people certain they had found what they were meant to keep.

They moved into the small third-floor apartment within the family home, a space William and Florence had long set aside for use rather than display. It had once been rented by the artist Shirley Tattersfield, a modest arrangement, no kitchen of its own, only light, quiet, and room enough for work and rest. Florence liked knowing the space would remain lived in, not emptied, carried forward rather than closed.

Donna made it her own quickly. Curtains were chosen. A small table placed near the window. Meals were taken downstairs, footsteps on the stairs becoming part of the household's shared rhythm. Florence noticed these changes without comment, recognizing the particular ache and satisfaction of watching a daughter settle into her own life under the same roof, yet newly apart.

With Donna married, Robert remained.

He was the last child still tethered to the daily life of the house, the final set of shoes by the door, the last voice answering from another room. The quiet arrived gradually now, not as loss but as completion, the closing of a chapter read carefully to its end.

Robert and Bernadette

Robert left for college with little ceremony, the way he did most things, steadily, without spectacle. His departure lacked the sharp edges Florence had braced for; there were no lingering pauses, no last-minute instructions repeated twice. He packed carefully, thanked her for the meals she sent along, and promised to write. He did. Often.

It was there, in that widened world, that he met Bernadette, studying to be a primary teacher at Cabrini College. Florence first heard her name folded into a letter, mentioned as if it had always belonged there. When she finally met her, it was on an unremarkable afternoon, the kind Florence trusted most. Bernadette arrived with Robert, paused just inside the doorway, and quietly took in the room before stepping forward.

Later, as Florence gathered plates, Bernadette rose without being asked and followed her into the kitchen. She rinsed her hands, then reached for the dish towel.

"You do this a certain way, don't you?" she said, smiling slightly as she waited. Florence nodded once.

Bernadette adjusted, matching her pace, her movements careful rather than hesitant. When they finished, she folded the towel neatly and set it back where it belonged. Florence noticed. She always did.

The rest revealed itself in time, the ease of conversation, the shared silences that did not ask to be filled, the way Robert listened more than he spoke when Bernadette was near. Their connection unfolded with the same quiet certainty Florence had come to trust in lasting unions, not hurried, not performative, but grounded. After graduation, they married, and Robert stepped fully into a life of his own making, one that carried traces of home without needing to return to it daily.

All eight of Florence's children were now grown and settled. Each had carried forward a household, a rhythm, a future that no longer required her steady hand to keep it aligned. Florence did not mark the moment with reflection or announcement. She simply noticed one morning that the house asked less of her and that she was ready to give differently now.

Matriarchy arrived without ceremony. It took shape in remembered birthdays, in advice offered only when asked, in knowing when to step forward and when to remain still. It was not authority she felt, but stewardship, the quiet responsibility of holding a family's shape even as its center widened.

Though Donna and Shenton still lived in the third-floor apartment above, their lives had separated in the way all lives must, close in distance, distinct in direction. Florence heard the rhythm of their days overhead, footsteps and laughter marking time that no longer intersected with hers in quite the same way. The house held fewer routines now, but more anticipation.

Grandchildren began to arrive, one by one, filling rooms that had learned how to wait. Cribs were set where desks had once stood. Toys replaced ledgers. The garden felt footsteps again, smaller and less certain, pressing new paths into familiar ground. Visits from children living farther away became occasions, planned, counted down, held with gratitude rather than expectation.

Florence found herself measuring time differently now. Not by departures, but by arrivals. Not by what the house released, but by what it gathered. What had once required her constancy now returned to her as gift, proof that what she and William had tended had learned how to endure.

CHAPTER TWENTY-FOUR — THE CENTER HOLDS

Traditions had a way of finding Florence even when she did not go looking for them.

They settled into the house slowly, holiday meals beginning at the same hour each year, chairs drawn from the same corners, serving bowls returned to the same shelves. Nothing about it felt ceremonial. It was simply the way life arranged itself when people stayed long enough to notice what worked.

William and Florence's anniversary arrived without fuss. No speeches were planned, no gathering called. The day passed much like any other, save for the way William lingered a moment longer at the door before leaving for work.

"You'll be late?" Florence asked.

"Not too," he said, then paused. "I'll bring something home for supper."

She smiled, smoothing the table after they ate that evening, aligning the placemats she would soon put away.

It was Estella who noticed.

Living in Florida with Stephen had not dulled her attention; distance, Florence suspected, had sharpened it. Estella had always known how to step in without disturbing the surface of things. What years apart had given her was clarity, an understanding of what could be offered gently, and what must be left untouched. When she called Philadelphia, she did so quietly, already aware of what her daughter would accept.

The front desk at the Bellevue-Stratford Hotel answered promptly. A woman named Genesis listened without interrupting as Estella explained—dates, preferences, an anniversary meant to remain intact until it arrived. She spoke with care, not indulgence, describing not extravagance but intention: a room with light, a dinner that did not rush, tickets that would place them close enough to feel the music without being swallowed by it.

There was no need to explain why this mattered. Or what it represented. Genesis understood the shape of the request. She asked the right questions, made a few notes, and promised nothing aloud beyond care. That was enough.

Estella had learned, early and thoroughly, what it meant to do without. Raised where restraint was virtue and beauty was permitted only in quiet forms, she had grown up knowing how to wait, but not always how to receive. The weekend Stephen had once planned at the Bellevue, when he asked her to marry him beneath chandeliers and velvet hush, had given her something she had not known she was missing: a moment chosen purely for joy. A tenderness not earned through labor or endurance, but simply offered.

It was that feeling she wanted to share now with Florence. Not spectacle. Not indulgence. Just the permission to step briefly into a world that asked nothing of her but presence—to sit in a good chair, to hear music rise, to be seen not as mother or keeper, but as a woman whose life had also been shaped by longing and grace.

Florence and William were told only to pack overnight bags. Estella did not explain further. She trusted that what she had arranged would meet Florence where she was, offering recognition. A pause. A gift carried carefully across generations.

"Do you know where we're going?" William asked, folding his jacket.

Florence shook her head. "And I don't intend to ask. Simply show up at 200 South Broad Street."

He nodded. "Good."

September held the city in a gentler way.

The heat had eased, the air no longer pressing, just cool enough to make walking feel deliberate. Florence drew her coat closer as they joined the quiet stream along Broad Street, the day carrying that particular mix of restraint and anticipation she had come to associate with Philadelphia at its best.

They had been given only a street address. William glanced down once at the slip of paper, then up again.

And then they saw it.

The facade rose before them in pale stone and carved ornament, lit from below so that its columns seemed to hold up the night itself. Arched windows, wrought-iron balconies, tiers upon tiers of symmetry and intention. The entrance canopy cast a golden wash across the sidewalk where uniformed doormen stood as if positioned there since another century.

Florence slowed without meaning to.

"The Bellevue-Stratford," William said quietly.

The Grand Dame of them all.

She had passed it before, of course — everyone had — but always at a distance, always with the sense that it belonged to another tier of living. Tonight it stood open, luminous, not forbidding but expectant.

"We're early," she said instinctively, as if they might not be meant for such a threshold.

William checked the number again. 200 Broad.

"No," he said. "We're exactly where we're meant to be."

Inside, the marble floors carried a softened echo beneath their steps. Chandeliers gathered light rather than scattered it. The air held that faint blend of polished wood, linen, and something floral, restrained but deliberate. Above them, the ceiling arched in quiet confidence, frescoed panels framed in gold leaf that did not apologize for their existence.

Florence felt something shift — not intimidation, not quite — but the awareness of scale. Of history layered into plaster and stone. Of conversations that had unfolded beneath these ceilings long before she had ever stood in this city as a young bride.

At the desk stood a woman whose composure suggested she understood both privacy and celebration in equal measure.

"Mr. and Mrs. Adams?" she asked with a knowing warmth.

"Yes," William answered.

"My name is Genesis. We've been expecting you." She smiled and produced a sealed envelope, cream and heavy.

"Your arrangements have been thoughtfully prepared," she said. "Your suite is ready. And after you've settled, a car will be waiting to take you to the theater. Dinner reservations follow. This evening is meant to be enjoyed fully."

Florence felt William glance toward her.

"For its own sake," Genesis added gently, as if reading the question she had not spoken.

Only then did she understand.

Estella.

Not merely a room, but an unfolding.

They were shown upstairs. The suite waited in quiet elegance: tall windows overlooking Broad Street, velvet draperies drawn back just enough to reveal the glow of the city below. A small arrangement of white flowers rested near the writing desk. Two theater tickets lay beside it.

Florence moved toward the window. From this height, the city felt composed. Contained.

"Well," William said softly, looking around. "This was thought through."

"Yes," Florence replied, her voice lower now. "And kindly."

They did not linger long. The evening had already been shaped.

The theater lay only a block away—a distance they knew by heart—and so they informed Genesis, with quiet confidence, that the car might wait until after the curtain fell. That detail, like the rest, had already been thoughtfully considered.

From the Bellevue, Broad Street carried them south at an easy pace. Florence had always liked this part of Philadelphia, how one place gave way naturally to another, without explanation.

Ahead, the lights of the Academy of Music glowed against the dark, its pale columns steady and unassuming. Florence slowed as they approached.

"This building knows how to wait," she said.

William smiled. "Like you."

Inside, the hall settled almost immediately. Voices lowered. Programs were folded and tucked away. When Eugene Ormandy lifted his hands, the room answered with stillness.

The music unfolded patiently, sound shaped by discipline and care. Florence felt the steadiness of it, the way it moved without excess, how each passage seemed to know exactly how much space it required.

"This," William murmured, leaning toward her, "is what order sounds like."

She nodded. "Like mornings," she said softly. "Before the first cup cools."

When they stepped back out onto Broad Street, the night had deepened into velvet.

The hotel's driver stood beside a polished black automobile, cap in hand, as though he had been there all along, part of the evening's quiet choreography.

"Good evening," he said warmly. "I trust you enjoyed the performance. It won't be long now."

William opened the door for Florence, and she settled into the leather seat, aware of the simple extravagance of being conveyed rather than conveying oneself. A luxury in and of itself.

The city moved past the window in softened light as they headed south, the buildings giving way gradually to the older bones of the waterfront. The driver turned onto narrower streets, where cobblestones caught the glow of the lamps and reflected it back in muted gold.

He slowed before a familiar name set in dignified lettering.

Bookbinder's.

Florence drew in a small breath. "I've read about this place," she said quietly. "More than once."

Located in Old City, its brick facade and tall windows held the weight of years without strain. Inside, candlelight rested on white tablecloths. The air carried the mingled scent of butter, wine, and the sea.

They were greeted by name and shown to a reserved table near the window. Outside, the cobblestone street lay hushed; inside, every table held a single candle, each flame steady and unhurried.

Menus were opened. Glasses poured.

Florence allowed herself the indulgence — oysters fresh and cold, a delicate bisque, fish prepared with a precision that honored rather than disguised it. The meal unfolded in courses, deliberate and generous, each plate arriving as though time itself had agreed to slow.

William lifted his glass. "To my beautiful wife on our anniversary celebration and to Estella and Stephen for this extravagant gift," he said.

Florence smiled. "And to being persuaded."

They did not rush. The evening was not built for that.

When at last they stepped back onto the cobblestones, the driver was waiting once more, composed and patient. He opened the door without commentary, as though evenings such as this were simply part of the natural order.

And in that small, gracious silence, Florence understood that opulence, when offered kindly, need not be resisted.

It could simply be received.

The ride back felt quieter, not from fatigue but from fullness. Broad Street shimmered in the late hour, the traffic thinned to occasional headlights slipping past like distant thoughts.

When the automobile drew once more beneath the canopy of the Bellevue-Stratford, the building seemed changed—or perhaps they were. Its facade no longer stood as spectacle, but as shelter.

The driver stepped out and opened the door. "Good evening, Mr. and Mrs. Adams."

William thanked him with a steady handshake. Florence added her gratitude with a nod that held more than courtesy.

Inside, the lobby had softened. The chandeliers glowed

lower now, their brilliance tempered into warmth. A pianist somewhere out of sight traced a familiar melody, restrained, unhurried, as though unwilling to disturb the hour.

Florence's hand drifted to the marble banister as they began the ascent. Cool. Solid. Smoothed by decades of touch.

She paused only a fraction of a second.

All evening she had been receiving, music, candlelight, careful service, the deliberate unfolding of someone else's generosity. But here, in the quiet curve of stone beneath her palm, she felt something more enduring.

This place had witnessed countless arrivals and departures, celebrations and reconciliations, beginnings disguised as anniversaries. Tonight, it had quietly held theirs.

William noticed her pause.

"Tired?" he asked gently.

"No," she said, her fingers resting there just a moment longer. "Remembering."

Upstairs, their suite waited as before, lights dimmed, curtains drawn. The city hummed faintly beyond the glass.

Florence removed her gloves and set them carefully beside her bag. She crossed to the window and looked out over Broad Street, now reduced to ribbons of light.

"Opulence," she said softly, almost to herself, "is not noise."

William came to stand beside her.

"No," he agreed. "It's intention."

She turned toward him then, the evening gathered between them like a well-folded letter, something to be opened again later, perhaps years from now, and still feel the weight of.

And for once, Florence did not measure the hour. She simply allowed it to be.

Morning arrived gently.

Light filtered through the tall windows in softened bands, brushing the velvet draperies and gilded frames without insistence. Florence stirred before the knock came—three measured taps, discreet but confident.

Room service.

William answered the door, and a white-jacketed attendant wheeled in a small, linen-draped table with quiet ceremony. Silver coffee service gleamed beneath a polished dome. Two porcelain cups rested beside folded napkins. The scent reached Florence before the lids were lifted — fresh coffee, warm bread, something lightly sweet.

"Good morning, Mr. and Mrs. Adams."

"Good morning," William replied, his voice still edged with sleep.

The door closed softly behind the attendant, and for a moment they simply looked at it all.

Bellevue style.

Florence moved closer, lifting the lid from one plate. Eggs prepared with precision, fruit arranged as though color mattered, pastries still warm. The coffee was poured from a silver pot that felt almost too elegant to touch.

William handed her the newspaper, neatly folded. "The world waits," he said lightly.

She smiled. "Let it."

They ate slowly. Coffee was refilled without haste. Pages of the paper turned and rustled in companionable quiet. William read aloud a small item of interest; Florence responded without urgency. Outside the window, Broad Street resumed its rhythm, automobiles moving below as though nothing extraordinary had occurred.

But inside, time stretched.

Florence leaned back in the upholstered chair, cup in hand, and allowed herself the rare sensation of lingering without agenda. No children calling from another room. No bread rising. No clock to consult.

Luxury, she realized, was not excess.

It was space.

William folded the newspaper at last.

"We should be heading home soon," he said.

"Yes," she answered. "Soon."

She rose and crossed once more to the window, memorizing the height of it, the view, the way morning light gathered on stone and glass. The suite had held them well, not as spectacle, but as pause.

When they finally closed the door behind them, Florence did so gently.

Some places you left.

Others you carried.

And this one, she knew, would travel home with them, folded neatly into memory, like a pressed flower saved between pages.

Decades later—long after Florence and William had walked these same streets hand in hand, long after the room at the Bellevue had returned to holding strangers—another woman would arrive, carrying only a notebook and careful attention.

She would sleep beneath the same high ceilings, walk Broad Street with the same deliberate pace, and pause where others had paused before her. She would not come looking for answers, only for resonance —for the feeling that something had once been held, and not let go lightly.

Some places, after all, remember us before we know how to remember them.

Florence did not know this, of course. She only knew that something essential had been preserved—not in the room, not in the city, but in the steady center they had built and kept.

Back home, the house received them as it always did. Chairs waited. The kettle found its place without being asked. Florence set her gloves on the hall table and stood for a moment in the familiar stillness.

Nothing had changed.

And yet something had been restored.

That afternoon, while William stepped out on a small errand, she took her seat at the desk near the window. She selected her good paper, not ornate, but weighty, and uncapped her pen.

She did not begin immediately.

The Bellevue had offered marble and silver, candlelight and height. But what remained with her was not the grandeur.

It was the thought.

She wrote carefully.

Dear Mom,

Your gift was received in the spirit in which it was given, not merely as a celebration, but as permission. We were cared for in ways both visible and quiet. The evening was beautiful, yes, but more than that, it was kind.

She paused, considering her next words.

There are seasons when one endures, and others when one is invited simply to receive. Thank you for giving us such a season, if only for a weekend.

She signed her name with deliberate steadiness.

When the ink had dried, she folded the letter with precision and sealed it. For a moment, her hand rested atop the envelope.

Gratitude, she knew, was not measured by extravagance.

Only by acknowledgment.

She rose, carrying the letter toward the front hall table where it would be picked up in the morning. The house moved around her in its ordinary rhythm, the clock ticking, a floorboard settling, the faint hum of late afternoon light across the windows.

William returned soon after, removing his hat.

"All settled?" he asked.

"Yes," she replied.

And she meant more than the letter.

The weekend had not altered their life.

It had simply reminded them of it.

She reached for the kettle without thinking. Some habits endured not because they were necessary, but because they had been earned. Some things, she understood, did not need to be named to be known.

William stood beside her a moment longer than usual, his hand resting lightly at the back of the chair. As the kettle warmed, Florence's gaze drifted to the front room, to the painting Shirley Tattersfield had left behind—the garden scene she had come to pass so often she no longer looked at it, only felt it.

Tonight, she paused.

The couple walked hand in hand along the painted path, their figures turned slightly inward, the world ahead softened by distance. Near the edge of the frame, almost incidental, rose the low stone wall—nothing grand, just enough to mark a place where one might stop, where a hand might be offered and accepted without audience. Florence felt the memory surface not as scene, but as sensation: the stillness of that moment, the certainty that had arrived before words ever followed.

William's eyes found the same place. She knew it without turning. His hand shifted, resting briefly against hers, the familiar pressure light and exact.

"We've come full circle," he said.

Florence considered it. "Not back," she said. "Just... returned."

He smiled. "With less to carry."

"And more to remember," she replied.

They stood there together, the house quiet around them, no longer shaped by departures or arrivals, but by choice. The years ahead felt unmarked, open. Time, once parceled out to others, now belonged to them again. Not urgently. Not loudly. Simply.

After tea, the house settled into its evening hush.

The cups sat rinsed beside the sink. The kettle cooled.

William stepped in behind her. "Come sit with me," he said quietly.

She turned, curious.

He crossed to the piano without further explanation and lowered himself onto the bench, adjusting it by habit rather than thought. The lid lifted with a familiar whisper.

Florence took her place in the chair near the window.

He did not announce the piece. He did not need to.

The first notes unfolded with restraint — deliberate, measured — the opening of one of her favorite Chopin nocturnes. The melody moved gently through the room, neither grand nor showy, but intimate, as though meant for walls that understood them.

Florence felt it at once.

The Bellevue had offered chandeliers and marble, silver coffee service and candlelit tables. But this — this was theirs.

William's hands moved with quiet confidence, the years between his early theater work and now braided into every phrase. He did not perform the music; he inhabited it. The notes rose and fell like breath, like the steady rhythm of mornings before the first cup cooled.

Florence leaned back, allowing the sound to gather around her.

Outside, the streetlamp cast its soft circle onto the pavement. Somewhere in the distance, an automobile turned, then faded. The house held the music as though it had been waiting for it all along.

When the final chord resolved, William let his hands rest lightly on the keys.

Neither spoke.

Florence rose and crossed the room, resting her hand briefly on his shoulder — not applause, not gratitude exactly, but recognition.

"That," she said softly, "is enough."

He closed the lid gently.

The night did not demand more.

And so it ended not in grandeur, but in familiarity. Music shaped by love, a house at rest, and two people who had learned that the finest rooms were those built quietly over time.

The center held.

PART VII — THE MATRIARCH YEARS

CHAPTER TWENTY-FIVE — TWENTY-TWO GRANDCHILDREN

Joy, Florence had learned, was not something to chase. It arrived when there was room for it.

The house understood this now.

It held laughter the way it once held worry—carefully, without spilling. The long kitchen table bore its familiar scars, softened by years of hands and heat and the quiet insistence of meals shared. Chairs were added without ceremony. Plates mismatched. Someone set out too many cups, and no one bothered correcting it.

Florence did not rush to greet the noise. She stood back for a moment, hands folded at her waist, watching the accumulation take shape.

Children everywhere.

They filled the front yard first—darting between garden paths worn smooth by decades of footsteps, ducking behind hedges, crouching beneath porch railings for games whose rules shifted mid-sentence. Their laughter threaded through the open windows, light and uncontained, yet somehow safe.

William crossed the sitting room and lifted the piano bench with the same ease he once lifted their babies. He played without announcing himself—something familiar, steady, meant to gather rather than impress. A few children paused mid-stride. One climbed onto the rug and listened with solemn attention.

"Grandpa's playing," a girl whispered, as if naming a rule.

Upstairs, Florence opened the cedar chest only long enough to slip in another photograph. Another name was added in careful script to the back of the family Bible. She never hurried the ink.

Each image was placed with intention, not by order of

birth, but by closeness, by how the years had folded them together. Twenty-two grandchildren now. She did not count them often. Numbers mattered less than the way their presence filled rooms without strain.

When she closed the lid, the scent of cedar rose briefly, then settled again.

Contained. Preserved.

The house learned children again, layered now, babies sleeping while older ones whispered beneath tables, shoes lined in uneven rows by the door. Florence noticed everything and corrected little. She knew the difference between disorder and life.

She allowed herself one quiet regret—that her mother could not come up from Florida—then set it aside with the others, safely held. She was grateful that William's mother, Lillian, had been able to come, her presence steady and familiar, as if she had always belonged to the shape of the day. Lillian's sister, Mae, came as well—Aunt Mae to everyone in the house—already seated at the piano with Sylvia nearby, her hands guiding, correcting, encouraging, as they always had.

Beyond the porch, the red maples stood tall now. Once planted in memory, one for each loss, each name spoken softly at the time, they had grown into something generous. Their branches offered shade where children rested and beauty where no one had thought to look for it. Leaves stirred gently above the yard, holding sunlight without urgency.

What had begun in sorrow now held peace. Joy, Florence knew, did not erase what came before it. It grew because of it.

They came from everywhere.

Bill and Donita arrived first, the car dusty with summer travel, children tumbling out before the engine had cooled. Gerry and Janet stopped in from Syracuse, their visit threaded between moves and obligations, their children quieter at first, observant. Ron and Lucy drove in from Colorado, road-worn and cheerful—the kind of tired that came from choosing the long way home.

Dale and Liz took leave when they could, Air Force schedules bending just enough to allow it. Their children moved easily between accents and places, belonging without explanation.

Dean and Jeanne were already there, as were Sylvia and Jack, Donna with Shenton, Robert and Bernadette, each arrival folding seamlessly into the whole.

They always seemed to arrive at Longwood Gardens without ceremony. No one announced the outing. It simply happened.

Blankets appeared. Baskets were filled. Someone forgot the napkins and laughed about it later.

The gardens received them as they always did, paths wide enough for wandering, benches placed just where rest was needed, beauty offered without demand.

They began in the summer gardens, where color announced itself before form. Heat lifted the scent of earth and bloom, and the air was heavy with sweetness—roses, lilies, something citrusy Florence could never quite name. They passed beneath the overreaching arbor, roses tumbling overhead in thick, fragrant ropes, petals brushing shoulders as if the garden itself were greeting them. Beyond it, the space opened into an oasis—contained, luminous, humming with bees.

The children surged ahead at once, shoes striking the brick path as they raced toward the fountain at its center. Their laughter echoed off stone and water, ricocheting back to the adults in bright, irregular bursts. Florence slowed, as she always did. She knelt beside a bed of deep violet blossoms, their petals veined with darker ink, and traced the curve of one with her eyes. Each visit gave her something new, an arrangement she would later try at home, a color pairing she would carry back into her own soil. The gardens did not overwhelm her; they instructed.

Each of them found something that day, something small enough to carry, something lasting enough to return to.

They walked on to the far end of the garden, where a rounded limestone bench rested against a towering wall veiled in ivy. The children discovered the whispering bench before anyone explained it. Secrets traveled its curve, arriving intact at the other end, and shrieks of delight followed each successful test. They bent close, cupped hands, traded nonsense and solemn vows, astonished that something so quiet could move so clearly.

From there, the path softened beneath trees and opened suddenly onto water. The Italian Water Gardens spread before them—formal and theatrical—stone steps descending in a cascade that caught the sun and shattered it into motion. Water fell, climbed, fell again. They crossed the bridge and climbed the opposite side, where woods closed in briefly before releasing them into the open-air theater. The lawn auditorium stretched wide and green, the stage backed by fountains and framed by trees and dark arborvitae.

Florence paused there. How beautiful it would be, she thought, to sit among all this living order and listen to music, sound braided with water, leaf, and sky.

This became their standard walk, a rhythm they would repeat until it lived in their bodies: garden to water, water to woods, woods to theater—ending always at the conservatory.

And that was only the beginning.

The conservatory rose like a promise of another world—glass and iron holding light in place. Inside, seasons dissolved. Rooms unfolded one into the next, each more extravagant than the last.

William disappeared, as Florence knew he would. He found the pipe organ and stood beneath its towering ranks, studying the geometry of sound, the logic of air and pressure and reach. Florence watched him once before turning away, smiling. This was his kind of wonder.

The others drifted room to room, voices hushed, eyes wide. They reunited at last in the water lily court, where the air cooled and widened. Circular pools held floating worlds—lilies from distant places, their round leaves like green shields, their blossoms rising clean and perfect above the surface. Pink. White. Yellow edged in red. Each child chose a favorite, naming it, claiming it, dreaming aloud of where it might have come from.

Florence thought it felt like Eden—not imagined, but tended. A living, breathing proof that care could create something enduring.

Hunger arrived gently, the way it does when a day has been well spent. They exited the conservatory and headed toward the Carillon Chimes Tower, its bells silent for now but full of promise. The children ran ahead again, racing up the hillside paths beneath century-old oaks and conifers. Beyond them, the land dipped into shade, trees arching overhead to form a natural room.

The picnic area waited.

Blankets were spread beneath the canopy. Baskets opened. Food was passed hand to hand. Stories layered themselves, one atop another, old ones resurfacing, new ones beginning. Florence sat while William stood behind her, his hands resting lightly on her shoulders, steady and familiar.

For a time, there was only the soft industry of eating —paper wrappings folded back, lids lifted, lemonade poured carefully into small cups. The hush that settles over true hunger fell among them, not silent exactly, but softened. Even the older boys lowered their voices between bites.

Then, without warning, the stillness was gently visited by sound.

From the nearby tower, the carillon began to ring.

The first chime drifted outward, clear and measured, as though testing the air. Another followed, then a fuller cascade, tones layering themselves across the lawn and into the trees. The bells did not rush. They unfolded deliberately, each note given its rightful space.

Heads lifted in unison.

"There!" one of the children exclaimed, pointing toward

the tower as though the sound itself were visible.

The younger ones froze mid-bite, listening with wide-eyed wonder. A few attempted to count the notes before losing track and laughing at their own effort. Even the adults paused, hands suspended briefly above plates.

The music lingered over them, over blankets and baskets, over crusts and crumbs, before drifting upward into the branches. It seemed to gather the day together and hold it suspended for just a moment longer.

And then, as gently as it had arrived, the bells fell quiet.

The children returned to their meal with renewed animation, recounting what they believed they had heard, a song or a signal meant just for them. Conversations resumed. Someone reached again for the mustard. Someone else passed the last of the lemonade.

The tower stood steady above them, its work complete for now.

And the picnic continued, threaded now with the memory of sound.

"They're all here," William said quietly.

"I know." Her voice was soft and steady.

After their picnic lunch, no one was quite ready to leave. The day still shimmered with possibility.

They had learned that the Main Fountain Garden would debut its first dramatic illuminated evening performance later that season, lights choreographed with water arcing high into the darkened sky. Though their visit was timed for daylight, the mere description of it had set their imaginations alight.

They meandered back toward the fountains, the sound of water pulling them like a familiar hymn. Streams leapt in steady rhythm, some delicate as lace, others bold and commanding. The children darted ahead, weaving between the patterned stonework, laughter rising above the steady rush.

"Can you imagine this in the dark?" one of the older boys asked.

Florence paused, her gaze stretching across the wide basin.

"The sky black as velvet," she said quietly, "and the water glowing like stars."

She stood a moment longer than the others.

Even in daylight, the fountains carried something theatrical, as though they were rehearsing for a greater unveiling. She imagined the darkness settling in, the sudden ignition of light beneath the surface, the water rising brilliant where only shadow had been.

Some things, she knew, did their most astonishing work against the dark.

There had been seasons when her own life felt unlit, when absence and uncertainty pressed in from every side. Yet here she stood, surrounded by children and grandchildren, laughter echoing in the spray. What once seemed buried had risen. What once felt dim had found its radiance.

She did not speak the thought aloud. She only slipped her hand into William's and squeezed gently.

They agreed then, almost ceremonially, that they would return the following year to see the fountains illuminated, a promise tucked quietly into the family's shared calendar of memory.

The magic of the water followed them as they slowly worked their way outward, the steady percussion accompanying their steps along winding paths.

The smaller children, at last overcome by sun and sweetness, began to fuss. Shoes scuffed more heavily. Little hands reached upward, asking to be carried. The day had given all it meant to give.

And so they found themselves gently ushered toward the exit.

Florence glanced back once.

For a fleeting instant — no more than a breath — she remembered another garden long ago, when she had been small and uncertain, holding tight to a world that did not hold her back. She remembered watching from the edges then, unsure of where she belonged.

Now she walked not at the edge, but at the center, children clustered near, grandchildren orbiting like bright satellites around her steady presence.

She did not name the symmetry.

She only felt it.

Water rose. Light would come. And she, once carried away, now carried them forward.

As they turned toward the gates, a breeze followed them, soft and warm, brushing the roses they had just left behind. The fragrance clung faintly to her sleeve. When she lifted her hand to settle a child's hat or smooth a small shoulder, the scent rose again, delicate and persistent.

She did not brush it away.

William reached for her hand as the youngest began to fuss, and together they stepped beyond the gates, carrying with them the promise of illuminated fountains, the echo of water, and the quiet perfume of a garden that had, once again, given more than beauty.

By the time they pulled out of the gardens, their departure resembled a modest parade. Automobiles lined up in loose succession, engines turning over one by one, windows lowered to allow for cross-car conversation and final head counts.

Nearly fifty in all.

Children were redistributed according to energy levels and patience. The youngest were bundled into back seats beside mothers. The older boys negotiated their placements carefully, angling for whichever automobile seemed most likely to include adventure.

They had not gone far along Route 202 when one of the lead drivers slowed slightly and leaned an elbow out the window, signaling to the car behind. A ripple of communication followed — hand gestures, grins, the universal tilt of a thumb toward the road ahead.

"Concordville," someone called from one open window to another.

That was enough.

The suggestion moved through the caravan like a spark catching dry tinder. Within moments, several of the automobiles peeled gently off together, the others following in cooperative succession.

They pulled into the lot at Jimmy John's — the beloved establishment opened in 1940 and known proudly as the oldest business along that stretch of Route 202.

Inside, they filled the space in cheerful waves—booths claimed, tables pushed together, children sliding onto stools, the room accommodating them in layers of laughter and motion.

And then, as if on cue, every gaze lifted upward.

Model trains circled the room on suspended tracks, engines humming steadily overhead. The tiny cars clattered along their routes with reassuring persistence, passing miniature crossings and painted stations. Every whistle brought renewed delight.

The older boys stood beneath the tracks, craning their necks to follow each engine's progress. A few of the men joined them, pointing out mechanical details, admiring the craftsmanship with appreciative nods. Fingers traced imaginary routes in the air, mapping distances not yet traveled.

Florence watched them, the way their faces tilted upward, intent and unguarded. There was something in that posture she recognized. Not merely fascination, but longing. A readiness to follow movement wherever it led.

She did not dwell on it. She only noted how naturally they studied the rails, how easily they imagined destinations beyond the walls.

Hot dogs were passed down long stretches of table. Mustard bottles were exchanged with solemn responsibility. Laughter rolled in easy waves.

It was a different music than the fountains.

There, water had risen in elegant arcs.

Here, steel wheels moved in steady circles.

Yet both carried the same quiet promise: forward motion.

Continuance. Return.

When at last they spilled back out into the light, children messy, men content, women gathering napkins and stray hats, the line of automobiles once again assembled like patient carriages awaiting instruction.

Engines started in staggered rhythm.

And as the caravan turned toward home, Florence caught one last glimpse through the car window, a few of the grandsons still glancing upward as they walked, as though listening for a whistle only they could hear.

She rested her hand lightly over her heart.

Some departures begin long before the journey is named.

Night had come gently by the time they returned, and the porch light cast its steady circle across the steps, no spectacle, no music, only the faithful glow that had guided them home for years.

The younger children were carried in sleeping bundles. The older boys moved more slowly now, sun-worn and thoughtful. The house absorbed them all, as it always had.

Some of the men drifted toward William's workshop, drawn by habit more than purpose. Tools were lifted and set down again. Ideas were discussed that did not require conclusions.

Florence moved through the rooms with practiced calm, refilling cookie tins, retrieving forgotten sweaters, guiding the youngest away from the stairs with a hand at the shoulder. She did not try to hold everyone at once.

She had learned better.

Joy stayed because it was given shape.

Because it knew where to rest.

Sometimes, when the house was still, Florence thought she heard the organ again—not loud, not calling attention, just keeping time so others could move forward. Stories were told, but not all at once. Some were repeated often. Others were held until the listener had grown enough to carry them.

Florence believed timing mattered as much as truth.

After the last child had gone to sleep and the house quieted, she walked the garden once more—checking ties and stakes, pressing soil back where it had been disturbed, making note of what would need thinning come morning. Growth, she knew, did not excuse neglect.

Beneath the maples, she listened.

The sounds were different now, cars in the distance, radios through open windows, but the rhythm remained. Children grew. Trees matured. What was planted with care returned it, season after season.

Florence and William rose while the house still held its breath. Coffee was set to brew without light, the familiar sounds enough to guide them.

"You're awake early," William said quietly.

"I didn't sleep much," Florence answered.

Outside, the garden waited, paths damp with dew, leaves holding the last of the night.

They stepped into the cool air.

"It will be warm later," he said, more observation than prediction.

"Yes," she replied. "It always is."

They walked slowly, side by side, saying little.

After so many years, words were rarely required.

William reached for her hand and they walked ahead.

When they returned to the house, the day had already begun to gather itself.

Bill, Gerry, Ron, and Dale sat around the kitchen table, coffee mugs in hand, voices overlapping as easily as they once had. The years fell away in that room. They picked up where they had left off, as if no distance or deployment had intervened—only a pause.

Footsteps soon sounded on the stairs.

One by one, then in clusters, the rest descended into the kitchen, drawn by hunger and noise in equal measure. Chairs scraped back. Someone reached for a roll before asking. Another laughed too loudly for the hour and was forgiven for it.

Serving bowls were chosen for durability. Spoons wandered. Flour dusted the counters more often than not. Florence moved through it all with ease, adding water where dough grew dry, setting timers she rarely needed. She had cooked long enough to know when something was done by how it felt.

The grandchildren learned her rhythms quickly—where to stand, when to speak, when to wait. Questions were welcomed; whining was not. Florence was not stern.

She was consistent. Children understood consistency.

From the doorway, one of the younger grandchildren watched without moving. He held his bowl tight to his chest, careful not to spill, careful not to interrupt. The kitchen felt bigger than it looked, too many voices, too much warmth, the kind of room that asked you to learn the rules before stepping in.

Florence caught his eye. She didn't call him forward. She didn't wave him back. She simply nodded once, toward the counter.

That was enough.

He stepped in when there was space, placed his bowl where she had cleared it, and waited. Later, he would remember this more than the noise, the way order lived inside kindness, and how being seen did not require being loud.

By the time the table filled again, the house no longer felt like it was hosting a gathering. It felt like itself.

Later that morning, those who lived nearby arrived with covered dishes to share. Lids were lifted and set aside. Familiar scents layered the air, warm bread, simmered vegetables, something sweet waiting its turn. The kitchen adjusted without effort, making room as it always had.

Sylvia arrived midmorning, and the room lifted.

She came through the door with boxes balanced easily in her arms, the scent of butter and sugar announcing her before she reached the table. Conversations paused. Lids were lifted with ceremony. Her pies were received with the quiet reverence reserved for things done especially well.

"The crust," someone said almost immediately, shaking their head in admiration. "No one does it like you."

A chorus of agreement followed.

Sylvia laughed lightly as she set the knife to the first pie. "Oh, I've had good teachers."

Florence had first shown her the feel of proper dough —how it should gather without surrendering, how restraint kept it tender. But after Sylvia married Jack, the education continued in his family's kitchen. They baked with conviction there. And Jack's oldest sister, Jessie, especially, insisted on standards.

"The water must be ice cold," Jessie would say, pressing a glass into Sylvia's hand. "Cold enough to bite your fingers. If it isn't shocking, it isn't right."

His younger sister, Mary Jane, would stand nearby, nodding approval, reminding her to turn the dough only once more—no more than that—before letting it rest.

What began at Florence's table had been strengthened and refined in theirs, until the work became something close to mastery.

"What's the secret?" one of the cousins pressed playfully now.

Sylvia paused just long enough to glance toward Florence —then beyond her, as though acknowledging other kitchens, other tables. "It was never mine alone," she said simply.

The knife slid cleanly through golden layers. The crust flaked perfectly.

Florence felt no possessiveness in it—only pride.

Some inheritances are passed hand to hand.

Others are perfected in the passing.

Music drifted in from the sitting room, Aunt Mae and William taking turns at the piano, one yielding easily to the other. Sometimes they played together, sometimes not. The sound settled over the house like a second roof, something steady and familiar.

Outside, children ran the length of the yard, disappearing and reappearing beneath the red maples. Others spilled onto the porch, perching along the steps, visiting, laughing, sharing stories they would repeat later as if they had always belonged to them.

The house did not strain to hold it all. It knew how.

By afternoon, the house exhaled.

Plates sat rinsed and stacked, waiting without urgency. Coffee cups cooled where they had been set down and forgotten. Somewhere upstairs, a door clicked shut, followed by the soft certainty of sleep. The piano lid was lowered halfway, as if even the music knew it was time to rest.

On the porch, voices softened. Conversations thinned into pauses that did not ask to be filled. A few adults leaned back in their chairs, shoes slipped off, eyes closed against the filtered light. Laughter arrived now and then, brief and natural, like a remembered thought.

In the yard, children's games slowed. Running gave way to wandering. Some lay beneath the red maples, tracing the leaves above them, letting the shade do its work. Others drifted inside, drawn by cooler rooms and the promise of nothing required.

Florence moved through it all with awareness rather than direction, straightening a folded blanket, collecting a stray shoe, setting aside a plate she knew would be wanted later. She did not call anyone to order.

The rhythm had already been established.

This, too, was part of the gathering.

Not the arrival.

Not the feast.

But the knowing pause afterward, when joy stayed because it was allowed to be quiet.

As evening approached, the house began to release its hold. Cars pulled away slowly. Goodbyes were unhurried, folded into promises that did not require dates. The yard emptied in stages, toys gathered into baskets, shoes reclaimed from unlikely places.

Florence and William stood together on the porch once the last door closed. The light had shifted, softer now, settling into the corners of the garden. Porch lamps clicked on one by one, their glow modest and sufficient.

"They did well," William said.

"They always do," Florence replied.

A moment passed.

"They carry it differently now," he added.

Florence nodded. "As they should."

Below them, the garden paths were worn but sure. The red maples held the evening, their leaves catching what remained of the sun. What had once been planted in memory now offered shelter without asking to be noticed.

"It holds," William said, his gaze moving across the yard.

"Yes," Florence answered. "It was meant to."

Inside, the piano remained closed. The kitchen was quiet, its counters cleared, the long table bare except for a single cup Florence had not yet moved.

"You'll leave that?" he asked, glancing toward the cup.

"For a little while," she said. "It reminds me they were here."

He gave a small nod. "It doesn't take much."

"No," she said. "It never did."

She would take care of it later. For now, she rested her hand in William's.

The house stood ready again, empty without feeling hollow, full without needing to prove it. What it held would return when called. What it had given would carry on, moving outward steadily.

"They'll come back," William said after a time.

Florence's fingers shifted slightly in his. "They always find their way."

Joy did not linger because it was asked to. It stayed because it knew where it belonged.

Later, when the house had fully settled, Florence returned

the last toy to its chest and closed the lid. Cookie tins were stacked, their contents diminished but accounted for. Nothing was hurried. Nothing was left loose.

"What's left?" William asked quietly from the doorway.

Florence glanced once around the room. "Nothing that needs tending tonight."

He watched her a moment longer. "You've kept it well."

She met his gaze, not lingering, but not turning away. "We have."

What mattered had been used, shared, and returned to its place.

She turned out the light knowing the containers would open again soon.

CHAPTER TWENTY-SIX — THE KEEPER OF STORIES

Stories behaved much like people, Florence knew. Some arrived breathless and demanded attention. Others waited patiently, content to be noticed only when the house was quiet and the light just right. She had come to respect the ones that waited. Those were usually the truest.

The scrapbooks lived on the lower shelf now, where her knees complained but her hands felt sure. She took them down one at a time, resting each on the table before opening it. The covers were worn smooth, the corners softened by years of use. Inside, photographs lay tucked beneath careful captions, dates written small, names spelled correctly, nothing hurried.

Florence did not record everything. She chose.

There were pictures of birthdays and graduations, of weddings and first communions. Newspaper clippings were folded into thirds and slipped between pages, their edges browned, the headlines still legible. Letters appeared too, some written in pencil, some in ink, a few read so often the creases no longer held. Florence smoothed them anyway, as if the paper might remember being cared for.

She paused at a photograph of Ron, younger than he would ever be again. The picture was newer than most, the paper still stiff at the edges. His uniform was folded just so, different from his brothers', the cut unfamiliar. Florence felt the familiar tightening in her chest, not pain, exactly, but recognition. She slid the photograph back into its envelope and returned it to its place without comment.

Not every chapter required a voice.

Across the room, the family Bible lay open on the sideboard, its thin pages lifted slightly by the afternoon air. Florence moved to it slowly, turning the pages with care. The front held births and marriages, the ink dark and confident in the early years, lighter later on, as though even the pen had learned restraint.

Near the back, the list continued. Several lines remained open.

Florence traced the blank space with her finger and smiled. She had learned not to rush what was still becoming. There would be more names. There always were. She closed the book gently and set it back where it belonged.

The house had grown louder over the years, then quieter again, then louder once more. When the grandchildren visited, they treated it like a place that could contain anything. Drawers opened and closed. Cookie tins rattled. Toy chests spilled their contents onto the floor and were gathered again before bedtime. Florence watched it all with quiet satisfaction. She had once measured everything carefully—portions, pennies, patience. Now the house held abundance without spilling.

At the end of the day, when the noise settled and the chairs were pushed back into place, Florence returned things to their proper homes. Photographs slid into albums. Letters back into envelopes. Stories back into themselves.

There were other items, too, kept not on shelves, but waiting elsewhere in the house. Things that had belonged to other lives. Other hands. Florence did not feel compelled to tend to them yet. She had learned that some histories announced themselves when they were ready, not before.

Some memories were shared easily, offered across the table with laughter and repetition. Others were kept, not out of secrecy, but stewardship. Florence understood the difference. Not every truth needed air. Some needed time.

She closed the last scrapbook and stacked it carefully atop the others. The weight felt right in her hands, substantial, balanced, complete. When she returned them to the shelf, she did not label them or count them. She knew where everything was.

And more importantly, she knew why.

She had just reached the doorway when she heard it—the piano, alive again.

She stepped into the hall and paused. William sat on the bench, shoulders relaxed, fingers moving with an ease that surprised her. He was playing an old Chopin nocturne, the one she loved, one that never asked for more than listening and one he rarely chose unless the house was truly quiet. The music filled the space between rooms, not loud, not tentative, shaped by feeling more than precision.

She came up behind him and watched without announcing herself. The way his hands lifted and fell. The way the melody leaned and returned. It sounded like memory—not fixed, but faithful.

When he finished, Florence leaned in and whispered, "Bravo."

William turned, startled only for a moment. He smiled and held out his hand.

"Will you walk the garden with me?"

She did not answer. She didn't need to. He stood, and they went out together, fingers entwined, the door closing softly behind them.

They followed the familiar path, pausing where they always did—at the small oasis they had made together. Florence glanced at the roses climbing the arbor, the trees they had chosen years ago now casting real shade.

They did not go far.

The garden held them the way it always had—quietly, without expectation.

What had once been saplings were now steady and full-limbed. The maple near the fence spread broad and confident, its leaves turning their pale undersides toward the cooling air. Boxwoods, long since shaped and reshaped by careful hands, stood in gentle symmetry along the path. The hydrangeas had grown dense and generous, their blooms fading now into softened blues and dusky rose, petals papery to the touch.

The earth still carried the warmth of the day. When Florence stepped from the stone path to the grass, she felt it through the thin sole of her shoe, a stored kindness, slowly releasing.

The air shifted as evening lowered itself across the yard. The scent of turned soil mingled faintly with lavender planted years ago along the border. Somewhere honeysuckle lingered, sweet but not cloying. Crickets began their patient rhythm, steady as breath.

William guided Florence to the small bench beneath the tree they had planted when the children were still young enough to climb its lowest branches. She could still picture scraped knees and laughter rising from the tree's early limbs, the boys competing to see who could climb higher. It had outgrown that need now. The trunk was thick, the bark deeply furrowed. Shade fell where it was needed, wide, dependable, unhurried.

They sat.

For a time, neither spoke.

Evening settled itself into the leaves, the light filtering through in softened gold before surrendering fully to dusk. A breeze moved overhead, carrying the faint rustle of branches adjusting to one another. Somewhere nearby, something small, perhaps a rabbit or field mouse, moved through the undergrowth and disappeared again.

Florence rested her hands in her lap. Dirt lingered faintly beneath her nails from tending earlier in the week. She did not mind. Gardens left their mark gently.

The house behind them murmured with the muffled sounds of dishes being cleared and children being called inside. But here, beneath the tree, there was only the layered quiet, soil, bark, leaf, breath.

Time had deepened this place.

It had deepened them, too.

"They're spread everywhere now," William said at last. "Hard to imagine them all in one place."

Florence smiled. “They come back when it matters.”

He nodded. “You made it possible.”

“No,” she said gently. “We did.”

William looked out across the garden—the beds they had shaped together, the trees that no longer needed staking. “You kept things,” he said. “When it would've been easier not to.”

Florence considered that. “I kept what could be carried,” she replied. “The rest had to learn how to wait.”

“And it did,” he said.

“Yes,” she agreed. “It always does.”

She reached for his hand, the same way she had earlier, as if it were simply the next right thing to do.

“I used to worry,” William said, “about whether we were doing enough.”

Florence tilted her head toward him. “You still do.”

He smiled at that. “Only about different things.”

They sat with the thought, watching the light slip lower.

“I think,” Florence said finally, “that what mattered most wasn't what we saved. It was what we made room for.”

William squeezed her hand. “Then we did all right.”

She leaned her head against his shoulder. “We did.”

The garden breathed around them, nothing hurried, nothing unfinished. What had been planted had taken hold. What had been lost had not been erased. And what was still coming would find its way, as it always had.

They stayed there until the light was gone, saying little, knowing much. Nothing needed to be said.

Florence had not been given a childhood that stayed intact. She had learned instead how to hold what mattered, how to preserve without display, how to make room for what was still on its way. She had learned that survival was not loud and legacy was not accidental.

That, she understood now, was the work.

The house settled behind them, familiar and full. Nothing misplaced. Nothing forgotten. Everything waiting.

She stood for a moment longer, listening to the quiet of it, and felt the old understanding return and how life moved forward whether one named its direction or not.

Like the river that has a thousand turns to take. It bends around the stone, refusing stillness, learning its own rhythm as it goes, finding a way without needing to name it.

What rushes forward eventually eases. Calm gathers. An island forms by patience. Few linger in the shade of the palm, yet roots hold fast where the water keeps moving.

The river does not argue with each bend, nor grieve the paths it never came to follow. It moves with trust that motion is enough and rests by yielding to the way it's led.

It follows where it is quietly drawn, without requiring sight to trust the course is sure. The river rests in hands it leans upon and ends its journey held—just as it began.

Florence did not think of endings. Only of how faithfully one was carried.

CHAPTER TWENTY-SEVEN — THE TRUNK

The house did not feel finished. Morning light entered as it always had, across the table's worn edge, over the piano's closed lid, into corners where dust and memory settled together. The garden continued without asking permission. New growth rose where she had not planned it.

This, Florence understood, was how things endured, not by holding on, but by continuing. Faithfully. One day into the next.

Her traces remained, though none announced themselves: a path worn smooth by passing feet, an extra chair set out without thinking, stories told again not for polish, but for keeping. What she had made—steadiness, welcome, faith practiced in small ways—moved quietly through those who followed.

August 1956

The trunk arrived three days after the funeral.

It was heavier than Florence expected—not in weight, but in presence. William carried it into the parlor and set it where the afternoon light fell clean across the floor. Neither of them opened it at once. Some things required a pause, simply to acknowledge their arrival.

William's mother, Lillian Adams, had kept her life carefully. That was evident from the exterior alone—the reinforced corners, the lock worn smooth from use rather than neglect. It had traveled. It had been closed with intention.

Florence waited until the house was quiet. When she lifted the lid, the scent of old paper rose—familiar, steady. Letters tied with ribbon. Journals stacked with precision. Certificates wrapped in cloth. Charts folded and refolded until their creases softened. A life gathered, not scattered.

Nothing inside felt accidental. Nothing misplaced. It had been kept with the expectation that someone would understand how to receive it.

Florence rested her hand lightly on the topmost bundle, not yet untied. She did not rush.

Some things were not meant to be opened all at once.

She moved slowly, lifting each piece just long enough to understand it before setting it aside. Nothing spilled.

It was the loose page near the bottom that held her. Not bound or labeled. Folded once.

Florence unfolded it.

I kept what could not yet be carried. I waited until there were hands strong enough to hold it without breaking. Nothing here was hidden from lack of courage. It was preserved for lack of safety. If this is being read now, then the waiting was right. What was entrusted has arrived.

Lillian had not chosen lightly.

Florence saw it now, not in a single moment, but across the years that had led here. The quiet watching. The visits that seemed ordinary. The way Lillian's gaze had moved through the house, taking in what was kept, what was mended, what was allowed to endure without display.

She had been measuring, not with doubt, but with patience.

Not for perfection. For steadiness. For hands that would not scatter what they held.

Florence remained standing.

She read the words again, recognizing the restraint in them. This was not confession. It was judgment exercised patiently over time.

She thought of the letters she herself had written and never sent. Of the box beneath her bed. Of truths kept intact, not out of fear, but out of discernment.

Women, she understood, often carried history this way—quietly—waiting not for permission, but for readiness.

Beneath the page lay the charts.

Names aligned in careful order. Dates. Places. A line drawn backward until it rested on two names written with deliberate clarity: Frederick Watts and Jane Murray. Scotland. Departure. A single word marking the crossing—*emigrated*—as if leaving one world and entering another required no embellishment.

Frederick Watts, who would join the Revolutionary cause and rise to brigadier general. Jane Murray, recorded beside him without explanation, as if her steadiness required none.

Together, whatever their relationship, they marked the beginning of the family's American story, an origin rooted not in comfort, but conviction.

Florence traced the line with her finger.

Exile, then building. Separation, then stewardship. War, then institution.

The pattern revealed itself, not as history, but inheritance. What began on a battlefield had moved, generation by generation, into classrooms, workshops, and households. The form had changed. The discipline had not.

Florence refolded the page and returned it to its place. She did not tie it. She did not conceal it. It belonged where it rested —kept, but not buried.

Some things, she had learned long ago, did not survive by force. They survived because someone kept them from scattering.

This story had not begun with her. It would not end with her.

What she had been given, she would guard. What she had built, she would leave. The rest would unfold in its season, as all things did.

She rested her hand once more on the cedar lid, feeling the grain beneath her palm.

She closed the trunk gently.

Whatever came next would be met as the rest had been—not beyond these walls, not in speculation, but here.

Then she rose and returned to the living hour.

Author's Note

The Matriarch's Legacy is a work of historical fiction shaped by documented family history, archival research, and lived memory. Florence is inspired by my grandmother, whose early life was marked by separation and the disciplined resilience of women who understood when truth could be spoken—and when it had to wait.

While the events of this novel are imagined, they rest within the lived realities of families who endured the Great Depression, sent sons to war, and carried forward the long, quiet aftermath of both.

I began this book believing I was writing about national rupture. In time, I understood I was writing about formation—about how moral architecture is constructed within kitchens and hallways while history gathers force beyond the door. Public events alter a nation. Private choices shape a lineage.

The genealogical discovery revealed in the novel's final chapter reflects sustained research into my eighteenth-century ancestors, Frederick Watts and Jane Murray, who emigrated from Scotland to America. Watts served in the Revolutionary War and later contributed to the civic and educational foundations of the early republic. Their inheritance, like Florence's, is not one of spectacle, but of stewardship.

In the process of writing, I became increasingly aware that history often survives in margins, in preserved letters, carefully kept records, restrained decisions, and stories safeguarded until they can be safely received. Many women before us carried legacy this way, long before their influence was formally acknowledged.

In December 2025, I returned to Philadelphia to walk the streets my grandparents once traversed. Research, for me, has never been confined to archives. It lives in place: in the weight of buildings, the rhythm of a city, the spaces that hold memory long after those who moved through them are gone.

It was there, in pursuit of the Prohibition-era world that

threads through this novel, that I was given access to details few records could provide. A generous guide opened the hidden architecture of a modern speakeasy, offering insight into how such spaces once operated, how they concealed, adapted, and endured. While William himself did not work within such a world, the spirit of ingenuity and quiet adaptation reflected something essential to his character.

Other moments of the story are drawn from memory more closely held. Valley Forge and the Soldiers' Arch mark not only a place of national history, but a personal one, where I first met my husband, an unexpected convergence of past and future. The small covered bridge that appears on these pages echoes one my father built by hand for my grandmother, a gesture of devotion that endured beyond his lifetime and later found its place outside my mother's bookstore, surrounded by wildflowers.

Even the grandeur described within the city's great hotels was shaped by lived experience, by the kindness of those who preserve such places and welcome others into them with care.

Florence does not set out to leave something behind. She builds something within.

If these pages cause you to pause—to consider the quiet architecture that shaped you—then the story has fulfilled its purpose.

— Beth Brubaker

Discussion Guide
The Matriarch's Legacy

1. The novel opens during the 1929 stock market crash, yet the story remains centered in the home. Why do you think the author chose to anchor national upheaval inside one family's kitchen and hallway?

2. Florence is not ambitious in worldly terms. She does not seek recognition or acclaim. How does the novel redefine strength through her steadiness?

3. Many pivotal moments in the book occur in silence — a footlocker closing, a letter held before opening, a chair left empty at the table. Why are restrained moments often more powerful than dramatic ones?

4. The theme of legacy runs quietly beneath the surface of every chapter. At what point did you realize the novel was less about events and more about formation?

5. The Passover and Easter scenes appear within the same spring season. What does the novel suggest about shared hope across traditions?

6. The sons leave one by one, each departure slightly different in tone. How does the author portray maternal release without diminishing attachment?

7. "Distance is not always measured in miles." How does this line shape your understanding of wartime separation?

8. Florence inherited endurance from Estella. In what ways does generational inheritance shape identity — both positively and painfully?

9. The novel suggests that legacy is not what we leave behind, but what we live into others. Do you agree?

10. After finishing the novel, what part of your own legacy felt newly illuminated?

Held Between the Pages

These poems were written alongside the story—not to explain it, but to remain with what lingered after certain pages were finished. They hold moments that asked for stillness rather than scene, for breath rather than narrative. If the chapters moved forward, these lines stayed behind, keeping watch over what could not be carried any other way.

Florence

Beloved lady whose presence is never so far away,
Often we catch a glimpse of you each passing day.
Whether in the beautiful garden where the flowers thrive,
Or high above, gliding upon butterfly wings, thou strive.

Her ethereal fragrance lingers beyond the rose bouquet,
Brought back to life in the glimmer of a morning sun ray.
Her endless love goes beyond sheer magnificence,
And for a moment, we see her true significance.

Beloved and cherished for her tender, loving heart,
You gave joyously the treasures that shall never part.
A kind encourager, filled with a beacon of streaming light,
Shone warmth and love in abundance before she took flight.

Vulnerable no more, she rests in the arms of all eternity,
Awaiting patiently in the realm beyond earthly modernity.
Kind lady shall always be in our hearts and near,
Still loved, still missed for all she held dear.

(From *The Philadelphia Matriarch*, Epilogue)

Sylvia

"Who is Silvia? What is she?"

She bore a poet's name
and kept its promise.

Named for a woman of verse and light,
for Shakespeare's Silvia—
beloved, steadfast,
worth defying fathers
and crossing boundaries for—

born of a mother who loved words enough
to give them flesh
and call them daughter.

You learned early
that language could live in the hands—
ten fingers finding what the heart
could not always say aloud.

The piano became your voice.
Not for performance,
but for truth.

Notes shaped by feeling,
by listening,
by staying when others wandered away.

You lived up to your name
the moment you met Jack—
when love arrived not as permission,
but as knowing.

Not long after, you chose him,
eloping against your parents' wishes,
faithful to the truth you recognized—
loving not lightly,

but with resolve.

You were melody and measure,
gentle and exacting,
able to soothe or summon strength
with the same unwavering touch.

Mother of four daughters,
you held us not softly,
but fiercely—
a protector whose love stood guard,
whose vigilance never slept.

You gave generously—
time, music, care,
your whole self—
never asking if there would be enough left.
There always was.

Even now,
your music has not ended.
It moves through rooms we enter,
through habits of kindness,
through the way we listen
before we speak.

Your melody remains—
heard not with the ear,
but with the heart—
and felt wherever love,
brave and chosen,
decides to stay.

White Illusion

She waits in stillness, masked in white,
A whisper soft, a bloom so bright.
No thorn, no hiss, no warning call—
Just grace that stands, serene and tall.

The breeze admires her silken sway,
She summons gently those who stray.
A petal's lure, a maiden's guise—
The nettle burns beneath the lies.

The curious reach, the kind bend,
The hand seeks what it can't defend.
A sting for trust, a mark for grace,
A lesson etched on skin's embrace.

And still she grows, in shade and sun,
The fairest face—the concealed one.
Not every beauty means you well;
Some saints wear thorns, and some a spell.

A Wish & A Prayer

Once rooted, once resting,
now lifted by air—
a life in transition,
becoming more than it was there.

It feels like only yesterday
you were new to this world,
small hands, first breaths,
a beginning barely unfurled.

Like the butterfly,
you move when the time is right,
trusting the wind,
learning the strength of your flight.

What you carry forward
was never meant to stay small—
every season has shaped you,
every fall taught you how to rise tall.

Something new is calling,
though its shape remains unnamed;
you've listened in silence,
and followed where peace remained.

My child, may God go before you,
steady your steps, and guard your way.
May grace meet you in the unknown,
and joy rise with each new day.

There are moments in life
when we don't need to name what's ahead to trust it.
We simply recognize the peace
that accompanies the next step.

When Winter Has Its Grip

When winter has its grip,
come—
follow my meandering path.
Step beneath the tall oaks,
into a cloak of shelter
draped in silvery Spanish moss,
soft as breath held between tides.
Even on blue-sky days
I'll surprise you—
a drifting butterfly,
a patient bee,
a brave new blossom
catching the light.
The freeze shrivels what bloomed too boldly,
petals surrendering
to a leaf-littered floor,
cushioning each careful step.
With every stride,
the forest releases itself—
salt-kissed air,
decaying leaves,
moss waking back into earth.
You were summoned here,
not by chance,
but by a Hand that knows
what must rest,
what must fall
and what will rise again—
in its appointed season.

Acknowledgments

This book was shaped by many hands, some present and some long gone.

I am grateful to the women who came before me, whose lives were lived without spectacle and whose strength was practiced daily. Their steadiness made this story possible, even before it was imagined.

To my editor, Emily, whose insight, precision, and deep respect for story elevated these pages beyond what I could have reached alone—your guidance sharpened not only the work, but the writer. For that, I am profoundly grateful.

To Mary, for her thoughtful beta read and discerning eye, my sincere gratitude.

To my husband, Scott, thank you for your patience, constancy, and unwavering belief in this work. You understood when the writing required quiet, and when it required faith. To our son, Eric, thank you for reminding me—by your way of moving through the world—that attention, care, and stewardship matter.

And to the faithful companions who kept watch during the long hours—Thelma and Louise, ever vigilant, and Bubba, who insisted on occupying whatever warmth could be found—thank you for the steady presence that made the work less solitary.

To the friends, readers, and fellow storytellers who listened, encouraged, and trusted this story to unfold in its own time, thank you for keeping it with such care.

And finally, to those who recognize themselves somewhere in these pages: may you feel seen, and may what you carry forward be lighter for having read.

About the Author

Beth Brubaker is a writer of historical fiction based in Fernandina Beach, Florida. She writes early in the morning, when the house is still, and is drawn to stories shaped by place, family, and the passage of time. *The Matriarch's Legacy* continues her exploration of how lives are formed not only by what is spoken, but by what is carefully carried forward.

Florence and William, circa 1924

In memory of those whose lives shaped this story.

The Matriarch Series

The Philadelphia Matriarch
Book One

The Matriarch's Legacy
Book Two

The Matriarch's Discovery
Book Three *(Coming Soon)*

Before Philadelphia.
Before the garden benches and red leaf maples.
Before classrooms, workshops, and careful hands.
There was a crossing.
A leaving.
A choice made under a Scottish sky that altered generations.
The discipline Florence recognized did not begin with her.
It began long before.
And the trunk she closed was only part of the story.

www.ingramcontent.com/pod-product-compliance
Lightning Source LLC
LaVergne TN
LVHW100516110826
845146LV00002B/663

* 9 7 9 8 9 9 9 1 3 6 2 2 0 *